T0304557

BRAD ABDUL

THE DEVIL'S ADVISOR

This is a **FLAME TREE PRESS** book

FLAME TREE PRESS
6 Melbray Mews, London, SW6 3NS, UK
flametreepress.com

US sales, distribution and warehouse:
Simon & Schuster
simonandschuster.biz

UK distribution and warehouse:
Marston Book Services Ltd
marston.co.uk

Thanks to the Flame Tree Press team.

The cover is created by Flame Tree Studio with thanks to Nik Keevil and Shutterstock.com. The font families used are Avenir and Bembo.

Flame Tree Press is an imprint of Flame Tree Publishing Ltd
flametreepublishing.com

A copy of the CIP data for this book is available from the British Library and the Library of Congress.

3 5 7 9 8 6 4 2

PB ISBN: 978-1-78758-845-5
ebook ISBN: 978-1-78758-847-9

Printed and bound in Great Britain by Clays Ltd, Elcograf S.p.A.

BRAD ABDUL

THE DEVIL'S ADVISOR

FLAME TREE PRESS
London & New York

For my love.

Thank you for sticking with me
through Hell and back.

CHAPTER ONE

Clocks don't tick anymore. Not when everything is digital. That means that there is no audio cue that suggests the passage of time. Time becomes arbitrary – it becomes relative. With a ticking clock, comfort could at least be found in the monotonous rhythm that accompanies the passage of time. However, when staring at a digital clockface, seconds can feel like hours. That was Brian's problem. The seconds of his day felt like hours. In the monotony, Brian would have killed for a *tick* here or there.

Brian jiggled his mouse to rouse his out-of-date computer to life and quickly tapped in his password. The glow of his seasonal affective disorder lamp brushed the trappings of his desk. The gloom of the not-quite morning just outside his office window tried desperately to suck the life from the room and its occupant. The light was a good defense against the drab, but coffee was Brian's sharpest weapon to slice through the early-hour cobwebs. He sipped at his mug as he skimmed his calendar and the hodgepodge of meetings that made up his day.

A soft knock rattled the office door before it opened and Amanda, Brian's assistant, stepped through. A blue pen was stuck behind her left ear, pinning the loose auburn strand that evaded the rest of her ponytail. She was in a plain white blouse that tucked into the waist of loose flowing black pants. Her pale blue eyes looked over the edge of her glasses at a leather planner in the hand that wasn't desperately clinging to her coffee tumbler.

"You've got some schedule changes," she said, eyes still on the planner.

"Good morning, Amanda."

"Your ten o'clock left a message saying he needed to cancel."

"My night was all right, how was yours?" Brian carried on, half listening to the agenda updates.

"The staff meeting was moved from first thing this morning back to this afternoon at one," she continued, not missing a beat.

"Well, that's too bad, I was looking forward to getting all that social interaction over as soon as possible," Brian replied, genuinely feeling disappointed.

Amanda's gaze slid upward to meet Brian's.

"Play nice, they're your colleagues," she prompted, using the mom voice Brian was sure, outside of her kids, she only used on him.

"They don't like me, Amanda. I'm aware of that."

She dropped the planner to her side and cocked a hip, turning up the volume on her scolding gaze.

"And why do you think that is?"

"Not this again, please," Brian pleaded.

"How long have you been in the firm?"

He sighed and rolled his eyes.

"Just under a year now," he replied, playing along with their familiar song and dance.

"And in that time, you've leapfrogged every one of your co-workers. They're all still pretty sour about you getting the Senior Business Advisor role over them."

"If they wanted it, they'd work harder," Brian said, stating the simple truth of the matter.

"Your attitude doesn't help, either—"

"Amanda, I don't need the lecture. I know. I rub them the wrong way. The feeling is mutual. Can we move on?"

Brian didn't exactly dislike his co-workers; he just never seemed to get off on the right foot with them. He overshadowed some tenured advisors while simultaneously setting a seemingly impossible bar for anyone who came after. Jealousy, it turns out, is a potent ingredient for a hostile work environment. However, the collective peer hatred didn't bother Brian. When he wasn't in his office, he made it a point to show as little face as possible. In hindsight, he thought that probably added to their disdain, but it didn't matter; he wasn't there to make friends. Amanda was the closest thing he had to an amicable relationship in the office. Even that was tenuous at the best of times.

She scolded him a moment longer before raising the planner back to her chest.

"Long story short," she said with a notable degree of annoyance, "your morning is free."

"Lovely. Thank you, Amanda," Brian said, jovially raising his coffee cup to her before taking a sip.

Amanda rolled her eyes and spun on the spot, exiting the room and closing the door behind her.

★   ★   ★

As he actively avoided any social interactions with his spiteful peers, Brian's only means of passing the time was checking his junk mail. The office firewalls were annoyingly inclusive of most other distractions, and browsing a phone looked too unprofessional. He wasn't overly sure of how he landed a spot on most of the mailing lists, but it was an entertaining, if mundane, way to pass the time. Thankfully, the filters of Brian's company email were lax when catching junk mail – malicious or otherwise.

Sometimes it was learning about a distant relative he'd never heard of who had left him a hefty inheritance. Other times it was discovering new and natural ways to enhance the length, girth, density, or performance of his genitals. Brief snippets of the outside world bled through the cracks of his boring office and provided him a temporary reprieve from the passing hours of his day. After a time, Brian had become familiar with the types of junk that would get through the filters. That made finding a chain letter, on this particularly dull morning, a treat....

From: Ms@tan.com
To: all@BSConsulting.com
Subject: If there is someone you hate...

Body:

"Is there someone you hate? Someone you just can't stand?

An old roommate, an ex-lover, a co-worker?

Reply to this email with their full name and something bad will happen to them.

Forward this message to everyone on your contact list to make the person you hate suffer an even worse fate."

Brian's eyes lingered on the message. It was a curious creation – certainly retaining the chain letter aesthetic but with a malicious twist. Still, it wasn't interesting enough to be the distraction Brian was hoping for. Just some poorly crafted prank that left him wanting.

Brian closed the email and sighed. The rest of his day would feel like an eternity now that all the decent distractions were eaten up in the first half.

★   ★   ★

In the back of a cramped conference room, Brian sat, enduring the palpable tension of his co-workers as they attended their monthly performance meeting. Their department head, Dianne, sat at the front of the room. She was a portly woman, squeezed into a frilly blouse and a black knee-high skirt that stretched across her thighs near to the point of stitches popping. She conducted the meeting, drawing the attention of the advisors to various projected graphs and figures that, more often than not, featured Brian's name – the primary reason for the tension in the room. He hated the attention, trying to draw as little of it to himself as he could.

"And again," Dianne said, referring to the projected graph, "our biggest contract of the month was closed by Brian." She beamed proudly in his direction, dragging the eyes of everyone to him. Scowls crossed every unremarkable face in the room as they stared him down in the back corner of the room.

It was an odd feeling, being hated because of his success. Brian felt that everyone could have a running chance at topping the sales charts if they tried at least a little – hell, Brian could do this job in his sleep. That was the exact reason he needed something more to throw himself into. So he bided his time until the awkward meeting was over to sneak in a quick chat with Dianne.

As the bodies all filtered out of the room, glaring at Brian as he passed, Dianne packed her things and readied her own exit. He approached her as she was slipping her laptop into its bag.

"Dianne," he said, "could I have a minute?"

"Of course." She looked surprised that he was still in the room. "What can I do for you?"

"The Regional Manager position, I saw that there was a posting from HR about a vacancy. I submitted my name for the position but the application requires supervisory approval in order for consideration."

Dianne nodded, a considering look on her face.

"I did see a request come through to my desk. I must say, I was taken aback. You haven't been with the department long."

"That's true, but I think that, in my time, I've shown what I'm capable of and that I'm ready for more responsibility – more challenge."

"You certainly have," Dianne chortled. "My team's numbers have never been this good. However, I feel like it's not the right time."

Brian's heart dipped. He swallowed, blinking rapidly while thinking what possible problem she could have.

"I've done a good deal for the department. If it's a tenure thing, I'm sure HR would have notified me."

Dianne shook her head. A faux-remorseful look crossed her face.

"No, no – nothing like that. I think you'd be a wonderful fit for the role, and the firm never stands in the way of self-starters like yourself over something silly like tenure. I just feel like you could benefit from staying in the department for a little while longer so you can really make a name for yourself with the figures you pull in."

"What's a 'little while longer'?" Brian asked, frustrated with the ambiguity.

Dianne's eyes drifted up in her skull as she pressed a pudgy finger to her chin in thought.

"I'd say around February would be a good time," she said.

How specific.

"That timeline wouldn't have anything to do with the annual performance bonuses, would it?" Brian asked through his clenched jaw.

"Oh my, I hadn't even considered that," Dianne replied, not at all convincingly. "You are making me the envy of the other team leaders though. Best numbers we've had in a long time."

Brian's pulse shot up at the reply. "Are you telling me that you're actively blocking me from advancing because you'll get a bigger bonus at the end of the year if I stay?"

"I never said anything of the sort," she snapped. "How dare you accuse me of something so petty?"

All words of rebuttal scrambled in Brian's mind. His mouth opened and closed several times. He wanted to scream but, despite his desire for a well-deserved outburst, he still needed her endorsement.

As if answering his dilemma, Dianne finished packing her things in a huffy manner.

"This conversation alone shows me that you need more time to grow in your role. I will not be approving the application. I will inform HR when I return to my desk."

She swerved around Brian, leaving him standing in the empty conference room, his own anger smoldering to frustrating defeat.

★　　★　　★

Brian returned to his office in a lingering fog of disbelief. Any motivation he'd had was siphoned out of him during his talk with Dianne. He needed a distraction. Instinctively, he returned to his junk mail, praying there would be something new to occupy his time. He did have new junk mail – all of them replies from his co-workers to the chain letter from earlier that day. All of them bearing Brian's name. In that moment of rock bottom, the only thing Brian could think was how unprofessional it was that they chose to Reply All.

His haze carried him through the afternoon and into the early evening. Having given up on his junk mail and reverting instead to his phone, Brian spent the day perusing jobs outside his consulting firm worth applying for. It wasn't until the sun had nearly set that he realized he should have packed up and left almost an hour ago. He sighed, switching his SAD lamp and his monitor off before standing up and pulling his sport coat from the back of his chair. He heard a click from the door as he pulled his arms through the sleeves.

"I figured you would have gone home by now," Brian said, assuming it was Amanda at the door.

Instead, he saw a man wearing a casual charcoal suit standing in his office. He was young with short, dirty-blond hair. His features were sharp and handsome, looking as though he were plucked from a magazine cologne ad.

Brian's brow furrowed. Was there a meeting he'd forgottten about? The man certainly fit the bill of a young entrepreneur with money to spend on a consulting firm. Brian's mouth started to open but he was cut short.

"Brian Lachey, right?" the young man asked.

Curiosity crossed Brian's face. "I'm sorry, did we have a meeting scheduled?"

"No, I'm here to collect you for an interview."

Brian's heart skipped at the answer. Had Dianne had a change of heart? He certainly wasn't prepared for an interview but he had a knack for winging things like that.

"O-oh, of course," Brian stammered excitedly.

He moved around his desk to follow the man from his office, shutting the door on the way out. The pair entered into the grid of cubicles beyond and made their way to the elevators at the other end of the floor.

"Oh, I forgot to introduce myself – my name is Dallas," the man said, spinning quickly to offer Brian a warm smile and a hand.

He took it and gave it a sharp shake. "Pleased to meet you," he said as he straightened his tie. "I don't think I've seen you around before. What department do you work in?" He stuffed his shirt into his belt.

They reached the elevator and Dallas pressed the down button.

"Oh, I don't work here," Dallas replied pointedly.

A dull ding chimed from the elevator. Instead of the car, the doors opened to a wall of brilliant, writhing white, like slow licking flames bleached of their color. The light spilled out from the elevator, blinding Brian for a moment. He stopped at the door. His brow creased and he reassessed Dallas and the scene before him.

"What the hell is this?" he demanded.

Dallas laughed through his nose. "Interesting choice of words," he replied. "I told you, I'm bringing you to an interview."

Brian studied the man. He seemed to be enjoying himself, toying with Brian.

"I think I'll take the stairs," Brian said, turning to the doors that led to the stairwell.

Dallas shrugged. "Works for me."

The door swung open as Brian approached, revealing the same wall of white beyond. Brian was unable to act quick enough, feeling a firm palm press him between the shoulder blades, shoving him through the screen of flames.

CHAPTER TWO

Brian tumbled forward, feeling as though he had been pushed through a sheer of curtains – if those curtains had been set on fire. Once he regained his footing, he looked up to see that he was standing inside a foyer the size of a private hangar. The floors were black marble with three ivory pillars on either wing, creating a perimeter for the room. The pillars connected in arches that supported the domed ceiling. There were no windows – only a small leather sectional couch to one side and a bare half-size magazine rack next to it. At the end of the room was a large, semicircular desk. A massive double door was on either side of the desk.

Brian felt a firm clap on his back. Dallas smiled warmly and nudged him forward into the foyer. Brian felt uneasy and confused; there seemed nowhere to go but forward. As the pair walked toward the receptionist's desk, Brian's head swiveled slowly to take in the whole room. It felt like a void had swallowed him whole.

"We late?" Dallas asked as they arrived at the desk.

The girl behind the desk snapped her chewing gum and looked at Dallas with wide, green eyes.

"Shouldn't you know that?" she replied with a sassy tone.

"You're the worst," Dallas said as he ushered Brian around the desk toward the double doors on the right. "That's my sister," Dallas clarified. "She's the worst."

Brian's gaze lingered on the girl as they strode past. Surprisingly, he noticed hers lingering on him in kind. They arrived in front of the doors and Dallas took a step back. Confused, Brian turned to look at him.

"What now?" he asked.

Dallas gave him a baffled look. "Go in," he said, motioning with his arm.

The doors opened into a crisp, white room. The space was brightly lit from seemingly everywhere and nowhere. The adornments were minimal. A small filing cabinet stood in the far-right corner behind a large white marble desk covered in papers. A white armchair with gold embellishments sat on the opposite side of the desk. In the chair was a woman dressed in business attire – a sport coat with three-quarter sleeves and a plain white shirt underneath with a single glossy black button at the collar – she hadn't looked up at all from her desk when Brian entered.

Still, Brian was stunned when he saw her. Her porcelain skin was flawless against the long, straight, chestnut hair pinned up, save for long bangs that framed her face. The woman looked up from the papers that she was buried in atop her desk. Her smoky gray-blue eyes caught Brian, making his heart skip for the briefest of moments. A curious smile crossed her face as though she could hear the arrhythmic fumble in his chest.

"You must be Brian," she said.

Her voice was like silk.

Brian swallowed the lump in his throat. "I am."

The woman smiled softly and placed the papers she had been examining onto the desk before her. She pushed her chair back and rose to her feet. Brian was treated to the remainder of her ensemble – a tight black skirt that fell just above the knee, completing her professional, yet alluring, business attire. The click-clack of her shoes across the floor echoed against the walls as she approached. Brian began to awkwardly shift his weight where he stood in an attempt to shake his nerves.

She extended her hand to Brian. "You can call me Lucy," she said as Brian took her hand.

"Pleasure. Now, can you please tell me why I'm here?" Brian asked, attempting to maintain his composure in the woman's presence.

Lucy's eyebrow cocked. She released her grip slightly. "Did Dallas not explain to you?"

"Not exactly," Brian said. "He said I was here for a job interview. One which I do not recall ever receiving any indication of or submitting my candidacy for."

"Stop trying to use so many words to look smart. It makes you sound pretentious," Lucy said. "That's probably why no one at work likes you."

Brian was taken aback. How did she know no one at work liked him?

Lucy sighed and walked back to her desk. She propped herself up on one arm while reaching to press a button on a small intercom on the desk. Brian noticed her figure was presented clearly while poised against her desk.

"Dahlia," Lucy said.

"Yess'um?"

Brian recognized the voice of the girl who sat in the main foyer.

"Is Dallas still there?"

"Yeah. Why, do you need him?"

"*Need* is a strong word. Can you send him in?"

"No prob, Bob."

The door behind Brian swung open once more and Dallas entered the room.

"Yes?"

"Sit," Lucy said as she pointed to a chair behind the desk that hadn't been there a moment ago.

Dallas sighed dramatically and hung his head, reluctantly plopping down like a scolded toddler.

Lucy's eyes left Dallas and returned to Brian.

"Apologies for the confusion," she said. "Part of the reason you're here is because it's hard to find good help these days." She shot a disapproving look backward at Dallas. "Please, have a seat."

She motioned behind Brian to another chair that also had not been there a moment ago. Brian's head whipped back around to look at Lucy, who motioned with her hand once more, seemingly understanding Brian's confusion about the sudden appearance of the chair. Brian slowly sat as Lucy walked to the front of her desk and leaned her weight against it.

"Let's try this again, shall we?" Lucy started. "You can call me Lucy. This," she jerked her head to motion behind her, "is my idiotic son, Dallas."

"Pleasure," Brian said.

"Dallas, would you care to explain to Brian why he's here?" Lucy said, her eyes refusing to leave Brian's.

Dallas let out a loud and obviously irritated sigh of reluctance from the corner of the room. "Your co-workers want you dead," he said bluntly.

It took a moment for the words to register under the weight of Lucy's eyes on his. As they sank in, Brian's blinking doubled in frequency.

The only words that he could formulate tumbled from his mouth as if they'd tripped accidentally on the way from his brain. "M-my... what?"

Dallas leaned forward in his chair and rested his elbows on his knees. He stared Brian directly in the eyes.

"Your co-workers.

Want.

You.

Dead."

"Why? What? That's ridiculous. How do you know?" Brian asked, still dumbfounded.

Dallas looked a mixture of annoyed and confused. "Didn't you get my email? They definitely did. Your name came rolling in *loads* of times."

Brian's head was spinning but finally landed on the only word that he'd heard in the last ten minutes that made sense – *email*.

"You mean that dumb chain letter?" Brian asked.

Dallas's face scrunched up in annoyance. "Dumb? *Dumb!?*" Dallas became flustered at the unintentional insult. "Well, it got you here, didn't it? How dumb could it be?"

Dallas's comment brought Brian to his senses once more.

"And where is here exactly?"

He looked at Dallas but thought better of it and directed his gaze instead to Lucy.

"Hell," Lucy punctuated.

Silence filled the room for an excruciating length of time. Brian attempted to swallow a lump in his throat. He then tried three more times after the first didn't take.

"Hell," he repeated.

His eyes connected with Lucy's, to which she responded with a carefree shrug.

"If this is Hell," Brian said hesitantly, "then who does that make you?" His eyes lingered on Lucy's.

She shrugged once more as if it was a silly question.

"Isn't that obvious? I'm the Devil."

So nonchalant.

"The Devil," Brian echoed.

Lucy rolled her eyes.

"The Devil, Satan, the Prince of Darkness, *Lucifer*. You people have given me so many names. Take your pick."

"Lucy?" Brian's head tilted slightly.

Lucy chuckled to herself.

"I thought you'd like that. Clever, isn't it? I've been using it for a few centuries now."

Brian was still lost amidst the seemingly obvious reveal.

"Aren't you supposed to be a man?" Brian blurted, with instant regret.

"I don't have a gender. My appearance is based entirely on what my perceiver would find most tempting."

Brian's face reddened as Lucy finished her sentence. No wonder he was so drawn to her.

Lucy saw the revelation dawning across Brian's face. She looked down at herself – bosom on display as she propped herself up on her desk. A venomous smirk crossed her lips.

"I have to say, the body and physical features your subconscious gave me to work with are nice, but I'm wondering where the business-professional-fetish comes from. Are you *that* consumed by work that you imagine 'sexy' as 'pencil skirt and blazer'?"

"Uhh…." Brian was at a loss for words.

Criticism aside, Lucy's words were right on the money. Brian was so wrapped up with work that he lost something inside him – a drive that was there, once upon a time, something that had been slowly replaced by the stifling day-to-day of his office and the people and building surrounding it. He no longer had a personality; he was just an employee number that called itself Brian.

Hot on the trail of his mortifying revelation came something he'd forgotten about long ago.

Passion.

He was once bright-eyed and passionate, but every inaudible second that passed within the walls of his office wore away at him like water on a cliffside, making him complacent. All at once, Brian was suddenly very unhappy with himself. He was unhappy with how his work had taken over his life. He was unhappy being made a tool for someone else's profit.

He was unhappy.

Period.

The pink drained from his cheeks and he looked up at Lucy, too busy still admiring her own assets to take notice.

"You mentioned I was here for a job interview, right?" Brian asked.

Lucy suddenly came to her senses and turned her attention to Brian. She pushed herself from the perch at the edge of her desk and walked to the chair behind, pulling the pin from her hair and letting chestnut locks fall. She looked down at her desk and shuffled some folders, searching for a specific file.

"Tell him about the email, Dallas," Lucy said, keeping her gaze on the desk.

Dallas stood from his seat and began to pace slowly.

"The email was a bit of genius on my part," he said with pride and a hint of spite laced into the word 'genius' directed at Brian. "We make good on our promise – something bad happens to the person named in the reply of the email. However, by naming someone, the respondent is willfully committing an act that would harm another human. That kind of act is money in the bank for us."

Brian's eyebrow rose.

"You mean money metaphorically, right? I don't see the Devil, or even Hell for that matter, suffering from financial dependency." Brian looked from Dallas to Lucy. Neither seemed to reject the notion. "Wait, you're kidding me. Hell runs on money?"

"It's not that simple," Dallas said defensively.

Lucy raised her hand to silence Dallas. "We do have a currency, of sorts. Something a bit more metaphysical than you're used to. Hell runs on the energy of corrupted souls."

She reached over to a folder that lay on her desk. She opened it and leafed through a few pages.

"You have an impressive track record, Brian," she said. "You've taken on some very menial projects and bolstered them to S&P 500 levels—"

"The fact that you even know what that is—"

"—and all for what?" Lucy said as she snapped the folder shut and directed her smoky-blue gaze at him.

Brian swallowed the lump that had been slowly reclaiming its territory in his throat.

"What do you mean?" he asked.

"You're good at what you do, but you get nothing out of it other than just being good at it. The work isn't rewarding anymore, I can tell. Why is that?" Lucy's question dug into him.

Brian hesitated but he knew the reason. He felt like she already did, too.

"My boss knows that I'm good at what I do. That means losing me to a promotion would mean she loses a strong performer on her team. It impacts her paycheck. The other advisors that work with me aren't nearly as good as I am. Not to boast, but they just don't see the details like I do."

"And that's why you're here," she said.

She opened the folder again briefly and slid out a single page before closing it once more.

"If we're counting your co-workers alone, there were fourteen responses to Dallas's email with your name on it."

Brian's heart sank. His department only had sixteen people in it, including him.

"Your file came across my desk to approve whatever terrible fate you had in store at the hands of those in your office. However, because of your talents, I am considering forgetting you were ever named – *if* we can come to some kind of…arrangement."

"What sort of arrangement?" Brian asked.

"A business agreement. More accurately, a job offer," Lucy said bluntly. "I want you to work your magic on Hell and get us running as efficiently and cost-effectively as possible. Better than that, I want Hell to be profitable."

"Otherwise I meet some terrible fate as it was intended?"

Brian was not thrilled by being blackmailed into working for the Devil.

"That goes without saying, but I think we can sweeten the deal for you," Lucy said.

She opened the folder once more and slid out a package of papers, handing them to Brian.

"What is this?" he asked as he took hold of the stack.

"Incentive," Lucy said. "Meaning. Purpose. Drive. Whatever you want to call it, really."

Brian looked down and realized that he was holding a contract.

"An employment contract?"

"The long and short of it is that I'm looking for a suitable heir. Someone who can handle the day-to-day. Show me you can do that, and I'll make you my successor."

CHAPTER THREE

Brian's mind went blank. Lucy leaned forward, trying to get into his line of sight. She snapped her fingers in front of his face. His vision scrambled in his head as it focused again. He looked at Lucy with a blank stare.

"I don't think I understand," he said feebly.

Lucy gave him a sympathetic, if not patronizing, smile.

"What's to understand? You do the job, you get to rule Hell. It's that simple."

"Isn't everything more complicated when dealing with the Devil? Isn't that how these things go?"

Brian flipped through the contract in his hands absentmindedly, pretending that he was scanning the pages for some clause that would include his eternal damnation or some such punishment upon completion. Realistically, he wasn't reading a single word – comprehending written language was a lot to ask of his brain at that moment.

Her hand rested on his to stop his frantic flipping of pages. He looked up to see Lucy smiling warmly.

"Let's take a walk," she said.

The pair left the office through the foyer. Brian caught a glimpse of Dahlia seeming overly curious about their impromptu adventure. Her green eyes lingered on them once more as they rounded the desk to the other set of massive double doors opposite Lucy's office.

★　★　★

The doors opened and, to Brian's surprise, sunlight slipped between the cracks. The pair stepped through to an open-air walkway that looked onto a lush, green courtyard. Beyond the wrought-iron arches that framed the walkway, white stones created three paths that led to the center of the courtyard, where a beautiful ivory fountain trickled gently in the fading sunlight. For Hell, this kind of serene beauty felt out of place.

The fresh air seemed to help Brian's thoughts straighten out. He resurfaced to find himself strolling casually, with Lucy looking as though she were also enjoying the fresh air and breeze. She turned to him and smiled softly.

"I know this might be a lot to take in," she said as they moseyed past the archways.

"I don't know if I'm the gullible type but everything you've told me seems plausible. I know in all reality that it shouldn't. Once you eliminate the impossible, whatever remains, no matter how improbable, must be the truth. I can't seem to find a good enough reason to deny what you've told me." Brian motioned to the fountain in the courtyard. "Except maybe this."

Lucy chuckled. "Good deduction, Sherlock," she teased. "Hell used to look a lot different once upon a time. Just like your world, however, times change. Besides, just because this is Hell doesn't mean it can't be beautiful. It's you humans who painted this place to be fire, brimstone, and corpses." She stopped and leaned on an open archway to gaze at the fountain. "Why would I want to see something like that every day? I'd rather experience beauty. "That's why I'm offering you this opportunity." She turned her attention to Brian. "I have run this place for longer than I care to admit but, like any business owner, I eventually want to retire. I want to enjoy other beauties out there instead of constantly having to worry about whether Hell is freezing over without me fanning the flames."

"So, this is your retirement strategy? Have someone you were supposed to kill run your company instead?" Brian asked skeptically.

Lucy waved the comment aside. "It was a stroke of fate that your folder came across my desk. After some review, I think you'll be the perfect man for the job."

She reached to Brian's hand, still grasping the contract she'd handed him. She lifted his hand up to his chest and firmly pressed the pages into his body.

"I understand your hesitation. If I hadn't seen the things I've seen and done the things I've done, I'd probably hesitate as well. Take the night. Read over the contract. Let me know in the morning how you feel."

The pair started walking back to the foyer in silence. Brian's head was still buzzing with all the possibilities. All the questions. All the fantastical things he had just been a part of. He wasn't sure if a night would be enough time for him to digest everything.

The sky above the courtyard had slowly tinted pink and orange by the time they reached the double doors again. Brian's eyes lingered on the contract that was still pressed at his chest.

"I guess I'll take this home and give it a once-over, then," he said.

Lucy smiled and pushed open one of the doors enough to bellow through the gap, "Dahlia, can you bring Brian to his room, please?"

As quickly as if she'd been waiting behind the other door, Dahlia came bobbing through with a bright smile. Her dirty-blonde locks glimmered in the setting sun. She was taller than Brian thought, though it was hard to gauge someone's height when they were sitting behind a desk. It's also hard to see someone's curves behind a desk – curves now very visible in a simple, tight black and white dress.

Brian curbed the thought as he remembered that she was Dallas's sister.

The Devil's daughter.

She too could be manipulating her appearance to appeal to him – though he wondered why she and Lucy would look so different if that were the case.

Brian's ears finally reconnected to his brain and registered Lucy's request to Dahlia.

"Wait, 'my room'?"

"You can stay here for the night. I've had a room prepared for you – clothes, toiletries, mini-bar – the works." Lucy slipped past Dahlia and made her way through the door back to the foyer. "I insist!" she said without a backward glance, anticipating Brian's refusal.

The door shut and he and Dahlia stood alone, bathing in the glow of the sunset.

Dahlia took Brian's arm and directed him down the walkway. They walked past the courtyard and into a building that felt like a mix between a church and a hotel. Dahlia's eyes had not left Brian through a sideways stare since they began their journey. He was unsure of what she found so fascinating.

"Is there something on my face?" he finally said.

Dahlia seemed to realize that she had been staring and went a shade of sunset that was impossible behind closed doors.

"Sorry, I didn't mean to stare," she said innocently. "It's not often you see humans down here. Well, not for long at least."

The sentiment brought Brian back to the reality of his current location.

"Right, this is Hell. Humans are probably carted off to some eternal damnation or evil pit of despair or something, right?"

Dahlia giggled, which, Brian found, was both off-putting and slightly endearing.

"No, humans don't come down here like that. We get souls, or fragments of souls. The humans we do get are usually overnight guests of my mother's. The others that are in for longer stays aren't humans for very long. They become Hellions shortly after."

"What exactly is a Hellion?"

"They're sort of like our…employees." Dahlia looked unsure whether that was a good way to describe them.

Brian's eyebrow rose. "I thought Hell would have *demons* or *ghouls* or something."

Dahlia seemed slightly offended by the comment. "A long time ago we did. That was before I was around. From what I've heard, they didn't make for good underlings; they were more of a hassle than a help. Hellions are different. They're humans that have pledged their services to work for Hell."

"Do they still look like humans?"

"Sort of," Dahlia said, struggling to explain further, "except... different. They are *humanoid* in a sense but they *feel* different." Her face scrunched up.

Brian was not sure if she was struggling to put words to their features or if she was irked by them. There was so much vernacular that Brian had to learn if, he thought, he was to take the job. The contract in his hand felt heavier at the thought, reminding him that it was still there.

"This really is Hell, isn't it?" he asked rhetorically.

Dahlia brightened back up at the question. "Not what you were expecting, right?"

"How could you tell?" Brian chuckled faintly.

Dahlia shrugged innocently and took in their surroundings. They had reached a heavy wooden door with a black iron knocker in the center. Opposite the door was a large window that overlooked the fountain in the courtyard. The sun had almost disappeared, bathing the hallway in a rich violet.

"I wouldn't expect it to look like this if I grew up where you did. Your world makes this place sound like a nightmare."

Dahlia nudged the large door open with surprising ease. Brian looked into the room. A large, fluffy bed framed by a small night table on either side took up the majority of the floor space. Off to the side was a large armchair, similar to Lucy's, next to a crackling fireplace that illuminated the room in a soft, welcoming glow. A heavy wooden wardrobe sat on the opposite wall next to the doorway for an en-suite lavatory.

"We have most things that the human world does. I even had a puppy when I was a kid. You'll see, it's not so bad here."

"I'm starting to see that," he said, staring at the inviting softness of the bed.

Dahlia smiled and stepped back from the doorway so that Brian could enter.

"Looks like you've got some reading to do, then," she said. "I'll leave you to it. The mini-bar is part of the night table, in case you need some liquid comfort."

Brian entered the room, turned and smiled at her. She beamed back brightly before tugging the door closed by the iron knocker. Her voice slipped through just as the door clacked shut against the frame.

"Sweet dreams."

★   ★   ★

Brian stood for a moment at the door. His weary form was being drawn in by the plushness of the bed and further enticed by the soft crackling of the fire. The smell of the burning wood lightly wrapped him in a comforting release. He turned and slowly made his way to the fluffy mound. His body felt heavy. He wasn't sure if he was really as tired as he felt or if his brain had overloaded and wasn't sure how to convey his proper state of being at that moment.

He took a single step before flopping face-first onto the mattress; the contract in his hand hit the foot of the bed frame. He looked down at the package with tired eyes. This was the first time he was able to fully take in anything that was printed on the pages. The longer he looked down at the cover sheet, the faster sleep peeled away from his eyes. An opportunity.

That's what he had in his hand. However, how legitimate of an opportunity was still to be seen. Brian got up and walked away from the bed. Finding the armchair next to the fire, he dropped down onto the seat and started doing what he did best – he got to work.

★   ★   ★

What felt like hours passed and Brian hadn't moved from where he first landed in the chair. He made the last few markings on the contract with a pen he had in his coat's breast pocket and closed the package of documents. It hadn't been the worst contract he'd seen before, but it definitely had some room for improvement.

The fire crackled softly in the background. Brian was unsurprised that he didn't need to put another log on during the hours he sat and delved into the contract. If this place could make chairs disappear and reappear, what's an additional fire log or two?

He stood from his seat, feeling the muscles in his legs groan back to life. He walked across the room and gripped the handle of the door, opening it to clear moonlight in the hall beyond. The window parallel to his door glittered in the light, casting intricate shadows of the wrought-iron frame that held the panes in place. The fountain of the courtyard below trickled calmly in the moonlight and, for just a moment, Brian had forgotten where he was. He chuckled to himself as Dahlia's words snuck to the forefront of his mind:

It's not so bad here.

CHAPTER FOUR

Inside Lucy's office, just behind her pristine white chair, through a passage in the wall, steps of black marble spiraled upward. At the top, a large penthouse sprawled out above the office and foyer below. A four-poster bed draped in white linens sat framed by five tall windows that curved around the cushioned headboard. The windows overlooked the courtyard and the tower where Brian's room was nestled. A large, oak wardrobe rested along one wall, opposite the door to a lavatory. The room was sectioned off by frosted French doors that led to three wide steps descending into a lounge. The semicircular room was part cocktail bar, part library. Immediately next to the steps from the room was a small countertop with two red leather barstools. Behind was an open cabinet filled with various glasses and bottles. The shelves came to a halt just above a stout refrigerator and a dumbwaiter behind the countertop. A wide walkway traced the perimeter of the room and ended at a large wooden door at the bar side of the arc. The curved walls were composed of shelves filled with books. The entire walkway sank two steps further to a small, cozy sitting area where Lucy rested on a plush, white couch in the center. A large-mouthed fireplace across from the couch crackled an ambient tune as Lucy took a sip from a tumbler, flipping the page of a rather large, rather old-looking book.

A knock bellowed from the wooden door and Lucy's gaze lazily lifted from her spot on the page.

"Enter," she said.

The metal latch of the door clacked as Dahlia opened the door and slipped in. "He's in his room," she said.

Lucy nodded, her eyes returning to the page in her lap.

"How does he seem?"

Dahlia shrugged as she stepped down from the walkway and sat on the arm of the large couch.

"Oddly complacent – he's either incredibly quick to adapt or is very good at hiding his panic."

Lucy corrected her posture on the couch, closing the book in her lap with the crackle of old leather.

"He's pragmatic. That's why he's a good fit for the job. He'll be able to roll with the punches."

Dahlia crossed the room to the bar and situated herself behind the counter. Lucy downed the remainder of her tumbler and extended her arm in Dahlia's direction. She shook the straggling shards of ice against the glass, signaling Dahlia to make her another.

"Have you seen Dallas since?" Dahlia asked as she fixed drinks for the two.

"No, he disappeared to wherever it is he goes when he's not working," Lucy replied with a carefree shrug. "Why?"

"I'm curious what he thinks." Dahlia returned to the couch, offering her mother a fresh drink.

"What's to be curious about? We both know your brother would much prefer Hell like it used to be in the old days. He's too concerned about appearances to see the forest for the trees." Lucy took a sip of her drink. "Frankly, I'm surprised he even brought Brian's file to me when he saw it."

"You don't give him enough credit. He's capable of change too, you know," Dahlia said before she took a sip from her own glass. Her eyes landed on the cover of the book in Lucy's lap. She nodded to it as she swallowed the oaky liquid. "Seems like applicable reading."

Lucy glanced down and brushed her palm across the cracked leather book cover. As her lounge might suggest, Lucy had a passion for reading. More specifically, she had a passion for history. Humans were curious creatures, and the free will of the living interested her to no end. As such, Lucy felt it her obligation to keep a record of the goings-on in the afterlife as well. In serving that duty, she compiled an abridged telling of the history of Hell. Documenting the days from when Hell was more rampant chaos compared to the structured bureaucracy that was presently sported, *The History of Hell* explained the evolution of the underworld as the human world above changed in leaps and bounds.

"Sometimes, to know where you're going, you have to know where you've been," Lucy said softly, lifting the book from her lap and placing it on a small table to the side.

"I'm curious," Dahlia said, taking a seat next to her mother, "why now?"

Lucy nearly choked on her drink at the question. She cleared her throat with a laugh and shot Dahlia a disbelieving look.

"The better question is, 'why not a hundred years ago?' Times were so simple then, it would have been easy to pass the torch."

"So then, why not a hundred years ago?"

Lucy took a sip of her drink, her memory slipping back as easily as the liquid down her throat. "Like I said, times were simple then. The job still had plenty of perks," she said into the dancing licks of flame in the hearth.

"Would those 'perks' happen to be what – or *who* – I'm thinking of?" Dahlia jabbed.

Lucy's gaze narrowed as it met the sight of her daughter. "That's enough out of you."

"Seriously," Dahlia pressed, "do you think Gabrielle will call it quits just because you do? That woman works harder than anyone I know."

"I don't know. I doubt she would hand over her mantle as Death to just anyone in order for us to be together but…."

Dahlia stared at her, waiting for the thought to finish. "But what?"

"But I'm done with not trying. If we're going to have a chance together, things need to change," Lucy said, mostly to herself.

Dahlia's eyes lingered on her mother. Lucy could feel the pity bleeding from her stare and she hated it. She didn't like feeling powerless, vulnerable.

"Don't fall into old habits then," Dahlia offered. "I can already tell that you like him. What's that saying about pen and company ink?"

Lucy laughed breathily at the assessment. "You're one to talk. I saw you staring. Besides, you can't blame me. He's interesting. I'm very curious to see what comes next," she replied, a sultry look crossing her face.

"Easy, girl," Dahlia said, before downing the rest of her drink. "We don't even know if he's going to sign the contract."

"Oh," Lucy said confidently, "he will."

CHAPTER FIVE

Brian awoke the next morning from the haze of a dream heavily laden with the images of Lucy in various provocative and compromising situations. Whether it was because Lucy stole her appearance directly from Brian's subconscious or she intentionally used some kind of Devil magic to burrow her way into his dreams, he wasn't sure. Both notions were equally unsettling. He shook the last clinging cobwebs of sleep from his head and made his way to the lavatory. After a quick shower and perusal through the wardrobe for some of the nicest clothes Brian had ever seen, he grabbed the marked-up contract and opened the door of his room to find Lucy standing there, admiring the view of the fountain below. An unintentional shiver went speeding down his spine as her unexpected presence prompted a brief flash of his nighttime run-in with her.

"I know that sound," she said, turning to face Brian with a wide, devilish smile. "You had dreams about me."

There was no point in lying about it; he could feel the heat emanating from his cheeks already.

"It's your own fault. You were the one who decided to dress up in a fantasy I didn't even know was up there."

Lucy looked slightly different. Her hair was a shade lighter than it had been the day before and her eyes were more blue than gray. Her outfit was still professional but less authoritative. She wore a tight black turtleneck dress with a thin leather belt cinching her midsection. More skin was covered but it felt no less provocative than her earlier ensemble.

"I have that effect on people. When I turn up looking like their wildest fantasies they didn't know they had, I leave a lasting impression."

She leaned in and shimmied her breasts onto his arm. "And just in case you're wondering, when I take a form for someone, I'm a custom fit in all the right places." She shot a wink at Brian and puckered her lips. "So, you can fantasize all you want about what I've got under this... turtleneck?"

Lucy's last few words seemed to indicate that she had just noticed what clothes she had transformed into.

Brian slipped his arm from the trap of her breasts and began to walk down the hallway.

"Forgive me if I don't find the prospect of getting off to the thought of the *literal* Devil overly enticing."

He hoped that Lucy hadn't noticed the redness in his cheeks intensify before turning away from her and making for the stairs. His hopes were dashed upon the sound of Lucy's venomous giggle.

"Look who's all 'Mister Big-Shot' this morning," she said as she quickly caught up to him. "Where were those cojones yesterday, mister?"

"I'm well rested, and I looked over the contract you gave me." He held up the pages. "I have some conditions," he said confidently.

Brian tried his best to remove all the unnecessary elements from the equation, fantastical or otherwise. All that mattered was that he was in the midst of a business transaction, one that would put him in the running to succeed the current CEO. This was terminology that Brian was comfortable with.

"Conditions, huh?" Lucy echoed skeptically. "Any one in particular?"

"Yes, actually," Brian said as he stopped at the door that led to the courtyard walkway.

He flipped open the contract to a page that was marked furiously with pen. He turned the page to face Lucy and handed it to her.

"This section here states that I will receive ownership and leadership of Hell once my role has been completed in full."

"Yeah...."

"Yet, nowhere in the contract does it state the definition of 'in full'. When do I know when I've completed this project of yours – how do

I measure satisfaction in order to track progress? With wording like that I could be working on this project for centuries and not get anywhere."

"How thorough," Lucy replied.

She flipped through the pages of the contract, taking note of the changes Brian had made along the way. "The other amendments I see pertain specifically to that lack of definition." She flipped the pages shut and handed them back to Brian. "Is it fair to say that, provided we make those adjustments, we have a deal?"

Brian looked at Lucy. He searched her face for a hint of deception. He had gotten used to looking for dishonesty in people when working with bigger companies, and the same applied in this situation. However, the only thing Brian could see in Lucy's eyes was anticipation.

"Provided that you make the changes I've requested in here, then yes, we have a deal."

"Excellent!" Lucy exclaimed. "What do you say to a seventy-percent increase in productivity as a meter stick for this little venture of ours?"

"Seventy percent? Seems steep." Brian thought on the contract's contents and how little it conveyed of the actual requirements he was shouldering. "Thirty-five."

"Fifty."

"Done," Brian said. Whatever the project, he was confident enough in his abilities that a fifty-percent increase would be manageable.

Lucy reached over to Brian's sport jacket and opened it to pull the pen from his breast pocket. She handed him the pen with a smile.

Brian's brow furrowed. "I said when the changes have been made."

"They have been," Lucy said. "Go ahead, take a look."

Brian flipped through the contract and saw that his pen markings had vanished. He scanned the pages and saw every single one of his amendments had been printed into the pages, including the fifty-percent target that was just discussed.

He looked up from the pages to see Lucy with an amused smile on her face.

"I hope I don't have to explain to you *how* I changed the contract that quickly."

THE DEVIL'S ADVISOR • 31

"Devil magic?" joked Brian.

"Something like that."

Lucy re-presented the pen to Brian, who took it and flipped over to the last page of the contract.

There was a dotted line underneath his name with another one underneath Lucy's name. She decided to call herself 'Lucy Fair' on paper.

"Don't I need to sign in blood or something?" Brian asked as he put the paper up to the wall and signed on the line.

"Are you kidding? That would be a health and safety nightmare." Lucy stepped forward and took the pen from Brian after he signed. "We already have enough— You know what? You'll find out soon enough."

She signed her name, clicked the pen closed, and smoothly placed it back in Brian's blazer pocket.

"Let's get started, shall we?"

★ ★ ★

Brian and Lucy walked through the double doors from the courtyard into the foyer. Dallas was sitting in the waiting room, thumbing through something on his phone.

"Good morning!" Dahlia's perky tone greeted them from behind the receptionist desk.

She smiled brightly at Brian. Her hair was done up in a loose bun. Dirty-blonde waves fell from the bun in an intentionally messy manner. She wore a burgundy long-sleeve shirt more akin to workout clothing than business attire. Brian smiled back at her.

"Morning," he replied.

"Sleep well?"

"Surprisingly, yes," Brian said, trying to figure out how much sleep he got.

There were no clocks anywhere and Brian's attention since arriving was occupied by various other things. The Devil at his side. The stark realization that he despised his career. The girl in front of him.

From the corner of his eye, Brian thought he could see Lucy smirking.

Dallas glanced up from his phone upon hearing the exchange and quickly got to his feet. He wore a simple gray casual suit and loafers, looking like he was more suited to board a yacht than work in an office.

"So? What's the verdict?" he asked as Brian approached.

Lucy smiled and handed Dallas the freshly signed contract.

"He's part of the family now," Lucy said.

Dallas chortled congratulations to Brian and gave him an awkward shoulder hug that was entirely too forceful.

"I need you to take those down to Records while I show Brian around the office," Lucy said.

With a nod and a friendly shoulder jab to Brian, Dallas turned and walked toward a large set of double doors opposite Dahlia's desk.

"'The family'?" Brian repeated mockingly.

"Big and happy, with squabbles a'plenty," Lucy said. "So, what do you want to see first? Where we punish the wicked? Where all the aborted fetuses go?" Her face twisted to illustrate the ridiculousness of her words.

"Do you have a Finance department?" Brian said flatly.

Lucy's teasing face dropped and was replaced with curiosity. "We do. Why there?" she asked.

"You suggested yesterday that Hell was in some kind of economic trouble. I'd like to get a picture of that from the source."

"Straight to business, huh? So, you're not curious about the... you know, *damnation* part of Hell?" Lucy seemed surprised and a little disappointed.

"I am, but that can come later. If I'm going to be running this place one day, I'll have to learn about everything eventually. Right now, however, I am your Business Advisor, right?"

He looked at Lucy, eyes filled with a passion he seemed to reclaim overnight. Not for her, but for his work.

Lucy motioned with her hand toward the door that Dallas had exited through.

"Right this way, then," she said.

★   ★   ★

The door opened and Brian stepped through. A familiar feeling of hot silk tickled his face before he found himself in a small office with twelve out-of-date, boxy computers, six on either side of the room. At the opposite end was another door with a small frosted-glass window. At each computer sat a person. Rather, they were humanoid, but they *felt* different. Brian finally understood what Dahlia meant when she attempted to describe Hellions to him. They looked like people; they had arms and legs; they had faces and bodies. They also wore clothing but, upon looking at them, Brian couldn't help but think he was being made to *see* humans while something else entirely different pulled their strings behind the façade.

"Boys and girls," Lucy said, getting everyone's attention, "this is Brian."

They all looked at Brian, though he thought he could feel them looking at him well before their eyes moved in his direction. He raised his hand and waved weakly at the Hellions.

"Brian has come on board to help us get Hell running a little smoother."

Lucy glanced sideways at Brian and nudged him with her elbow.

"Right," Brian said, prompted from the unease he felt around the Hellions. "I'm excited to work with all of you and learn from you what I can."

Brian hoped that the quiver in his voice wasn't too noticeable. Then again, he felt like he'd been put on display in every way since being pushed through the doors the day before. What was one more foible?

"How reassuring. Deborah," Lucy said, waving over one of the workers in the back. "Deborah runs our Finance department. She can give you a good run-down on how things work down here."

The Hellion named Deborah walked over to Lucy and Brian. She looked to be in her mid- to late thirties with a shoulder-length dark bob and honey-brown eyes that felt closer to holographics than real irises.

She was petite and wore a dark blue and white polka-dotted dress, as though she were plucked directly from the seventies.

"Pleasure to meet you, Brian," Deborah said and extended her hand.

Her voice was soft but Brian could swear that he heard a slightly lower-pitched voice overlaying it.

"Same to you," Brian said uneasily.

As he took Deborah's hand, she gripped his firmly. Firmer than he was expecting, and certainly firmer than any handshake he'd ever had. She released her grip and smiled pleasantly. Brian attempted to dampen any unnecessary uneasiness by taking things to his playing field.

"So, Deborah, from what Lucy's told me, Hell runs on some kind of energy produced by souls. I'm going to need a crash course in damnation economics."

Deborah nodded and smiled politely. "It's not too difficult a concept to grasp. I'll do what I can to help."

She motioned for Brian to follow her back to her computer.

Brian walked over and crouched next to Deborah's desk.

"Why don't you have a seat?" she said, motioning to a desk chair that had not been there a moment ago.

Brian looked at Lucy as she snickered at his surprise.

"I'm never going to get used to that," he said and pulled the seat closer to see Deborah's screen.

"Now, as you described, all of Hell is made possible from the spiritual energy that's extracted from souls."

Deborah clicked her mouse a few times and opened an empty pie graph.

"When humans are born, their souls are of neutral standing. As they grow and develop, they delve into acts of altruism or acts of corruption. When a human commits certain acts that are deemed undesirable by their society, a portion of their soul is assigned at death to Hell." Deborah clicked a few more times and the pie graph filled in with slices of color. "Gray slices are the parts of the soul that remain neutral. Red slices are the percentages that are assigned to Hell, and blue are the percentages that go to Heaven."

"So, Heaven works on the same system as this?" Brian interjected. He looked back at Lucy, who shrugged in response.

"It's been a long time since I've seen their operation. They get their designated percentage but I couldn't tell you how they use it," Lucy said.

He stared at the pie graph for a moment while he digested the concept of souls having a numerical value.

"How is each percentage calculated?" he asked.

"Each percentage is based on actions taken by the specific party. Murder, theft, genocide, all of it carries a weighting based on the individual's average life span in their area of living."

Brian blinked hard in disbelief. "Wait, you're telling me that you have a way to measure the weight of any given sin based only on statistical averages? Don't you have some way of knowing what an individual's life span is?"

"Not here," Deborah replied.

"Then in which department?"

"None of them," Lucy said, seeming disappointed.

Brian looked up at her with curiosity. Lucy crossed her arms over her chest and shifted her weight.

"Death and her Reapers are the only ones who can access an individual's exact life span," she said.

Brian stared at her blankly for a moment trying to understand what she had said. "Is that another department?"

Lucy paused, pursing her lips as if being scolded. "Not exactly," she said finally.

"And why are we not able to get that information?" Brian pushed.

"The only interaction we have with Death these days is essentially the same as getting a check in the mail for the soul percentages we're due from humans," Deborah explained. "We used to work closely with the office of Death, but—"

"But we don't now," Lucy said simply.

Brian felt like he could cut the tension with a knife, provided one materialized from thin air like the chair he sat in. He thought he would drop it for the time being.

"So, who comes up with what each action is worth in soul percentage?" Brian asked Lucy, attempting to change the subject and bring her back to the conversation.

"The Actuarial department," Lucy replied. She seemed to appreciate the attempt to change focus.

She motioned to the door on the opposite wall.

Brian smiled. "Thank you for the info, Deborah. I still have a lot more questions but it might be a better idea to get a broad overview of the operation before I delve into specifics."

He stood from his seat, which he was annoyingly surprised to notice was no longer there.

Deborah nodded curtly before returning to her screen.

"I can already feel that brain of yours working away," Lucy said. "What are you thinking?"

"That there's money being left on the table if we don't have exact numbers to work with. I'll know more when we talk with the actuaries," Brian replied.

"Best prepare yourself," Lucy advised. "No one really visits them, and for good reason."

Brian threw a curious look back at her as they made their way down the short row of computers. "How bad could they be?"

"Your funeral," Lucy said with a snicker.

CHAPTER SIX

The pair entered the small office at the end of the Finance department. Inside, only two Hellions were present. They sat at respective desks on opposite sides of the office. Stacks of paper were piled high from the ground, rising past the height of the desks.

"Gentlemen," Lucy said as they entered the room.

The Hellions did not stop their work. Their heads remained buried in the papers on their desks.

"This is Brian. He will be helping us out from here on." The Hellions grunted in response. "Brian, these are the Twins."

Brian looked to the men working frantically at their desks. After learning what the Hellions were, he couldn't help but wonder what sort of thing these men would have sold their souls for.

"We're not twins," the one on the right shouted with a Cockney British accent.

"We've got names," the one on the left shouted with the same accent.

"That's not the point, you twat, we're not rela'ed," the first one yelled at the second.

"Aye, and we still 'ave names, ya cunt," the second one yelled back.

Brian tried to hide his genuine astonishment at the exchange he witnessed.

"Boys, play nice now," Lucy warned.

The pair grumbled once more and returned to their work.

"The one on the right is Peter and the one on the left is Paul. We call them the Twins because they're both assholes. Also, they look alike." Lucy motioned with her hand as she introduced them respectively.

"Sod off, ya bloody witch," Peter yelled.

"Oh, she's a woman to ya now, ay Peter? Last time you saw 'er she was a dog, wasn't she?" Paul yelled back at Peter.

"On'y cus I was thinkin' a' your mum." The pair of them began giggling like school boys.

Watching them bicker, Brian saw how their familial relations could be confused. Aside from the obvious behavioral similarities, physically, they were both stout with dark hair and dark eyes. It would be easy to mistake one for the other.

"Nice to meet you, gents," Brian said to the Twins. "I was hoping you could help me understand some things."

Neither of the Twins responded. Lucy rolled her eyes.

Lucy forcefully cleared her throat, followed by a vicious glare at the Hellions.

The Twins finally looked up from their desks with disgruntled expressions on their faces.

"I said play nice," Lucy said.

The Twins both directed their dissatisfaction to Brian now. This wasn't the first time Brian had to deal with difficult employees. He just wasn't sure how much he could push when dealing with literal residents of Hell. He decided to take the friendlier road first and see where that led him.

"You fellas look like you've got a lot on your plate," Brian said.

"Wha' you talkin' 'bout?" Paul said sarcastically, "this 'ere is jus' a walk inna park, ay, Peter?"

Peter rolled his eyes.

"Yeah, lovely day at the beach," he added.

Okay, unfriendlier path then.

"I bet you could cut your work down by at least half if you pulled your heads out of each other's asses once in a while." Brian fired a warning shot – a declaration that he could play, too.

Lucy choked in the background as the Twins' looks became noticeably more putrid. Peter seemed as though he was about to rebut, likely with something much viler, now that the first stone had been thrown. Brian didn't give him the chance.

"What would you say if I could lower the amount of work you do, so as to maintain your current head-to-ass locale?" Brian asked.

Peter and Paul looked annoyed. Brian assumed that they wanted nothing more than to spit horrendous things in his direction, but they also didn't want to lose the possibility of less work. The two glanced at each other for the briefest of moments and returned their seemingly omnidirectional eyes to Brian.

"Awright, Nancy, watchu got?" Peter said, his words laden with skepticism.

Brian held back a smirk of satisfaction – *can't show them any weakness now.*

"First, I need to know *how* you do your adjudications."

The two scoffed as if Brian had told an off-color joke.

"Supposed to be simple, innit?" Peter started.

"Supposed to be tha' each time some 'einous act is commi'ed, it's assigned a value," Paul continued.

"On'y prollum is tha' you lot seem to think up new an' exci'in ways to fuck wiv people," Peter finished.

Brian considered. "Give me an example," he asked.

The Twins burst with laughter. Brian imagined that if the two were close enough, their outburst would involve much more knee-slapping and shoulder-hugging.

"Awright, Einstein. Murder," Peter said. "Murder is straight fo'ward, right?"

Brian shrugged. Murder seemed like a simple enough concept to grasp. "Sure, I suppose."

Paul smirked nastily. "Now, would you say that murder wiv a gun is worse than murder wiv yer fists?" he posed. "What about when it's a man who's been murdered? Or a woman? Or a child?"

"Each murder 'as elements. Each element 'as variables. Each variable 'as a value," Peter clarified.

"Add in drugs an' alcohol, times o' war, and mental illness. 'Murder' gets fucked two ways to Sunday."

"And you two adjudicate each case?" Brian asked. "*By hand?*"

The Twins puffed out their chests proudly. "Ev'ry single one," they replied in unison.

Brian figured that this was the first time that anyone had ever considered how much work they do and how ridiculous of a task it was. Their pride was noted, yet disregarded.

"That is incredibly inefficient," Brian stated simply.

The Twins deflated slightly at the jab. Their faces went cherry red.

"You can do it better, ay?" Peter asked. He seemed very perturbed that their hard work had come under fire.

"Nope," Brian replied calmly, "but *you two* definitely could." Brian walked over and snatched a file each from Peter and Paul's stacks. "With the right equipment and motivation. You don't mind if I have a look at these, right?"

He turned on his heel and walked toward the door.

The pair were fuming. *Good.*

"What sort of budget do we have for office equipment?" Brian asked Lucy as she turned to walk out with him.

She shrugged. "Good question. I don't think we've bought office equipment in decades," she replied, seemingly carefree of the inefficiencies.

Brian shook his head in disbelief. "How has this place stayed running all this time?" he asked.

Lucy snorted. "Your guess is as good as mine. Hell is home to depraved hedonists. What sort of workforce do you think that makes for?"

Brian chuckled, offering his arm to Lucy as the two exited the office.

★   ★   ★

The door to the foyer shut behind Brian and Lucy as they walked in with arms still linked. They walked past the reception desk and Brian smiled at Dahlia. She returned his smile with a dead stare. Her eyes flicked from his to the arm linked to Lucy's at his side, and then back to her work. It was an awkward exchange but maybe she was just busy. He couldn't imagine what sort of administration requirements Hell had. He found it so absurd that the underworld staffed regular office workers. Well, office Hellions. *Hellions....*

"Hey, I was meaning to ask—"

"What the Hellions are?" Lucy said.

He frowned at having his mind read again. "Yeah. They look human, except...different."

"Hellions used to be humans who sold their souls," she said and stepped forward.

"I thought everyone's soul belongs partially to Hell. At least, based on how much it's corrupted?"

"True, but Hellions are the rare few that sell their entire soul's worth for a specific goal. When you get a full soul, you basically get a whole person. What you see of them is just a projection of what they used to look like."

"So they're kind of like ghosts?" Brian asked.

Lucy shrugged nonchalantly. "Kind of, but 'Hellion' sounds cooler, don't you think?"

Admittedly, Hellion *did* sound cooler.

Lucy walked over and sat on a chair in the waiting area. Brian sat in a seat adjacent to her. She looked Brian up and down.

"That was fairly impressive," she stated.

Brian's brow raised in confusion. "What was?"

"The way you handled the Twins. Not many people know how to work with those two. That's why they're all on their own."

"I've seen all sorts when dealing with the businesses I've dealt with. I've developed a knack for knowing how to break down walls and, in the event that I can't, scaling them instead."

A smug smile crossed Lucy's lips. "I knew you would be good at this. So, what did you get out of our little field trip?"

Brian paused and considered what he had learned. The value of a soul's corruption. The judgment of heinous actions. *Death.*

"There's a lot more that I need to understand," Brian finally replied. "But first things first. At least in the departments I've seen, there are clear gaps in efficiency that can be closed. Provided, of course, that we have the funding to do so." Brian's brow furrowed at the thought of funding. "How does the energy gathered from corrupted souls work as currency?"

Lucy crossed her legs and leaned back in her seat.

"The energy is banked in a single point and is repurposed and redistributed for whatever we need here. Everything you see came from using soul energy." Lucy motioned with her hand in a loose gesture to the entirety of the foyer.

"So, the chair thing," Brian asked, starting to put pieces together, "happens when soul energy is repurposed to materialize a physical object. Then when it de-materializes the energy returns to the original bank?"

Lucy's eyelids dropped and her eyebrow rose into a pleased, yet sultry, look.

"Very good, I'm impressed."

Brian was too lost in thought to notice her look.

"Who has control over this energy?"

"Everyone, pretty much," Lucy said, eyes drifting up in thought. "I don't like micromanaging, so Hellions having access to the bank is handy when keeping the paperwork under control."

"You mentioned that you were in a bit of a financial crisis. I don't understand how that can be if anything that is created by the soul energy is recyclable. How can you be running out of energy with a steady flow coming in?"

Lucy sighed. "It's not just physical objects that require the energy. The existence of everyone in Hell is dependent on that energy. Mine included."

That was it.

"The salary of the personnel is more than the business can sustain. Options are to: a) lower the salary, b) downsize the workforce to create balance, or c) increase revenue to sustain the current personnel and salary." Brian spoke as if he were reading a textbook.

This was something he had seen many times before. Each option available was a difficult one.

"Problem is, the 'salary', as you call it, is non-negotiable. The Hellions, me, Dahlia, Dallas – we don't die, and most of us don't require additional sustenance. There is no less that we can accept without it impacting…let's call it our 'quality of life'."

Options b or c, then.

Brian went silent as he considered the outcomes. Increasing revenue would be the most ideal scenario but that would involve a further look into the operations of Hell. It would also mean actively pursuing the corruption and damnation of human souls. A momentary moral dilemma flashed in his mind – one he quickly compartmentalized for later. He was having too much fun to get sidelined by nitpicking. However, the thought of further delving into the inner workings of Hell suddenly made Brian realize how worn out he felt. Realization dawned that he hadn't eaten anything since first arriving and had slept only a few precious hours the night prior after amending his contract. At least, he thought it was a few hours. Brian was finding it difficult to grasp on to the sense of time in Hell. He felt as though he had only just begun and yet his body screamed like he had been working nonstop for days on end.

"Like I said, there's a lot more that I need to understand before I can create a complete strategy to act on. Before that happens, I need to eat something," Brian said, succumbing to the pang in his stomach.

"Right, I forgot you still need to do that." Lucy uncrossed her legs and stood. "Why don't you take the rest of the day and get some rest. I'm sure the files you took from the Twins will keep you busy if you still want to push forward."

She started toward her office at the end of the foyer.

"Tell Dahlia what supplies you need. She'll make sure they're ordered."

Brian nodded silently and slowly rose to his feet. The doors to Lucy's office closed behind her as Brian reached the receptionist's desk where Dahlia sat, staring into the contents of her phone.

"Hey, Dahlia," Brian said.

"Hi," Dahlia replied.

"So, I can order supplies with you?" he asked. Dahlia hadn't looked up from her phone at all.

"Nope," she said bluntly.

He recoiled. "Okay, why not?"

"Busy." Dahlia stood and walked around the desk. "Besides, I don't think I'm going to have what you're looking for."

Brian watched as her body swayed down the foyer toward the double doors that led to wherever they needed to.

"Right," he said to himself as she disappeared through the doors, white flame swallowing up her silhouette.

CHAPTER SEVEN

Lucy entered her room at the top of the stairs from her office. Her mind was buzzing with the excitement of watching Brian work. It was impressive how quickly he latched on to the concepts of Hell. Though it was still early, she had to admit that Dallas had made a good call when he gave her Brian's file. She made her way into the lounge on the other side. She crossed the floor, tugged open a door, and stepped into a small rectangular room.

From the ceiling hung an intricate and impressively large chandelier. The light that glittered through the crystal shimmered down onto a black and white marble floor. Two padded benches upholstered in burgundy velvet sat parallel to one another in the center of the room. The walls were adorned with paintings. Lavish golden frames captured Baroque scenes on the walls. Lucy loved Baroque and took full advantage of her position as the Devil to commission several pieces from Caravaggio when he was still alive. The paintings here were of nothing and no one in particular, aside from one – the only Renaissance piece she owned. The bright colors against the heavy contrast of the other pieces made it feel as though it illuminated the room with a sfumato glow. The piece was the only thing she commissioned from Leonardo da Vinci – she couldn't justify any more from him. Keeping his work private was a disservice to the man's brilliance. The painting was titled *The Snake and the Maiden* and depicted the fabled story of Eve accepting the forbidden fruit from the Devil. The only difference was that it depicted the snake as a woman. With a head of fiery red hair and her lean, porcelain figure draped in liquid smoke, she extended the apple to Eve. Cradled in both hands and extending from her breast as if it were her own heart, the apple was the most vibrantly colored part of the painting.

As Lucy crossed the gallery her eyes lingered on the apple. It called to her as it had thousands of times before but the sting it elicited dulled with every passing. Nostalgia, in its purest definition.

The hallway made a ninety-degree turn to the right and ended with two doors facing one another on either side. Lucy came to a halt at the door on the left and gently rapped her knuckles on the wood. After a few moments, the door opened up and Dallas appeared in the gap.

His eyebrows rose at the sight of Lucy.

"This is a surprise," he started. "Is everything okay?"

"More than," Lucy said, tilting her head past his figure and into the room beyond. "Can I come in?"

Dallas shot a nervous glance over his shoulder and back to Lucy.

"Now isn't a great time," he said.

The corner of Lucy's mouth curled into a suspicious grin.

"The gallery, then. Five minutes."

★   ★   ★

Lucy sat on one of the benches with her leg crossed over her knee. Her gaze swung from frame to frame, all the while ignoring da Vinci's brushstrokes practically clawing at her back for attention.

"So, to what do I owe the pleasure?" Dallas asked, announcing his arrival in the gallery.

Lucy swung her legs so she could face Dallas.

"Believe it or not, I came to thank you," she replied.

Dallas's face scrunched in confusion as he took a seat on the bench opposite Lucy.

"You're welcome?" he said. "What for?"

"Credit where credit is due, you made a good judgment call with Brian."

Dallas's face relaxed. "So, the pup has had his first field test, then?"

Lucy paused, feeling the sharp edge of Dallas's words.

"He did. With a little more exposure and time, I think he will do very well."

She watched him go rigid as the conversation proceeded.

"Well, that's disappointing," Dallas muttered.

"You realize I'm trying to give you credit for this, right? This is a win for you."

"It's the opposite, actually."

Lucy's confusion mixed with annoyance on her face as she straightened her posture on the bench.

"You know, you're making it very difficult for me to retain the sliver of desire I had to give you some positive reinforcement. Want to tell me who pissed in your cereal this morning?"

Dallas mimicked his mother's posture correction while running his fingers through his hair. He took in a deep breath and let it out in a huff.

"This was supposed to help me prove a point."

"I don't have time to play twenty questions – say what you mean."

"Brian wasn't supposed to be an actual viable solution to your retirement. He was supposed to prove to you that no human can do what you do."

Lucy groaned in exasperation. She perched an elbow against her knee, and rested her forehead in her open palm.

"Dallas, I have been doing this longer than I care to admit—"

"—And I'm not saying you don't deserve to retire. You've done your time and deserve some of your own now. All I'm saying is that the legacy that you leave behind shouldn't be left to a human. Brian was supposed to show you that even the most qualified and capable human still isn't up to the monumental task of ruling Hell."

Lucy was tired of this argument. She and Dallas had it almost monthly recently. It was the same each time, and the repetition was beginning to bore her.

"Look, how many times have I read *The History of Hell*?" Dallas pressed, seemingly sensing his mother's building annoyance.

"More times than me. That hardly makes you qualified to take over in my stead."

"I beg to differ. I know what Hell is. I know what Hell used to be. I know what Hell needs to be again," Dallas retorted, his words being carried by a palpable heat. "Hell isn't bureaucracy and paper pushing. Hell is damnation."

"This isn't the old days. The Hell you are so infatuated with was a symptom of the times. A chaotic pit of despair and eternal damnation is only functional up to a point. The amount of humans we had back then was only a tiny fraction of the population of today. If we want to survive, we need to change, not regress."

"Or is it that you just don't trust me to do it right?" Dallas spat back.

A flame ignited in Lucy's chest at the question. This was Dallas's problem – when he got emotional, all sight of logic was lost and he became childish. In a way he was right: Lucy didn't trust him to run things properly, and this was exactly the reason why – but that was hardly the point.

"I came here to congratulate you on a job well done for once. I didn't come to start an argument. You and I have talked about this before, at very great length. I didn't change my mind then, I won't change my mind now. Grow the fuck up and get on board or get out of the goddamn way."

Lucy rose to her feet and made for the other end of the gallery. It was rare that her temper flared up these days but it never failed to be her children that brought it out when it resurfaced.

As Lucy disappeared from sight, Dallas stood rooted to the spot. His body trembled with rage and his skin stretched tight across his face and knuckles. His fingernails dug into the flesh of his palms as he shot daggers after Lucy, each one cued by the climbing beat of his heart.

CHAPTER EIGHT

Brian made his way back to his room, where he found what looked to be a Room Service menu and telephone sitting on his bedside table. His hunger was in no mood to peruse a selection of items, so Brian ordered a cheeseburger and French fries, which happened to be the first thing on the menu.

There was a knock at his door as he hung up the phone and he was greeted by a Hellion pushing a lobby cart.

The Hellion was a mousey young man, probably in his early twenties, wearing proper bellhop attire. He was lean, almost fragile-looking, with a mess of brown curls under his hat.

"Room service," he squeaked when Brian opened the door.

Brian moved out of the doorway and extended his arm to invite the boy in. He couldn't take his eyes off him. It seemed such an odd concept for Hell to have hotel services. How often could they possibly host guests? The boy lifted the lid of the platter and the room filled with the aroma of fresh, hot food. Brian's body shivered at the sight of the meal but his curiosity got the better of him.

"What's your name?" Brian asked.

The boy lifted his gaze from the lobby cart looking very surprised. "Me, sir?" he replied.

Even with his Hellion dual-toned voice, he still sounded nervous.

"Well, there's no one else here, is there?" Brian jabbed and then immediately thought of the possibility of someone else *actually* being in his room without his knowing. The boy looked sheepishly around the room. "Jeremy," he said.

Brian wondered what he was so worried about. He smiled warmly and extended his hand to Jeremy.

"I'm Brian."

Jeremy hesitated again briefly before taking Brian's hand for a fraction of a second and recoiling.

"Tell me, Jeremy," Brian said as he made his way to the lobby cart, "how many people do you think are in the hotel?"

He grabbed a French fry and took a satisfying, salty bite while waiting for the response.

Jeremy's head shook like a frail branch in a stiff breeze.

"Th-there's no hotel, sir. You're the only one," Jeremy replied. "This tower was constructed specifically for your stay." He answered as though he were being asked a trick question.

Brian's brow furrowed at the response.

"Why do you have a bellhop outfit and lobby cart, then?" he pushed.

Jeremy's body remained tense.

"I guess because we have to look the part, sir. It's good practice."

Brian still didn't understand. He grabbed another French fry and took a bite, talking between his chews.

"What do you mean 'look the part'? Who is 'we'? The Hellions?"

Jeremy shook his head in the same manner as before.

"Not all of us, sir. Just the Reps."

Brian simply replied with a curious glance.

"Reps – representatives – are Hellions who go back and forth to the human world. They are the ones who meet with humans to make contracts for souls and to influence the corruption of souls."

It was a very matter-of-fact response. Jeremy looked down at his clothing.

"We take on whatever appearance we need to make deals. We can be anything."

Brian couldn't help but notice Jeremy's repetitive use of the word 'we'.

"So, you're a Rep, then?" Brian assumed.

Jeremy nodded nervously.

"In training, sir."

That explained Jeremy's nerves. He considered what Jeremy had said as he reached for a few more French fries that were suffering the impending fate of room temperature. Brian couldn't shake the feeling that Jeremy's unsureness seemed out of place.

"Can I ask a personal question?" Brian said gently.

Jeremy looked up at him with a wide-eyed stare. "Sir?"

"How long have you been here? In Hell, I mean," Brian asked, unintentionally keeping his voice low.

Jeremy swallowed hard. "Three months," he replied.

Brian exhaled hard; he needed to know more.

"What happened? I mean how did you become a Hellion? How does it work?"

Jeremy's face began to turn scarlet.

"I sold my soul," he said bluntly. "I met a Rep at school. He brought me here and I sold it. I vowed eternal servitude upon my death."

"What did you sell it for?"

Brian was sure that he'd crossed a line at that point. Anyone who felt strongly enough about something to sell their soul for it might be protective of it. He was about to recant his question when he was stopped short by Jeremy.

"A girl. She went to the same school as me."

Went.

The past tense made Brian cringe.

"What happened?"

"I asked for her to fall in love with me," Jeremy said, a quiver in his dual voices. "And it worked."

Silent tears started rolling down his rosy cheeks. Jeremy smiled an unsteady, nostalgic smile.

"I was so happy. *We* were so happy."

Brian's heart tightened as Jeremy spoke. If he owed his servitude upon his death, Brian knew there wasn't a happy ending to the story.

"What happened, then?"

Brian almost didn't want to know the answer.

Tears rolled faster and larger down Jeremy's cheeks. He wiped them with the sleeve of his bellhop uniform.

"There was an accident. We were driving home from our third date. It was a drunk driver."

Jeremy's chest began to heave silently. Brian understood now why Jeremy stood in front of him.

"You both died in the accident?" Brian assumed.

Jeremy shook his head frantically.

Brian's heart sank.

"Jesus Christ. She died in the accident," Brian started.

Then what, Jeremy died of a broken heart? Of guilt? No, the truth felt closer, and far simpler than any of that. "You killed yourself after."

Jeremy's body went still. He was no longer heaving or quivering. The tears had stopped. His head hung down from his tensed shoulders. Suddenly, the young man in front of Brian wearing the bellhop outfit wasn't a resident of Hell. He wasn't some eternal creature. He was just a kid.

"The worst part is that I'm reminded of what I've lost every single day." Jeremy's words were filled with such sorrow.

Brian could swear he also heard resentment between the notes of his speech.

"Something like that would be hard to forget."

"No," Jeremy said. The resentment started to rise in his voice. "I'm reminded of what I've lost every day I see *her*."

Lucy.

She takes the form of whatever her perceiver desires.

"Oh my god," Brian said.

He didn't have any words for Jeremy's story. The tension in his chest refused to subside. It was as though he could feel Jeremy's emotions in his own body.

Jeremy, it seemed, had enough of telling his story.

"Enjoy your meal, sir," he said bluntly.

He lost his nervous demeanor and headed for the door.

"Hey," Brian stopped him before exiting. "It was nice to meet you, Jeremy. I'm sorry for your loss."

He hesitated before completing his thought.

"Come by anytime. You know, if you feel like it."

Jeremy looked up at Brian. His eyes were wide with surprise. He stared for a moment and smiled a frail smile. He nodded and exited the room.

Brian turned to the lobby cart in his room with his now cold cheeseburger. Part of him wanted to say that he was in no mood to eat after his meeting with Jeremy, but his stomach screamed in protest at the very thought. Brian closed the door and devoured the cold meal.

★ ★ ★

After eating, Brian resumed his seat at the fire and took to the folders he'd pinched from the Twins. The information within detailed the profile of the soul, the actions that had corrupted it, and the varying circumstances around the actions. Brian could see how Peter and Paul would have so much trouble on some files – the complexities were numerous. They were, however, not impossible. Brian recalled software he'd seen used by insurance companies that could assist in adjudicating souls based on specific parameters set. This idea solidified just how important it was to get the equipment ordered.

A soft knock came from the door. Brian looked up from the folder sitting in his lap. He put it on the bedside table closest to him and crossed the hearth-warmed floor. He opened the door and found Dahlia waiting on the other side.

Her hair was fully down, cascading in relaxed waves. She'd also changed from her burgundy long sleeve into a tight white tank top and a loose-fitting black hoodie. The baggy parachute pants she wore did nothing to hide the curves underneath.

Brian's eyebrow rose at the sight of her.

"Funny, I was just thinking about you," he said, referring to being thwarted with his equipment ordering.

"Only good things I hope," she replied.

Brian wasn't sure how much of her comment was a jab and how much was sincere. It was hard to tell from her tone.

"Can't you tell? I thought you read minds," he replied in the safest way possible.

Dahlia shook her head slowly. "I can't do that. Mom is the only one around here that can."

Brian was relieved to hear it but still felt as though he should be cautious, just in case.

"Well, what can I do for you?" he asked.

She raised a large, frosted bottle up alongside two glasses.

"I came with a peace offering," she said. "I feel shitty with how I acted earlier."

Brian was surprised to hear her being so genuine with her reasoning. Amazing, the honesty you find in Hell.

He looked at her sympathetically.

"I appreciate the offer but I'm not a big drinker," he said.

She smiled and moved past him and into the room.

"I know," she said as she plopped down onto his bed, "it's ice water."

She placed the glasses on the bedside table that wasn't taken up with folders and poured two misty glasses of water.

Brian swallowed hard. His thirst screamed at him for forgetting it earlier among the burgers and suicide. He closed the door behind him as Dahlia extended a glass to him. He eagerly took it and tried not to drink it all in one gulp.

"So, there is ice water in Hell, huh?" he said, half joking, half thankful.

Dahlia chuckled. "I thought you'd like that," she replied as she sipped at her glass.

"How did you know I don't drink?" Brian asked.

"I read your file."

"Jesus – job satisfaction, drinking preferences, what else is in that file?" he asked sarcastically.

Dahlia put a finger to her chin, cocking her hip as she recalled what she saw.

"Loads of stuff. Blood type, childhood crushes, sexual history—"

"Please tell me you're joking," Brian said, nearly choking on his water.

Dahlia smirked devilishly, to which Brian couldn't help but be reminded of Lucy.

"Subject change. You're here to make peace? I didn't know we were...not at peace, I suppose," Brian said, attempting to lose the awkward tone in his voice.

"We weren't, I just overreacted," she said as she motioned for him to hand her his glass.

Brian obliged and sat on the bed next to her.

"Overreacted to what?"

"Seeing you all cozied up with Mom," she replied as she poured.

"Trust me, there's nothing there that you can call 'cozy', though I'm surprised you would care."

No sense in hiding the truth. He didn't quite trust her confession of lacking psychic abilities.

Dahlia shrugged and took another sip.

"It's not often we get new faces down here, and when we do, they're Hellions. Which, that is to say—"

"They're fairly unsettling faces to get, new or otherwise. I got that impression today."

Dahlia nodded and looked at him.

"I just didn't want you to get sucked into the void that is my mother. She has a way of doing that to people. I guess it's her nature."

"How do you mean?"

"She has a way with people – with their temptations. She is the purest of hedonists. Hell pretty much has parties every night, most of which end in her fucking half the guest list. Plus she's got the whole... changing-into-your-deepest-desire thing. Not many people can get around that kind of combination," Dahlia said, sounding slightly jealous. "I was just worried about losing an actual person I could get to know down here to her."

Brian shook his head. "It's just a costume that I'm looking at. I don't know what she...*it* really looks like. Besides, aren't you able to do the transformation thing too?" he asked, genuinely curious as to what powers she shared with her mother.

Dahlia cracked up slightly.

"Why, do I look like your deepest desire right now?" she said, motioning to her outfit before taking another sip.

Brian unintentionally scanned her up and down as she asked. The redness in his cheeks followed quickly after. He got up from the bed, suddenly very interested in the fireplace.

"So, she's a bit of a party animal, huh?" Brian said as he tried to force the blood out of his cheeks.

Dahlia smiled as Brian dodged her question. She took a sip of her water and reclined slightly on the bed.

"Understatement of the year. She's incredibly promiscuous as well, so if you actually have no interest, watch out. She's got her eye on you." She put her empty glass on the bedside table next to the bottle.

Brian laughed and turned to look at her.

"You're joking," he said in disbelief.

Dahlia shook her head. "You're new. She respects you. You're not a Hellion. Those are three major attributes that I can guarantee she's pining for."

"Good to know. Even better knowing she respects me. That means I can at least get some honesty out of her when it's necessary," Brian thought out loud.

He considered Lucy wanting him for reasons other than business matters being beneficial for their venture.

"Oh, she's always honest. Sometimes too much so."

"I don't know, she seemed pretty cagey today at the mention of Death," Brian replied.

Dahlia's head bobbed side to side, an unsure look on her face.

"That's a bit of a touchy subject. Mom and Death were something of an item way back when."

Curiosity got the better of him.

"How does that work?"

"You ever read the Bible?"

Brian shook his head.

"If I wanted fiction, I'd read Tolkien."

Dahlia nodded.

"Honestly, most of it is bullshit, from what I understand. What isn't, however, is how vengeful God was back in the old days. Plagues, floods, general flexes of power – God killed a lot of people, most of whom were deemed sinners." Dahlia took another sip before continuing, "That's how she and Mom got so close. They worked very closely with one another and, well, things happened, I guess."

Brian nodded along as Dahlia shared the story.

"So, what happened between them?"

"Population boom. Eventually, everyone got busier, Death takes sinners and saints alike, so the time she spent with Mom dwindled until, eventually, they just sort of became estranged to one another."

"That sounds depressing," Brian commented, taking a swig from his own frosty glass.

"Yeah, Mom never really got over it. Honestly, it's probably the reason why she's as promiscuous as she is. Just looking for something to fill the void."

Brian shuddered. "Please tell me that pun was unintentional."

Dahlia chuckled, downed her glass and stood from the bed.

"I never shy from a bad pun."

Dahlia held out her hand for Brian's glass. He drained it and handed it to her as she made her way to the door. She opened it and threw a sultry look over her shoulder.

"Well, this was fun." She left the room. "We should do this again. Thanks for the drink."

Brian followed after her.

"Apology accepted, by the way," he said teasingly.

He leaned against the doorway and watched her sway down the hallway.

"I'm forever grateful. Sweet dreams," she yelled back as she rounded the corner to the staircase down to the courtyard.

The hallway outside Brian's door was tinted orange as the sunset over the courtyard flooded in through the window. Brian found himself lingering in his doorway long after Dahlia had left. He realized that he was unconsciously waiting to see if he could catch a glimpse of her walking the courtyard. He wasn't lucky enough to see her swaying figure in the lush green below. Still, her words from the night before seemed to protrude once more from his mind.

It's not so bad here.

CHAPTER NINE

After Dahlia's visit, Brian couldn't seem to get back into the working mood. He was in need of a distraction. In an absurd dawning, Brian realized he had forgotten his phone was in the inside pocket of his blazer when he arrived in Hell. He hadn't seen the blazer since, but he got the sneaking suspicion that, if he concentrated enough, he would find it hanging in the wardrobe. As expected, the shabby article hung on a hook inside, and Brian searched his pockets, retrieving the phone. He unlocked it and glanced down at the screen. He had no bars, which wasn't at all surprising. What was, however, was the time displayed. By the looks of things, the internal clock of the phone must have malfunctioned, as it was only displaying thirteen minutes past when he was last in his office. Brian tapped into his calendar, just to be sure. His phone was still set to the same date Dallas had collected him.

Brian's mind flashed to Jeremy and their conversation earlier. He thought of Jeremy's personalized Hell every time he saw Lucy. The current of his mind took him to a dark stream where he considered how fitting of a personal Hell this would be – working with a client on a never-ending project. Never getting to close the book on it, never getting to move on from the mundanity that he was now acutely aware he despised – one that likely didn't care that he had disappeared from it. A world that Brian was feeling glad to be rid of, despite the handful of meaningful connections he'd left behind. Parents, the odd friend, a fish that Brian figured was surely dead at this point. Even Amanda, though, truth be told, he wasn't sure she would reciprocate the feeling.

The thought was enough to send shivers through his whole body. His phone, it turned out, was not an effective means of distraction. Instead, he decided to grab a shower and take a stroll out to the courtyard.

★   ★   ★

As he exited his room in anticipation of the crisp, fresh air, he caught sight of the courtyard below. More specifically, his gaze locked on to the sheer amount of people who gathered in pockets on the grassy section.

Brian was greeted by the sound of muffled conversations as he left the tower and stepped out onto the stone of the walkway. As he slowly made his way through to the courtyard, he realized that the people gathered were actually *people* and didn't have the same look as the Hellions he'd met earlier.

The sound of a familiar voice caught his attention, and he saw Lucy, laughing amidst the crowd closest to the fountain. Her look was drastically different from how Brian had seen her so far. A tight, black cocktail dress clung to her frame. A deep plunge neckline showed off the porcelain curves beneath. Her hair was pulled into an eloquent up-do that showed off the smoky shadow on her eyes and the vicious crimson on her lips.

As if she'd sensed that she had been spotted – which, in all likelihood, was a possibility – she smiled warmly at Brian and motioned him over. His face scrunched awkwardly as he made his way to her.

"What's all this?" he asked, arriving at Lucy's side.

"Just a little gathering of sorts," Lucy replied with a smile.

She introduced Brian to the three men she was conversing with; a DJ from California, a young politician, and a fairly famous actor Brian recognized from a slew of blockbusters, before excusing herself and taking Brian's arm.

As Brian looked closer, he began to notice familiar faces. The courtyard was filled with people in positions of power, celebrities, athletes, and everyone in between. Waiters made their way around, offering drinks and hors d'oeuvres to the attendees. Dahlia mentioned to Brian that Lucy had parties every night, but he never expected them to be cocktail socials.

"So, let me guess, these are all potential leads – people likely willing to sell their soul for some kind of personal gain?" Brian said softly as the pair made their way around the courtyard.

"Not all of them," Lucy answered. "Some have already sold their souls, others are potentials – some are just here because the invitation allowed for a plus one."

Her words were weighted by a slight slur. Brian looked at her with surprise.

"Are you drunk?" he asked in an excited whisper.

Lucy giggled breathily. "Only a little tipsy, but the night is young."

"How is it even possible for you to be tipsy?"

Lucy shrugged, grabbing a champagne flute from a passing server. "When I take a form, it's fully human. I can turn off the annoying bits of humanity like mortality and hunger, but inebriation and sex drive are perfect just the way they are."

She squeezed Brian's arm, emphasizing the end of her sentence. Brian was starting to see the truth behind Dahlia's earlier claim of Lucy's interest in him. He was also beginning to feel incredibly uncomfortable because of it.

"You need a drink," she said, reacting to Brian's stiffening demeanor. "There's champagne, wine, and beer out here. If you want the hard stuff, it's inside." She motioned to the double doors.

"Inside?" Brian asked.

Before he knew it, he was being dragged toward the foyer. A dull pounding sound started to rise as they got closer. Lucy pushed the doors open and a wave of sound hit Brian's eardrums hard.

Electronic dance music avalanched from inside. Dahlia's reception desk had been raised onto a platform and was being used as a DJ station for a bored, edgy-looking young man. The waiting area was completely gone and the ivory pillars that accented the room had somehow been converted into ivory dance poles encased by cages – each one sporting a different, yet similar-looking dancer in various stages of undress. Additional dancers were suspended from above on aerial hoops across the entirety of the room. Lights in various colors strobed across the ceiling and bathed the writhing crowd of dancers below. The doors to

Lucy's office were blocked by a pop-up bar where two tenders were stationed and frantically filling drink orders.

Brian's head swiveled in all directions, taking in the sights and sounds of the foyer-cum-nightclub. He reconsidered his cocktail party thought from earlier as he and Lucy made their way to the bar.

The crowd seemed to part as they moved through and arrived in front of the bartenders. Lucy snapped her fingers, which was surprisingly audible over the thrumming bass of the music. One of the bartenders turned around and greeted Lucy with a smile.

"Yes, madam?" he said kindly.

Lucy downed the remainder of her champagne flute and placed it on the bar.

"A martini – you know how I like them," Lucy said, quickly showing the signs of her last drink.

"And for the gentleman?" the bartender asked, gesturing to Brian.

"Water is fine," Brian said.

Lucy frowned. "That's no fun." She propped herself up on one elbow against the bar. "Have a drink with me."

The bartender placed a glass of ice water in front of Brian. He took it and tipped it to Lucy.

"I am," he said, smiling awkwardly before taking a sip.

Lucy's frown deepened along with the shade of red that flushed her cheeks. She plucked the martini glass from the tender and pulled it in for a swig.

"So, are all these people human or are there Hellions here too?" Brian asked as he took another sip.

Lucy snorted and shook her head. "No Hellions allowed. We might have a good working relationship, but they're still my employees, and they're definitely still damned." She turned to Brian. "Can't be fraternizing with the staff." She playfully walked her fingers up Brian's arm as she spoke.

Brian rolled his eyes and pulled away from the flirting, inebriated Devil.

"You were saying not everyone here is a potential lead for souls, so what's the occasion?" he asked.

A wry smile curled Lucy's lips as she glanced over the pulsating crowd. "Who needs an occasion?"

Brian's brow creased in response. "Not to be a buzz-kill—"

"Yet you're going to."

"—but how much of a drain is this on the bank?"

Lucy let loose an audible "ugh" at the question.

"I know this is Hell but that doesn't mean that *everyone* needs to be suffering. I'm allowed to have a little fun," she snapped and drained the martini glass in her hand.

Brian had seen this before – CEOs who were too wrapped up with their own pleasure to consider the impacts on their business. These kinds of self-indulgent habits were always the hardest to break, and straining on future relationships when they finally did.

"I get where you're coming from, but you hired me to do a job – this is me doing it." Brian directed her attention to the club behind him. "If all the people here aren't potentially offering you their souls, then they don't need to be here. Throw your parties, but have Hellions working the room. Round up additional contracts and make these soirees of yours bankable."

"Not everything has to be about work," Lucy said, nearly losing her martini glass as she raised it to the crowd beyond.

Brian sighed hard. Talking to Lucy while she was well on her way to being plastered was not the best way to be pitching business ideas.

"Look, I know you can turn off the feeling of being drunk. Can I ask you to hear me out for five sober minutes in your office?"

Lucy's eyebrow cocked at his request. She grabbed his hand and pulled him back in the direction of the bar. She waved at the tenders and they nodded, parting to either side of the pop-up, allowing Lucy to swing a section of the bar up to pass through.

Brian opened the door of Lucy's office, letting her slip through first. He shut the door behind them, immediately dulling the thumping of the music on the other side. As he released the handle and turned to face Lucy, he was pinned against the door with surprising strength.

Lucy smashed her lips into Brian's. Her breath was heavy as she kept Brian secured.

For a fraction of a second, Brian got carried away by her forwardness. However, the fraction passed and Brian pushed past the sweet taste of vanilla and honey on Lucy's lips. Summoning up a considerable amount of strength, he grabbed her shoulders and forced her off him.

She stumbled back, heels clumsily clacking against the marble floor. A glimpse of annoyance was quickly replaced by a coy eyebrow raise as Lucy's hands gingerly grasped the edges of her neckline, pulling her dress off her shoulders.

Brian quickly turned away, averting his gaze before the dress fell to the floor.

"This isn't why I wanted to talk to you in your office, Lucy," Brian said in a mixture of annoyance and pleading.

"I'm sure it's not what you had planned, but it's what you want, isn't it?" Lucy's words dripped like candle wax as the slow clack of her heels approached Brian's back.

Brian turned to face her before she could pin him against the door again. His face was stern and his eyes only met hers, which sported a look of surprise at the gesture.

"The real question isn't what I want. I'm trying to do my job – the job you hired me to do. If you really want to enjoy your retirement, things have to change. Throw your parties, but make them work for Hell. Make a profit, even a small one, on these kinds of gatherings. Have your fun, but do it in a way that still guarantees the continuance of Hell, and another chance for you to get alone in a room with who you *really* want to be with."

Brian wasn't sure whether it was his stern words, or the subtle mention of Death, but Lucy stepped back and turned away from him. She clicked her right heel down on the ground and the dress that had puddled on the floor where she stripped it off melted into the marble. She made a quick sweeping motion down her body with her hand and the dress reappeared on her body.

"Who told you?" Lucy demanded.

Brian's throat tightened. "Dahlia."

Silence lingered in the room for an eternal moment, prompting an acidic regret to bubble in Brian's chest.

"Fine," Lucy said, still facing away from him, "you've made your point."

Her words echoed through the room and Brian couldn't tell whether she was pouting, angry, or genuinely interested in making her social activities profitable. More specifically, he couldn't tell if she'd sobered up, which he felt was important to alleviating the awkwardness of the previous few minutes.

"Tell you what," he said, attempting to appease her, "let me work up some ideas on how to make these get-togethers of yours functional. I'll bring you a few when I've gotten a better understanding on how things run down here. You enjoy your night."

Brian moved to open the door, hoping to leave the conversation there.

"Brian."

Shit.

Brian turned to see Lucy facing him. Her expression was scarily neutral, leaving him with no chance of reading her or preparing for what she would say.

"I hired you to do a job because you're good at what you do. You've shown me that much in the short time you've been here. Though it might be against what I want in the short term, you've still got the long term in mind for the both of us. I'd like to thank you for that."

Brian exhaled a quiet sigh of relief.

"However—"

The sigh of relief crawled back into Brian's chest and shut all the doors and windows on its way back in.

"—if you *ever* use her against me like that again, our arrangement will end very abruptly, and very messily."

Brian swallowed hard but kept his eyes trained on Lucy. His heart pounded in his chest and, for a brief moment, Brian thought that the DJ outside had upped the bass on his music.

"Understood."

"Good," Lucy said. "Not a word about tonight will be spoken again. Get the fuck out of my office."

CHAPTER TEN

Morning broke the next day and Brian woke from what he swore was the worst sleep he'd ever had. After the tense exchange he and Lucy had, he couldn't seem to turn his brain off. His mind played with ideas on how Lucy's parties could work in favor of Hell, memories of the threat Lucy ended the night with, and grim fantasies of what tortures a love-scorned, pissed-off Devil could have in store under the correct circumstances.

He dragged himself from his bed and reached over to the Room Service menu on the bedside table. He flipped it over and scanned the card for a breakfast menu. His stomach groaned for bacon and eggs. He reached for the phone on the table and suddenly remembered Jeremy, the bellhop.

Rather, Jeremy, the Rep.

His desire for food diminished at the thought but his stomach roared in protest. Brian decided maybe a lighter breakfast would be an acceptable compromise.

After ordering just a simple bagel and coffee, and meeting a new Hellion bellhop named Robyn, Brian showered quickly and got dressed.

Brian opened the door to his room, half a bagel wedged between his teeth, coffee in hand, to find Dallas leaning against the window across the hall. Brian's throat tightened at the sight of his unexpected guest. Quick flashes of his flirtation with Dahlia, and his topless moments with Lucy skipped along the inside of Brian's skull. Brian shut his door and tore a bite from the bagel in his mouth.

"Sleep well?" Dallas asked cheerily.

Brian swallowed his bite. "Well enough."

Dallas looked at him for a moment. It felt like he was hesitating.

"I spoke with Jeremy," he started.

Brian suddenly felt empty inside, despite three-quarters of a bagel and coffee. He wasn't sure how to respond so he chose to remain silent.

"Seems you guys had a little chat last night."

"Briefly," Brian said. "I asked him about his bellhop uniform."

Dallas nodded. "I heard. I also heard that you asked about a couple other things."

Jeremy must have told Dallas the whole story. Brian was not excited about that. He felt as though he had overstepped boundaries during their talk but he was too curious for his own good.

"Yeah, about that—"

"Jeremy's taken a bit of a liking to you," Dallas said.

He swung his arm over Brian's shoulder and squeezed him.

Brian's face wrinkled in confusion. "I don't see why. I definitely thought I crossed a line with him."

"You did, but that's the point," Dallas said as he began to usher Brian down the hall toward the staircase. "It was a line that needed to be crossed. Jeremy isn't a big talker, so the fact that he spilled his story to you is kind of a big deal."

Brian awkwardly tried to take a sip of his coffee while within Dallas's grip.

"I'm glad I could help, then," Brian said.

He wasn't sure how exactly to react to the information. Dallas rocked him back and forth aggressively within his shoulder squeeze.

"I wasn't sure about you, Brian," Dallas said as they got to the edge of the staircase.

Brian couldn't help but feel like he was about to be thrown down it.

"But it looks like you've got a good heart."

Dallas awkwardly patted Brian's chest, just in case he forgot where his heart was.

"The Reps are my responsibility. I work closest with them. They're like family to me. Hearing that you made such a good impression on Jeremy makes me very happy, so I wanted to thank you," Dallas said, patting Brian's chest once more before releasing him from his forcible bro-hug.

"No problem. In fact, this works out. I was hoping I could understand the Reps a little more. What do they do? How do they do it?"

Brian tried to lead the conversation back toward the safety of work. He couldn't shake the feeling that Dallas's appreciation wasn't what it appeared to be.

Dallas, however, looked ecstatic.

"I can give you the grand tour. The Reps are part of the Sales department, so you can get a feeling for the whole operation this way."

He gave Brian a reaffirming clap on his back and made his way down the staircase toward the courtyard.

"Lovely," Brian said under his breath as he followed after.

★   ★   ★

The main entrance to the office building was located adjacent to the foyer. Dallas led Brian down the courtyard's opposite walkway and through a hall made entirely of windows. The view looked out onto lush greenery on either side. Brian wasn't sure how it was possible.

"I didn't think this compound would be so deep in the forest," Brian commented.

Dallas shot a confused glance over his shoulder. "It's not. We're smack dab in the middle of a barren wasteland."

Brian's brow furrowed. "What's all that, then?" he asked, gesturing out the window.

Dallas glanced to the greenery beyond the glass. "There are bits of different terrain scattered all through Hell. Pockets of different environments dotted here and there outside the gates of the compound. There are canyons, jungles, a shoe store – loads of different places. That's just one of them."

The explanation flew right over Brian's head, but he was also far too underslept to continue probing. Past the hallway was another foyer, similar to the main one but much smaller. The black marble and ivory pillars were replaced by granite and limestone; however, the overall structure and build were the same. Where Dahlia's large desk would be in this lobby instead sat a small office desk with a Hellion perched behind it. There was a large line that queued at the front of the desk and went all the way back to the main doors that Dallas and Brian entered through. The feeling immediately reminded Brian of being in the D.M.V.

The inhabitants of the line were like nothing Brian had seen before. Hellions of all shapes and sizes stood single file, waiting for their turn at the front desk. Brian was surprised to see that some of them looked more like out-of-focus photographs than people. Others resembled how Brian imagined human-shaped radio static would look.

"What is all this?" Brian asked.

Dallas glanced over at the line briefly. "Reassignment appeals," he said bluntly.

"Reassignment, as in…?"

"They want to change what it is they do in Hell. Doing the same job for eternity isn't exactly thrilling work."

"Why do some of them look like they're not all there?"

"You heard how Hellions *become* Hellions, right?" Dallas stopped and turned to Brian.

Brian nodded. "Sell your soul, the whole thing gets corrupted. You arrive in Hell as, basically, a whole person."

"Essentially. Thing is, a Hellion's soul still gets banked with other fragments so that its energy can be used for whatever it needs to."

Dallas nodded to a Hellion in the line that looked as though he was flickering in and out of existence.

"Eventually, the original soul has chunks taken out of it and replaced with other fragments it's been banked with. That happens over and over to the point where, sooner or later, most Hellions don't look like how they used to. Or rather, their souls can't project an image of their old selves. There isn't enough of their original soul intact to remember what their appearance used to be."

Brian thought of Jeremy. That explained why he seemed so different from the other Hellions he'd met. He was still mostly *Jeremy*.

"What about their memories?" Brian asked.

"Memories and personality are usually the first things to go. Those are already fragile concepts, even when they were still human and alive. Hellions retain some kind of personality, but it's more of a patchwork personality created from fractions of souls floating around in the bank. Whatever the original pieces of their soul can grasp on to, really."

The idea sounded awful but Brian was somewhat relieved. All he could think of was Jeremy and the pain his memories caused him every day of his eternal damnation. Eventually, he supposed, Jeremy would forget the pain because there wouldn't be enough Jeremy all in one place to remember the pain.

The thought was both horrendous and merciful.

Brian, however, still wasn't sure of one thing.

"So, what happens when a soul forgets what it originally looked like entirely?" Brian asked.

Dallas cringed. He looked at Brian sideways.

"That's a different field trip for a different day," he replied.

His answer was not at all satisfactory, yet Brian was comfortable with it. Something that made the son of the Devil cringe probably wasn't something Brian wanted to experience.

The pair made their way to the front of the line, ignoring the mass of Hellions waiting behind them. Dallas leaned on the desk and smiled at the young Hellion sitting behind it.

"Marie," Dallas said in a cheesy macho voice.

Marie giggled in reply. She tucked her pitch-black hair behind her ear and smiled a wide, blushing smile.

"Hi, Dallas," she said sweetly.

She was of Asian descent, possibly Japanese, and Brian thought she could have still been in her teens. She seemed the right level of schoolgirl smitten with Dallas for it to fit.

Dallas threw his arm back in a dramatic flourish, as if presenting Brian. "My companion and I require guest badges for the day," he said.

Marie craned her neck up past her desk to catch a glimpse of Brian. He smiled warmly and gave her a friendly wave. Marie's mouth dropped open slightly. She quickly leaned in closer to Dallas and whispered, albeit very loudly, "Is that him?"

Brian assumed that news of his employment traveled through Hell rather quickly.

"Now, now – it's not polite to stare," Dallas said to Marie. "Brian, come meet Marie."

He waved Brian over to the desk.

"Hi, Marie, I'm Brian," he said warmly, extending his hand to the young girl.

She took his hand gently and with a slight blush.

"Nice to meet you," she said in a mousey dual-tone.

Dallas snorted. "See? He doesn't bite. Now, guest badges. Please and thank you."

"O-oh, of course!" Marie said, releasing Brian's hand and scrambling for something inside the drawers of her desk.

As she searched, Dallas greeted some of the Hellions who stood in line behind him. From what Brian could tell, Dallas was fairly popular with the workforce – something Brian found entirely surprising. Marie finally pulled what looked like an old Polaroid camera from her desk alongside two lanyards.

"Smile!" she said to Brian as she pointed the lens toward him.

Stunned, he quickly smiled before the flash went off. A rectangular badge ejected from the front of the camera, which Marie retrieved and clipped to the end of the lanyard. She handed it to Brian with a smile and turned to point the camera at Dallas. Brian looked down at the photo on the badge. His lack of sleep and sudden surprise resulted in a blurred version of his face staring up at him from the photo. Brian felt a firm clap on his shoulder and looked up from his badge.

"That is a terrible photo of you," Dallas said as he directed Brian off to the left of Marie's desk. "Right this way."

Brian smiled and gave a quick wave to Marie once more as he was ushered past her. She smiled before returning to the queue waiting for her.

The two made their way down a hallway to what looked like an empty shipping bay. On the far wall was a wide length of mirror that ran adjacent to a small, enclosed office. Directly opposite the office was a large bay door that was pulled open. The bay door, however, didn't open into the greenery that surrounded the building as Brian saw on the way over. Instead, a soft, white light emanated from it. The light danced gently and resembled small, white tongues of flame twisting in the wind.

Dallas walked over to the small office and knocked on the door. Annoyed grumbling and shuffling could be heard from the other side. The door opened and a short, stocky Hellion answered. He was balding and looked to be in terrible shape. He had a pen sticking from his mouth and was clad in very shabby dress clothes.

"Dallas, how you doin', kid?" the man said warmly with a thick Brooklyn accent.

Dallas embraced him in a half-hug, patting him on the back. "I'm good, Sal. How you been?"

Sal took the pen from his mouth and tucked it behind his ear. "Same ole same." He jutted with his chin toward Brian. "Who's the tax man?"

"Nice to meet you," Brian said, extending his hand. "I'm Brian."

Sal looked at him sideways. Brian could practically feel the skepticism leaking from Sal.

"So, you're Brian, huh?" Sal finally said. He gripped Brian's hand, shaking it violently. "Jeremy was talkin' the world of you last night."

Brian was genuinely surprised at the level of camaraderie he found with the Reps so far. He smiled warmly, trying to keep his shoulder from being dislocated by Sal's violent shaking.

"Come in, grab a seat," Sal said, releasing his grip.

He turned and waddled back into the office, waving for the two to follow. Dallas offered Brian one of the chairs at the front of Sal's desk. Brian sat and scanned the contents of the room. The office was claustrophobic. Half a dozen tall filing cabinets lined the perimeter of the office. Brian wasn't sure how Sal reached the top halves of them. There were overflowing folders on every surface of the office and a whiteboard parallel to where Brian and Dallas were sitting with figures scribbled across in red dry-erase marker.

Sal navigated through the disaster space and finally slumped down in his chair with a relieved, dual-toned wheeze.

"So," he started, "to what do I owe the pleasure?"

Dallas waved a hand to Brian, signaling him to begin.

"I was hoping to get an understanding of how the Sales department operates," Brian said.

Sal nodded and spun his chair around to flip through a stack of files. He retrieved a single sheet of paper and placed it on the desk in front of Brian. The sheet was organized in tables. Various names were scrawled on it along with what looked to be desires for each entry.

"These are humans who have expressed some kind of inclination to sell their soul for a particular wish," Sal explained.

Brian looked down and saw an assortment of wishes – from money and fame, to crime and murder.

"How is the information gathered?" Brian asked.

"Hellions," Sal replied. "We have groups of Hellions stationed all over the world listening for the requests of humans."

"How does that work? They just try to pick up on someone saying they want to sell their soul as they pass them on the street?"

Dallas shook his head. "Canvassers have the ability to listen, both physically and psychically, across long distances covering a wide radius. They don't listen to everything, but when certain key words have been said or thought, they are able to focus on the location and the person who said it," he explained.

Brian was immediately put off by the thought of a Hellion psychically listening to his thoughts for some hint of soul-selling desire.

"Hellions will canvass areas and send us back reports on prospective candidates," Sal said, pointing to the page in front of Brian. "That's a lead sheet."

Brian looked down at the sheet, re-examining it within the context he'd just been explained.

"How do the Canvassers know what leads are good leads and which ones aren't? I'm sure that people out there say things like 'I'd sell my soul for' whatever. Hell, I've probably said it in the past," Brian said.

The operation seemed lacking, but he wasn't sure how just yet.

"Canvassers know who's serious by the strength of the signal," Sal explained.

"When someone is *really* willing to offer up their soul for something, the voice that the Canvassers hear gets…*louder*, for lack of a better term," Dallas continued.

Brian considered the approach of generating leads. It wasn't a terrible one and seemed relatively efficient.

"How do the Reps fit in, then?" he asked.

"When a lead gets sent back to us, a Rep is assigned to the request," Sal said. "The Rep has to do what they can to secure that lead. They infiltrate the lives of the lead. Disguise themselves in whatever way is necessary to get closer to the lead and make the sale."

Brian thought of Jeremy's bellhop outfit. It made sense. In fact, it was a brilliant strategy. He still felt, however, that there was something missing from the equation.

"Are there any Reps that try to reach out to humans that aren't actively considering selling their soul?" Brian asked.

Sal shook his head. "Cold calling is a hard game. We tried it before but it wasted too many resources and there was too little return to keep it going." He shrugged, scratching the stubble on his second chin.

There was a gap. The souls that Hell took in were all inbound from people who had reached their limit with trying to attain something. Brian recalled his conversation with Lucy the night before and how the people at her party weren't being approached for contracts. Hell wasn't being proactive enough.

"Dallas, is there a Marketing department in Hell?"

Brian had a feeling he knew the answer.

"There is – sort of," Dallas replied in an unsure tone. "It's not a large department. In fact, it's only one Hellion."

Brian turned once more to Sal to clarify the missing piece in his currently formulating strategy.

"Sal, are there limits to what people can sell their souls for?"

Sal's eyes rolled upward as he thought. "Needs to be specific. We can't grant vague wishes like 'I wanna be successful'. Success looks different to lots of people. We also look at how much it'll cost to grant a wish, but that's more Finance's department, not mine."

"So, Finance approves what wishes can be granted and what can't?"

"You got it," Sal said, snapping his fingers into a wink-and-gun.

The business of damnation was starting to piece itself together in Brian's head. He needed only a little more information. Whether he could fill the gaps of those pieces with a strategy, or if he had to cut certain pieces to make them fit, that was the challenge.

CHAPTER ELEVEN

Next, a few floors up from the shipping bay, Dallas led Brian to a single door in the center of a massive wall. Dallas stepped forward and knocked on the door. Brian wasn't sure what it was but he could hear a very high-pitched hissing on the other side.

"Come in," a voice called from the room.

Dallas turned the handle and stepped inside. Flickering light came flooding out of the room. Brian followed behind and entered to find a giant wall of screens. He couldn't help but think that he'd been brought to Hell's security office. He then noticed what was playing on the screen. *Commercials.*

Television commercials were playing nonstop. Various languages, products, even decades – the commercials were displayed on every screen in the room. In the center was a single Hellion sitting cross-legged. She was hunched over with her head craned upward and looked as though she were wearing pajamas.

"Danika, this is Brian," Dallas said as they entered.

Danika didn't shift her gaze or move at all. Her focus was directed entirely on the screens before her.

"Hi," she said briefly.

She seemed uninterested in the fact that there was a human standing in the room.

Brian took a step forward to try to get within her view. He stood to the side so as to not entirely obstruct the screens.

"Nice to meet you, Danika," he said.

Brian was able to see her now. She looked tired and sickly. Her dark hair was matted and unkempt, and she was, indeed, wearing pajamas.

"Dani," Dallas chimed in, "can we have a minute?"

Danika let out an irritated sigh and got to her feet. She slipped a slim remote control from the pocket of her pajama pants and pointed it at the screens. The pictures all flickered for a brief moment and then receded into the center of their respective screens. The lights in the room rose, though Brian was not sure from where. With proper lighting, Danika looked much gaunter than she originally appeared. She seemed to be in her mid- to late thirties with a medium build. Her bagged eyes looked from Dallas to Brian and back with annoyance. She raised her arms quickly to prompt one of them to speak.

"Well?" she said.

Brian cleared his throat and thought he'd try again. "I'm Brian."

Danika threw her hands onto her hips with attitude.

"I'm not deaf. What do you want?" She gave Brian an up and down appraisal and the look on her face changed.

She shifted her weight so it was dispersed evenly.

"You're human," she said.

Brian patted himself down. "Last time I checked."

For some reason, Brian's mind snapped back to the blurry photo that Marie took of him in the office lobby. A subsequent uncomfortable crawling feeling set in under his skin.

Danika looked frantically at Dallas. She pointed a finger at him, then to Brian, then back to Dallas.

"Explain. Why is there a human here?" she said with a quiver in her voice.

Brian started to get the idea that Danika didn't like humans. Dallas put both of his hands up.

"Calm down, Dani," he said, "there's plenty of time to—"

Danika squealed and grabbed Brian's hands, pulling them up to her chest.

"What is the human world like, lately!?"

Her high-pitched voice was almost enough to burst Brian's eardrums. The sound shook all the questions from his head and left him with blank confusion. Danika beamed at Brian with a wide smile. The bags under her eyes seemed to disappear, though her hair seemed to become more tangled at the same time. Brian wasn't sure how he should reply. Thankfully, Dallas inserted himself to provide some clarity.

"Dani is a bit of a fanatic when it comes to the human world. Hence all the, uh…." Dallas pointed to the screens.

Brian assumed that the monitors were all meant for marketing research. He looked back at Danika, who still held his hands and looked at him with starry eyes.

"Uh, the human world is good, I guess?"

Danika's face split into a wide, toothy grin.

"Where are you from? Where do you live? What kind of clothes are you wearing? *Are those designer?*"

Danika railed off question after question, entirely bombarding Brian. He wasn't sure how to interrupt her without being rude.

"Dani!" Dallas yelled from the side.

Danika's smile shrunk as she shot Dallas a dirty look for his intrusion.

"What?" she said venomously.

"Brian is here to talk marketing with you. He's a Business Advisor from the human world. He was hired to pull Hell out of the red."

Dallas spoke quickly as to not be interrupted by squeals Danika built up after every detail. She looked at Brian with wide, hopeful eyes. Brian nodded wearily in confirmation. She gripped his hands tighter before letting them go.

"What do you want to know?" she asked excitedly.

Brian let out a breath he hadn't realized he was holding since Danika's first outburst. He nodded to the monitors in the room.

"Are you using these for marketing research?" he asked.

Danika's head wobbled back and forth. "You could say that," she replied. "I like to get an idea as to what sort of marketing strategies work on humans. I also love seeing all the *stuff* you humans come up with."

Her voice was full of glee that didn't quite match the gauntness of her face.

Brian nodded. "So, have you applied any of what you've learned to anything in Hell?"

Danika's eyebrow shot up at the question. She shook her head very quickly.

"Hell hasn't marketed anything in...oh jeez, I can't even remember when," she said, drumming her fingers against her chin as she tried to recall.

"Sal in Sales said there used to be a Cold Calling initiative. Were you part of that?" Brian asked, hoping to push Danika into the direction he wanted her to go.

She shook her head slightly. "Not really. Legal was more involved with that campaign. Our team just came up with some pitches that the Reps could use to acquire more contracts."

Brian cocked his head. "'Our team'? I thought you were the only one in Marketing?" he asked, terrified at the thought of a team of Hellions just like Danika.

"Used to be a few of us," Danika replied. "We just downsized after the Cold Calls weren't a thing anymore. There's not many other ways to market Hell effectively, so they were reassigned."

"How come you got to stay? Why not get rid of Marketing entirely instead of downsizing it to one person?" Brian asked, thinking out loud.

Danika visibly considered the question.

"I guess to keep the faith and attempt to create some opportunities to rebirth the Cold Calling with a better plan. No one ever listens to my ideas on it though," Danika said, sounding a little scorned.

Brian's eyebrow rose. "You've got some ideas?" he asked.

Danika's face lit up with excitement – which Brian found absolutely terrifying coming from a Hellion.

"*Yeeeesssssss!*" she replied in an exclamatory hiss.

She grabbed Brian's hand and tugged him to one of the screens in the wall. She pulled the remote from her pocket once more and pointed it at the screen. The picture flickered to life as they approached.

"We need to make Hell *sexy*," Danika started as she directed Brian to the monitor.

The screen flashed with images of bikini-clad women and shirtless men from various commercials.

"For humans, sex sells. Everything from perfume ads to razor blades, there's always some level of sex appeal. That's what we need for Hell."

"How exactly do you propose making Hell sexy?"

Danika perked up. "There's lots of ways. Pop culture is laced with dreamy icons that can be roped into being poster children for Hell. We could also make up a couple of our own by using the Reps."

She rattled off the answer like it was the first thing to pop into her head but Brian's brain was going a mile a minute. Danika wasn't wrong – adding sex appeal to Hell could definitely work in its favor. He stroked his chin as he looked at the screen.

"I like the idea. Sex appeal has worked for a number of brands and companies in the past. It has potential," Brian said tentatively.

He looked at Danika, unsure of how his next question would be received.

"I'd like you to expand your research beyond the televisions you have. Tell me, Danika, have you ever heard of the internet?"

Brian hesitated when speaking the word as if he were a child uttering a curse word. Danika stared blankly at him. He wasn't sure what that meant. Her mouth hung open slightly as silence filled the room.

"Dani?" Dallas said from behind the pair.

Danika shrieked like a teenager going to a boy band concert. She grabbed Brian by the shoulders and shook him violently.

"*You're giving me internet access?!?*" Danika squealed as she continued her assault on Brian.

Dallas moved quickly to restrain Danika. Brian was confused as to what had just happened.

"I'm glad you're excited," he said, unsure of whether or not that was the emotion she was feeling.

Danika's chest heaved and excitement scrawled on her face in a fervor he'd yet seen thus far.

"I'm going to arrange to get you access. I'd like it if you could research this further. Television is becoming a dead medium and online marketing is a completely different game. I'd like you to get up to speed with how we can combine an online strategy with your sex appeal approach. Maybe even look into that poster child idea you mentioned."

Danika nodded quickly, tussling her hair more than it already was. Dallas released her from his grip so her violent nodding didn't backfire on his nose.

"One more thing," Brian said. "You mentioned that there was a Legal department?"

He wasn't sure why Hell would need to abide by legal requirements. Danika nodded once more, much slower than before.

"Underwriting and Legal, technically," Danika said. "They're in charge of drafting the contracts that humans sign when selling their souls."

"I'll need to get them involved with this," Brian mumbled, again, thinking out loud.

Dallas's ears perked up. "Get them involved in what?" he asked.

Brian shook his head slowly. "I've got some ideas, but I need Danika's data before I can present it."

He looked at Danika once more.

"Thank you, Dani," Brian said, "I look forward to seeing what you come up with."

Danika beamed. Brian waved goodbye and indicated to Dallas that they were leaving. The men left the room and Brian was already deep in thought. Dallas glanced at him as they descended the stairs to the entrance.

"What've you got in mind?" Dallas asked.

They walked back to the lobby where the line of Hellions seemed as though it hadn't gotten any shorter.

"Who reassigns Hellions?" Brian finally asked.

"Mom. Me. Dahlia. You, maybe?" Dallas answered.

He didn't sound sure of the process. Brian was surprised to hear that he was included in the list.

"I can reassign them?" he asked to clarify.

Dallas considered as they exited the office. "The contract you signed looked like it gave you some pretty free rein over whatever you need."

"Perfect."

★　　★　　★

The doors to the courtyard opened and Brian and Dallas entered the foyer. Dahlia stood talking with Lucy at the receptionist's desk. Dahlia wore her hair down; loose waves framed her smiling green eyes. She was dressed in a plaid button-up with a white undershirt slightly visible at the bust. Brian hadn't noticed that his eyes drifted to the black tights that she wore. He also hadn't noticed that he was staring.

"Ahem," Lucy said, startling him back to reality.

Her look had returned to the business-attire fashion in exchange for her evening wear that Brian had last seen her in (and out of). Her appearance still differed slightly from before – her hair was another shade lighter and was much less straight than it had been previously. Her eyes were now a deep blue with flecks of green. She was wrapped in a tight, scoop-neck black dress.

Brian's eyes adjusted and caught hers. She gave him a suspicious look.

"What have you boys been up to today?" she asked.

Brian cleared his throat. "Introductions with the Sales and Marketing departments," he replied, trying to reclaim his professionalism.

"And through the main lobby, no less." Lucy took a few steps forward and leaned over to inspect the guest badge that hung around his neck.

"That is a terrible photo of you."

"Thanks," Brian said awkwardly.

He wasn't sure if the tension in her words meant that she still harbored some resentment about the night prior. Lucy straightened herself and placed her hands on her hips. She looked at Dallas and Brian.

"So, did you learn anything important from Sal or Dani?" she asked.

"I didn't," Dallas chirped. "Dani is crazy as usual."

"I wouldn't call her crazy, she's just a bit fanatical," Brian said. "That kind of thinking is good for what I have in mind."

Lucy's eyebrow rose at the comment. "Sounds like someone has a plan," she prodded.

Brian shook his head. "Only ideas. Some of which I'm not sure will go over well with the staff," he replied.

Lucy seemed interested by Brian's vagueness.

"Oh? Something *gruesome*?" she said, appearing unapologetically hopeful.

"No, something *racy*. Right up your alley, I think," he shot back.

Lucy's eyes widened. "Do tell," she said, sounding very intrigued.

Though he was happy to find their dynamic was slowly returning, Brian shook his head once more.

"Like I said, they're only ideas. I'll know more when Dani gives me her feedback. Speaking of which," Brian said, turning to Dahlia, "can I order supplies now?"

Dahlia beamed at Brian. "Dunno, I might be too busy again," she said with a heavy dollop of sass.

Dallas groaned in exaggerated fashion. "As thrilling as supply ordering is, I assume you don't need me escorting you anymore?" he asked in an exasperated tone.

Brian shook his head. "No, thanks for all your help today," he replied.

"I didn't do anything. You did all the talking."

His voice sounded slightly annoyed. Brian assumed that the afternoon was much more boring for him than he thought it would be.

"You did plenty," Brian said, attempting to inject some positivity. "You'll be a big help when we move forward into the next stages."

"It looks like you've got this all under control, but whatever you say," Dallas said. He turned on his heel and gave a half-hearted salute.

He walked to the gateway at the other end of the foyer.

"And where are you headed off to in such a hurry?" Lucy called to Dallas as he approached the gate.

The doors opened and Dallas's figure was bathed in the white flickering beyond.

"Do you tell me where you go every time you leave?" he shouted over his shoulder as the doors closed behind him.

Lucy scoffed. "I should never have made that boy," she said.

Brian's eyebrow rose.

"'Made'? You mean you didn't...you know, *birth* him?"

"What?" Lucy replied, scrunching her face in disgust. "Do you know how long it takes to birth an actual human?"

"Approximately nine months? Wait, he's human?" Brian said in shock.

Lucy turned and made her way toward her office. She motioned with her head to Dahlia behind the desk as she passed.

"They both are."

Brian looked to Dahlia as Lucy's words sunk in. The surprise he felt was outweighed by the sadness drawn on Dahlia's face.

CHAPTER TWELVE

Before retiring to his room, Brian wrote down a list of supplies for ordering. His heart fluttered slightly as he included something that he hoped would be delivered much sooner than the rest of the items. He gave the list to Dahlia with a smile before making haste toward the courtyard doors.

Brian returned to his room and, after washing up, made his way to the wardrobe, which seemed to always be stocked with the right type of clothing he needed. He found a pair of comfortable pants and a loose-fitting t-shirt to slip into. He was surprised at how at home he was starting to feel.

A soft knock rumbled the door to his room as he finished getting dressed. He opened it to find Dahlia standing in the doorway, still dressed in the same outfit from earlier. She held up the list of supplies he'd handed her before leaving for his room. She turned the note over revealing the words:

Drinks tonight? – B

"Very smooth," she said as she stepped into the room.

Brian smiled innocently.

"To be clear, I still definitely need these supplies."

Dahlia smirked and walked over to the bedside table.

"No ice water tonight?" he asked.

She leaned over and opened the mini-bar that hid inside, pulling out a small bottle of chilled vodka.

"If you want, we can pretend it's water." She cracked the seal of the bottle and looked around the room. "Shit," she said as she scanned the room, "you don't have any glasses."

Brian frowned. "Can't we just Devil magic up some glasses?"

Dahlia's shoulders slumped as she took a sip straight from the bottle. She cringed at the taste and handed it to Brian.

"I don't like using soul energy for menial shit like that," she replied. She sounded slightly offended at Brian's suggestion.

"Sorry," he said, taking a sip from the bottle, "I guess we're roughing it tonight."

He handed her the bottle once more as she made her way to the armchair in front of the fire.

"So, what's with the sneaky invite? Not that I don't appreciate some discretion in front of my mother," Dahlia said, taking another cringed sip.

Brian sat on the edge of the bed facing her.

"What the Devil doesn't know won't hurt her. Besides, I wanted to ask you something."

"Let me guess," Dahlia said, throwing her legs over one arm of the chair and reclining on the other, "you want to know about me and Dallas being human?"

"You sure you don't read minds?" Brian asked, leaning forward for the bottle.

Dahlia handed it to him with a smirk. "Well, apparently I can read yours, but that might be because you're *incredibly* transparent." Her eyes sunk slightly as she considered Brian's question. "It's not a topic I like to discuss very often."

Brian took a sip of vodka and extended his hand to her. He shook the bottle and smiled warmly. Dahlia gave a disapproving, yet amused smirk and took the bottle from him.

"If you prefer, we can finish the bottle and I can ask again?" he said, half-serious.

Dahlia shook her head slightly before wobbling it back and forth in consideration of the idea. She tilted the bottle straight back and downed the remaining contents. Brian's eyebrows rose in surprise.

"Okay," Dahlia said as she choked back another cringe, "ask me again."

Brian chuckled and took the empty bottle from her.

"So, you're human?"

He wasn't sure how best to start his line of questioning. Dahlia made a flowing gesture with her hand over her body.

"A very fetching one, if I do say so myself." She smiled smugly at her own joke.

Brian noticed the redness that started to tint her cheeks.

"So, how does that work?" he asked.

Dahlia's eyes dropped. She directed her gaze to the fire. Brian couldn't help but notice that she and Lucy both found something else to focus on when they spoke seriously.

"I was made using soul energy. Dallas too."

She didn't take her eyes from the fire but pointed to the mini-bar. Brian placed the empty bottle on the bedside table and reached in to grab a small bottle of champagne.

"I didn't realize that was possible," Brian said, unwrapping the foil from the cork.

Dahlia nodded. "Apparently Mom could have made a completely new Devil if she'd wanted to. Same abilities, immortality, the whole schtick. Creating humans was just more cost-effective and easier to manage," she said, her words laden with resentment.

Brian popped the cork and took a sip of the fizzing liquid before handing it to Dahlia.

"Why would she need another Devil?" he asked.

"The same reason she needs you."

Something clicked in Brian's mind. "She was trying to create an heir?"

Dahlia nodded. "Both Dallas and I were created to assume the throne," she said as she sipped at the champagne.

Brian's brow furrowed.

"So then, why am I here?"

"Dallas took to the idea. He got on the ground level of Hell and started working with Sal and the Reps. He's good with the Hellions and great with his people, but ultimately, Dallas doesn't have the brains to run Hell the way it is now. Mom knows that, and I think he does too.

He is incredibly jealous of you. If he were in your shoes, Hell would be chaos and damnation in its purest like the old days," Dahlia said as her attention wandered away from Brian's and found the fire once more. "Mom thought that I could fill in for what Dallas was lacking. She thought that we could be a team. She was rather unimpressed when she found out that I had no interest in it."

"Why not?" Brian asked, leaning his elbows onto his knees to get closer to Dahlia.

She shrugged. "Mom has run this place since before time began. She lost love because of it, and she's never exactly been thanked for it. I have no intention of wasting my existence doing the same thing. She wants to retire for the same reason that I refuse to take her job. We both know there's more out there to explore." She swigged back the champagne. The redness in her cheeks continued to deepen as she spoke. "Besides, I'd rather spend my time with humans than Hellions." She raised the bottle in a cheers gesture to Brian.

"Sounds like you've spent some time with humans already?" Brian suggested.

"I like to adventure. I used to spend a decent amount of time outside of Hell, especially when Mom and I were at odds with each other – which was fairly often. She was pretty furious when I told her that I didn't want to run Hell, so I bailed and decided to go to school in the human world instead," Dahlia said with a smirk.

Brian was surprised. "You went to school? Like, university?"

Dahlia bobbed her head. "A few of them, actually. Last time I graduated Berkeley for Political Science."

Brian frowned. "'A few'? How is that possible? You look like you're in your twenties at best." He did the mental gymnastics trying to make the math work.

Dahlia smiled sweetly, batting her eyelashes against her rosy cheeks. "One of the benefits of being immortal, I suppose."

Brian thought it would be rude to ask how old she was and decided to refrain. At least, until she'd had a few more drinks.

"So, what part of this story is the one you don't like to discuss?"

he said, circling back to the beginning of their conversation before the alcohol fully derailed him.

Dahlia paused as she brought the bottle up to her lips. She exhaled slowly before taking another drink and handed it to Brian.

"Dallas and I are the reasons that Hell is in such a shit state," she said reluctantly. "The energy Mom used to create the two of us was a huge drain on the bank. Not to mention the fact that our lives still pull from the energy just like hers does. Since we were born, Hell has been in a deficit. We're immortal humans who serve no purpose in Hell. We're a waste of time and resources."

Dahlia's words were sharp. Brian wasn't sure if her spite was directed at Lucy or herself. He took a drink from the bottle, now feeling a little light-headed.

"Playing devil's advocate here—"

"Har har."

"—why keep you around if you're a 'waste of time and resources', as you so eloquently put it?"

"Who knows." Dahlia sounded as though she had considered the question before and came up stumped every time. "To torment me, most likely. This is Hell, after all."

Fair point.

"Do you think that maybe it's because she likes you?" Brian asked, unashamedly patronizing. "You are her kids, after all. Sure, she's not happy that you don't want to take over the family business, but that doesn't mean you're not still her daughter, right?"

"I really doubt it. We were a means to an end that just happened to assume the role of her children. There was no other definition for us. It was the signifier that fit best."

Dahlia's words drifted on notes of longing. Brian sighed and handed her the remainder of the bottle. She took it and downed the last swig.

"So, why stay?" Brian asked as he reached over for the mini-fridge once more.

Dahlia paused to consider before handing Brian the empty champagne bottle.

"I can't stay away from Hell too long. My lifeforce comes from the soul energy banked here. If I go adventuring for too long, I start to get weak. My human body would eventually die if it was cut off from the bank for too long. She doesn't even want me and yet I'm still trapped here."

Her look suggested that she was disgusted by the idea. Brian grabbed a bottle of some clear liquid he wasn't familiar with and cracked it open. He sniffed it to be sure it contained alcohol before taking a small sip.

"Lifeforce? Does that mean you don't have a soul?" Brian said as a shiver took his face after the sip hit his tongue.

He passed the bottle to Dahlia, who accepted it happily, downing a large gulp.

"My soul is one-hundred-percent corrupt. It was born in Hell using pieces of corrupted souls, so I didn't exactly have a chance. In essence, the soul inside me is closer to a Hellion than it is to a human. Hence I can't leave Hell for too long. I'm bound to the bank. It provides me vitality."

Dahlia took another large gulp and handed Brian the bottle. He downed the rest of it in one go, a solution his inebriated brain thought was the best one to avoid the awful flavor from before.

"So, to summarize," Brian said, trying to find words in the fuzz that was now his brain, "you're human."

"Yep."

"And you're immortal."

"Uh huh."

"And you have a soul."

"Kinda."

"But you're stuck in Hell."

"Sad to say."

Brian pondered the information for a moment. The fire crackled gently as the two fell silent. Finally, Brian snorted as he realized what Dahlia was describing.

"That sounds a lot like what I'm going to be once I finish this job. We'll be the same."

He recalled the contract he signed. The details explained that he would remain human but he would be granted immortality. He could only assume that working for Hell would corrupt his soul beyond repair, if it hadn't already. Strangely, he didn't find himself bothered by the idea, which, in and of itself, concerned him slightly. Was this place already affecting him in ways he wasn't aware? Dahlia's concern that Lucy was torturing her, just like she was everyone else in Hell, started feeling a bit more palpable.

He looked up and saw Dahlia staring at him. Her eyes were wide and Brian wasn't sure if what he'd said had upset her. She signaled with her hand toward Brian's. He reached out to hand her the bottle.

"It's empty," she said.

Brian forgot he had downed the contents already.

"Sorry," he said as he attempted to turn to the mini-bar once more.

Dahlia grabbed his wrist and tugged it toward her. The bottle dropped from Brian's hand and he nearly tumbled on top of her. He stopped himself with the back of the armchair, coming to a halt nose to nose with Dahlia. Her hand moved from his wrist and grazed gently behind his ear. She pulled her body close to him and pressed her lips against his. Brian melted at the sensation. His free hand found the small of her back and pulled her up out of the chair. She rose up with surprising ease, wrapping her legs around his hips as she came up. Brian tumbled back onto the bed, lips still locked firmly with Dahlia's. She pulled back and softly opened her eyes, staring deep into his. Her hair draped around both of their faces. Brian felt as though her dirty-blonde waves curtained out the rest of the world.

"Please tell me we're not just doing this 'cus we're drunk," he whispered.

A bemused curiosity crossed Dahlia's face.

"I'm not drunk, are you?"

"Entirely."

"What happened to you not being a big drinker?" she asked with a smug look.

"This is exactly why I'm not. I'm a lightweight. You'll have to be careful, this could be considered harassment in some courts."

"I'll take my chances," she said, cupping his face with her hands and pressed her lips deeply into his once more.

★   ★   ★

The embers of the fire glowed softly, barely illuminating the edges of the room. Brian and Dahlia lay under the sheets, still recovering their breath. Her head rested on his chest. His arm wrapped snugly around her shoulder and down to the crook of her waist. The buzz in his head was mostly gone and replaced by a tingle in his toes and fingers. She looked up at him, her green eyes just visible in the dark. He placed his lips gently on her forehead and she smiled softly before resting her head once more on his chest. Her skin felt warm on his. Not hot like Lucy's, but a healthy warmth.

A human warmth.

The embers finally died, cloaking the two in darkness as they lay, wrapped in each other – just two humans drifting off to sleep in Hell.

CHAPTER THIRTEEN

Weeks passed in Hell. Or, at least, what felt like weeks. Brian had no success in finding a functioning clock or calendar. Not that it really mattered.

After Brian and Dahlia's alcohol-fueled encounter, the two began spending more time together. Their relationship was secret, but almost every night Dahlia made her way to Brian's room. The two would talk until what Brian assumed to be the early hours of the morning. They would tell stories about school, people they used to know, awkward experiences – things normal people would talk about when first getting to know one another. It wasn't intentional, but Brian found himself softening to the idea that she was less a resident of Hell and more a captive of it. It made their companionship a bit more level.

Interestingly, as the weeks passed, Brian noticed that Lucy's appearance shifted a little more each day. He mentioned as much one cloudy afternoon after another meeting with Deborah in Finance.

"You know, you look a lot different than you did when I first got here," he said, attempting to make idle conversation as they made their way through the courtyard.

"Gee, you think?" Lucy feigned surprise.

The two seemed to get over any residual awkwardness from their exchange at Lucy's party, and had developed a fairly amicable working relationship. He considered her appearance of late. Her hair seemed shorter and much wavier than he recalled on their first meeting. The color was more of an auburn than a chestnut brown, and her eyes were green on some days, hazel on others. Her clothing was also much more conservative – usually sporting a professional, yet still fetching, dress in varying cuts. Brian couldn't help but think she and Dahlia now closer resembled mother and daughter.

"I'm not blind," Lucy said, interrupting Brian's thought process, "I know what I look like."

The two strolled the courtyard, silently in agreement on killing time.

"I would imagine you do. You own a mirror I suppose?"

He wasn't sure if she had been reading his mind again.

Lucy snorted. "Not exactly what I meant."

Confusion wrinkled Brian's brow. "Well, what *did* you mean, then?"

"Let me rephrase – I know *who* I look like."

Brian gulped hard, making Lucy smirk.

"How long have you known?" he asked tentatively.

Lucy gave a small shrug. "A while. It's obvious, really. When I start looking like my daughter, it's a safe assumption that it's not just lil' ole me keeping you here in Hell anymore. You've got other interests that have you sticking around."

Brian wasn't sure how to respond. Dahlia was right; she always seemed to be honest with him. Or rather, just honest in general.

"What makes you think I need a reason to stick around at all? I signed a contract, right?"

"True, but there's a difference between *having* to be here and *wanting* to be here. Not that I doubt your abilities, but I thought it would be enough incentive for you to go that little extra mile if you had a reason to stick around. You know, other than the obvious."

She was good, Brian had to admit. Lucy had a talent for analyzing and dissecting people. She had done it with him plenty of times in the past weeks and she continued to find new pieces of him to flay for fun.

"So, how do you feel about it?" he asked nervously.

Lucy smiled softly as they reached the foyer doors.

"I'm glad that you two found each other; however, please try to remember that I am the Devil. If you do anything to hurt my daughter, all bets are off with that contract. I will find lots of new and exciting ways to – how did you put it? *Flay* you?"

Brian would have been worried, and slightly more annoyed at the mind reading, if Lucy hadn't confirmed in her statement that she had maternal feelings toward her daughter.

"I've been wondering, actually," Brian said, attempting to change the subject by latching on to an earlier thread Lucy dropped, "how do your transformation powers work? Does everyone see you the way I do when you're around me? Is it involuntary, or can you control it?"

Lucy put a finger to her chin as she thought.

"I control it to a degree. There are some souls in here that would be tormented more by the sight of someone particular, at which point I take that form. Only they see it and it's totally involuntary."

Brian nodded, remembering Jeremy's account of Lucy's form.

"And what about me? You mentioned you take on the form of someone I find desirable or attractive. Is that intentional?"

"That is intentional. I can turn on the charm when I want. It's sort of like an evolutionary trait to entice temptation and such. I allowed access to that same skill to the Sales Reps, considering I rarely go out into the field to bargain for souls anymore."

"So, a little while back at the party, I saw you in more or less the same form as when I first got here. Was that for my benefit, or did your other guests see you differently?"

Lucy laughed through her nose. "Actually, that was an intentional appearance. Despite my razzing of you, I actually got a taste for the attributes your subconscious gave me."

Brian shook his head in disbelief. It was a strange thought, him influencing the Devil.

"I feel so honored," he said with a smirk. "So, do you have an original form at all? Something that's entirely, you know…you?"

"I do, but it's something few have seen," Lucy replied in a melancholic tone.

"Do I at least get a description?"

"You wish," she said with a sideways grin.

The two walked in silence for a moment longer. Their partnership felt ever closer.

"So, have you ever stopped reading my mind at any point?"

"Maybe for like…a day. Then I realized how dull Hell is without the weird shit I find inside your head."

★ ★ ★

The supplies had finally been ordered and doled out to their awaiting parties. Danika got her computer with internet access, resulting in a highly uncomfortable expression of gratitude toward Brian. Peter and Paul were also graced with new computers equipped with adjudication software that Brian commissioned from a developer in the human world. The pair were skeptical but slowly warmed to the idea after Brian explained the process, using the folders he took from them upon their first meeting. Though their gruff demeanor did not change, they were much friendlier with Brian afterward. Well, as friendly as the Twins could get.

Brian spent more time with Dallas, Sal, and the Reps, officially meeting the team in full a few days after his first visit. Brian, it seemed, was something of a celebrity with the Reps due to the respect he showed Jeremy on their first meeting. They welcomed him with open arms and showed him their operation, including how they adopted different appearances for their role in the human world. It was both astounding and terrifying watching the men and women before him twist and contort to adopt new features, figures, and voices.

Eventually, Brian made his way to the Legal and Underwriting team, led by a Hellion named Stephanie. The petite redheaded firecracker of a woman was sharp with her words and respected Brian for the way he was able to verbally joust with her using nothing but industry jargon. Out of all the Hellions Brian had met until that point, Stephanie was the one that reminded him most of his old life. She was a little like Amanda, just a little less disgruntled – an interesting notion considering one was a literal captive of Hell. The pair frequently discussed terminology that was drafted for contracts, the requirements and attributes of wish fulfillment, and everything in between. Lucy was typically left scratching her head at the end of most meetings involving Brian and Stephanie.

Deborah also became more familiar with Brian as he frequented the Finance department. He would discuss what wishes were fiscally responsible risks to take, how each wish was calculated for cost, and how the balance sheets looked after each wish was fulfilled. Brian was surprised to learn that wish fulfillment involved a fair amount of soul energy in order to manipulate certain humans or entities involved. Whether it was embedding ideas into an employer's head about promoting a specific person, or slightly changing someone's views on attraction for another human, each manipulation and suggestion had a cost. As long as the costs could be justified and there was still a profit to be made at the end of the wish, Finance would approve the request.

The weeks flew by as Brian built his understanding of Hell. His gestating strategy was seeming to be more viable than he originally thought, and he was greatly anticipating Danika's marketing research in order to present it to those involved.

★   ★   ★

Brian stared at his blurry reflection in the fog of the lavatory mirror, his features obscured by the condensation and undulating vapor from the shower. His reflection stared back at him. He looked tired but happy. He hadn't felt this satisfied since – he couldn't remember when, if it had ever even happened before. The steam slowly dissipated through the open door of his room where Dahlia was still lying in bed. He had forgotten what it was like to live in the human world; whether that was because so much time had passed, or that he really didn't miss any of it, Brian wasn't sure. Hell was starting to feel like more of a home than anything else in his life before it. He wrapped a towel around his waist and made his way into the room, catching a glimpse of Dahlia flipping through a file folder.

"What's that?" he asked as he opened the wardrobe.

"Dani came by when you were in the shower and dropped it off," she said casually while she leafed through the pages. Brian's head whipped around.

THE DEVIL'S ADVISOR • 99

THE DEVIL'S ADVISOR • 99

"Did she see you?" he asked in a panic.

Dahlia shook her head. "She knocked on the door and then slid the folder underneath." She gave Brian a snide, sideways glance. "Why? Ashamed of someone catching me in your bed?"

"With your hair in that state? You're damn right," he joked as he pulled a plain t-shirt over his head.

Dahlia dramatically stuck out her bottom lip as she smoothed the mess Brian made of her hair earlier in bed.

"What have you been getting her to research?" Dahlia asked and turned her attention back to the folder.

Brian finished getting dressed and sat at the foot of the bed.

"Online marketing strategies mainly. Also, how to apply sex appeal to Hell," he said.

Dahlia's eyes narrowed suspiciously as they lifted from the page onto Brian. His brow creased with concern.

"Why?" he asked.

"I think she might have gone a little overboard." Dahlia turned the folder to Brian.

He flipped through the pages enclosed, scanning each. He laughed lightly as he perused the report.

"I think that's a fair assessment."

Shabbily made digital collages of various pornographic photos were laced through the report. Clearly, Brian should have considered the necessity of internet browsing and the concept of filtered content. Then again, he doubted that would have stopped Dani for very long. Brian turned the page and found a sheet that held what looked like statistical information. He paused as his eyes lingered on the page.

"Yet," Brian said as he slipped the page from the stack, "she always seems to be on the ball."

Dahlia chortled.

"I hope that's not a pun on what's in that folder."

"It wasn't, but it definitely is now."

★ ★ ★

Brian looked over the oval conference table that had materialized in the center of the foyer.

Lucy. Dallas. Dahlia. Sal. Deborah. Stephanie. Dani.

Everyone seemed to be in attendance. This was the first time Brian had seen all of them in one place. It looked like everyone shared that same notion as they all awkwardly shifted in their seats, eyes darting from one face to the next. Hell was so compartmentalized in its organization, a gathering of disciplines like this was likely uncommon, if it had ever really happened before. As such, no one seemed to know where they stood with the other attendees. There was an underlying presence of an 'us' and 'them' mentality between Hell's management and the Hellions. Brian had a hard time placing himself in either camp. He felt like a hybrid of the two – part management and part...something else. The thought gave him a bit of a shiver and an uncomfortable feeling behind his eyes. Brian cleared his throat, directing everyone's attention to him.

"Thank you all for coming," he said.

Despite the unease of his standing, this was his domain – he felt the most confident when talking business, even more so when presenting it. This was the reason he'd got so far so fast back in the human world. The reason he was abandoned to mundanity just as quickly. He refused to let that happen here, especially after all he had been through. It was time that Hell learned what Brian Lachey was capable of.

"I hope I don't have to explain to you why you're all here?" Brian took a quick scan of the table. "Lovely."

Brian reached down to the table in front of him and grabbed several folders. "With the inefficiencies greatly reduced in the actuarial department, Hell is now processing corrupted souls at a faster pace than before. We need to see it out 'til month end but we're already trending to process more souls now than in the last quarter."

Brian motioned to Deborah, who nodded happily in response.

"Just from the numbers we've seen coming through our department, we can assume it will be the best month we've seen all year," Deborah chirped, smiling back at Brian.

He made his way around the table, handing out folders as he went.

"Now, I had a lot to consider when looking over the structure of Hell. With how much energy is taken from the bank to keep all of you alive, we would tap the well dry in the next two hundred years at the latest." Brian resumed his position at the front of the table. "So now we need to look at how to intelligently invest the energy into something that can generate more in the long run." Brian signaled to Dani, who shot out of her seat excitedly. "Dani, tell them what we've discussed."

"Right!" she piped loudly.

The whole table seemed unhappy that Dani had the spotlight. Brian assumed they were worried about her getting carried away. However, when Dani got carried away, that was when she was most brilliant.

"Hell hasn't seen any major influx of souls since the Crusades. Why is that?" Dani's attempt at audience participation was cringe-worthy. "Because," she continued, not missing a beat, "Hell has a bad name."

Lucy choked back a laugh.

"Of course it does, Dani. It's *Hell*," Dallas chimed in. "Most people who believe in Hell don't want anything to do with it. I mean, there are the Satanists but—"

Lucy raised her hand, interrupting Dallas's obvious point. Brian nodded to her in thanks.

"Dani, please continue," Lucy said.

Dani acceded and turned to address the table once more.

"Like I was saying. Hell has a bad name, but humans *love* to sin. Think about it – drugs, drinking, violence, sexual promiscuity; all of these things have booming industries backing them in the human world. All of them are associated with sin; humans just don't think of them like that."

"We want to capitalize on what humans are already doing," Brian explained further.

"So," Dani continued, "if you could all turn to page six of your folders."

Pages shuffled around the table.

"What the hell is S.I.N. Industries?" Dallas asked skeptically.

"I'm glad you asked!" Dani chirped. "S.I.N. Industries is the new name that Hell will operate under for the foreseeable future. We need to get away from the negative public image people have of Hell."

"So, does it stand for something? Or is it just a pun for pun's sake?" Dahlia asked, glancing at Brian.

"Social Interest Network. We are going to rebrand Hell as an industry involved in the production and distribution of recreational assets," Brian answered.

"We're gonna be pushing smut and booze," Dani clarified in a less professional manner.

Lucy sat forward in her seat, visibly intrigued. "Care to explain?" she said.

Brian couldn't tell if her tone was skeptical or curious.

"The goal is to produce alcoholic beverages, recreational substances, adult content, and gaming establishments that focus on exploiting the most common of human addictions. The products will be infused with a corrupting influence so that anyone partaking will become more susceptible to commit sinful acts. Other sections, like our adult entertainment initiative, will be subject to terms of use that include the surrender of a specific percentage of the user's soul."

"No one reads the terms and conditions anyways," Dani said.

"Regardless, we had Legal draft up a small clause that could be included in the Terms and Conditions that looks innocent enough but is still binding by the clicking of a mouse."

Brian was confident that he had thought of every angle when developing this idea with Dani. He finally realized, however, that the look on Lucy's face was, indeed, skepticism.

"So, you plan to corrupt souls by having them buy your products?" Lucy said.

Brian could tell that she wasn't impressed.

"Dallas had something with his chain letter attempt. I believe he was trying to tap into people's innate desire to hurt others. Humans, as a species, have a violent history. It's not unfair to consider that violence

THE DEVIL'S ADVISOR • 103

is part of who some of us are." Brian nodded to Dallas, who seemed incredibly pleased with himself.

He shot Brian a gun and wink in thanks for his recognition.

Brian nodded and turned his attention back to Lucy.

"We can offer them products that will influence susceptible humans to commit acts they are already considering – violent or otherwise. We're simply giving them a nudge in the direction we need them to go."

"This won't be an easy undertaking, financially," Deborah piped up. She also didn't seem pleased. "The cost to start and maintain a large-scale company in the human world is not an easy ask on the bank. Not to mention the creation of consumable products."

Brian hadn't realized how tough of a crowd Hell's management staff would be.

"Agreed, that's why we decided to go with adult entertainment as a starting block. There's very little cost associated and upkeep is simple. We can generate income that way until we're ready to expand."

Brian could tell that both Deborah and Lucy were still not satisfied with his answer.

"By 'adult entertainment', you mean porn, right?" Lucy's words were layered with speculation and a hint of intrigue.

Brian nodded. "We don't need any additional staff. The Reps are perfectly suited for this job. They can take on any appearance so we only need a few of them to make content that will appeal to a wide array of audiences." Brian gestured to Sal and Dallas. "You two know them best. Do you think this would fly with them?"

Sal snorted. "I can already think of a few of the Reps who wanna pork each other," he said.

Brian cringed at Sal's choice of words.

"I think it could work too," Dallas contributed. "The Reps are required to take on human forms and infiltrate the lives of humans to work leads. That, sometimes, includes getting on a physical level with the lead, right Sal?"

The stout man opposite him nodded. "They do what they gotta to get the lead. Like little, undead spies," he said.

Deborah silently considered the idea.

"So, everyone who accesses the adult content would be surrendering a portion of their soul. Do they lose more of their soul every time they go back to the content?" she asked.

Brian assumed she was preparing to crunch the numbers behind her multi-eyes.

"No, we want to minimize the amount of full souls we get in this strategy. We don't want another Hellion in the process. It's just another mouth to feed, in a sense. In this strategy we need a large quantity of small pieces. That's why Dani and I suggested this avenue to start. It's already a large industry with millions of subscribers," Brian said, seemingly assuaging Deborah's anxiety.

Dani nodded. "And trust me, there will be *a lot* of pieces. Do you know how much porn is on the internet? That's basically all the internet is used for."

Lucy snickered at Dani's innocent remark.

"So, what happens after that?" she asked, sounding less hesitant.

Brian pointed to the folder in Lucy's hand.

"There's a proposed growth strategy in the folder. In short, we start with porn, then we move up to alcohol, marijuana, casinos, and so forth. We need to use energy from the bank for the start-up of these initiatives, but once they start turning a profit, they'll be able to sustain themselves."

"So, to summarize," Dahlia said softly from the back, "we're going to ask people to sell part of their soul to watch Hell-porn. Then, when we've made enough money from that, we sell them, essentially, spiked alcohol and weed to get them to commit crimes and condemn themselves?"

Brian and Dani looked at one another and both shrugged in unison.

"Yeah, essentially," Brian said.

A venomous smile crossed Lucy's lips. "I love it."

"Yeah," Brian said, unsurprised, "I had a feeling you would."

CHAPTER FOURTEEN

The meeting with Hell's management team concluded after Brian explained the expansion strategy and the details of the project kick-off. He explained to each department what their roles would be in the upcoming changes. Everyone left the meeting in agreement of the plan and Brian felt there was a high level of anticipation through the group.

The attendees dispersed from the table as it dematerialized into the foyer. Lucy caught Brian's gaze and signaled for him to follow her to her office. Brian glanced at Dahlia, who responded with a confused look.

"You had me worried," Lucy said as the doors to the office closed behind Brian.

She took a seat on a leather sectional sofa that materialized adjacent to the doors. Brian took the seat opposite her.

"I know, the strategy is a bit unorthodox," he said, attempting to gauge what the impromptu meeting was about.

"That's being modest. I never thought you'd suggest starting a porn studio in Hell," she scoffed. "I have to admit, though, I love the idea."

"I knew you would. Hell, I was half expecting you to say you wanted in on the productions." He chuckled.

Lucy shot him a sultry smirk.

"Oh Jesus, please tell me that's not what this meeting is about."

Lucy laughed and threw her arm over the back of the sofa as she reclined.

"Sorry to disappoint you but that's not exactly my cup of tea." Her eyes started to wander, a surefire sign that she was about to get serious. "I just wanted to talk to you one-on-one about this." She paused, seemingly considering her words carefully. "I want to make sure you've got your head on straight."

Brian grimaced. "What makes you say that?"

"Just the oddity of your strategy. I suppose that I'm surprised you thought of something so…racy. It's not very *you*."

"Don't read too much into it," Brian said, feeling a little underestimated. "I simply looked at some of the factors involved in souls entering Hell and started basing the plan off that. It was part of the reason I got the Twins new software. Analyzing data to formulate the strategy became easier." He couldn't help but wonder what the reasoning behind the sudden interrogation was. "What's the deal? This is the first time that you've really dug into anything I've put together."

Brian stared at her, refusing to let Lucy's eyes wander again. The look she returned was one of concern.

"Have you been feeling well lately?" she asked.

The question was clear but Brian was still confused.

"Of course. Why, do I not seem well?"

A sour look crept onto Lucy's face. She poised her palm upward and tensed her fingers, materializing a round mirror with an intricate golden frame. Brian's head cocked as he watched Lucy position the mirror on her lap with the glass facing him.

"What the fuck!" he screamed.

Brian shot out of his seat toward the mirror. His reflection stared back at him but his eyes seemed to look in multiple directions all at once. His heart lurched in his chest as he stared at the reflection of his Hellion eyes. He looked up at Lucy, who returned his gaze with one of concern.

"What the hell is this, some kind of joke?"

Lucy shook her head before nodding to the mirror.

"Look again," she said softly.

Brian hesitated – he was afraid to see those strange eyes looking back at him. His gaze slid slowly toward the mirror in Lucy's lap. The reflection staring back at him, however, was not the same as the one he'd just seen. It looked normal.

"I don't understand," Brian said weakly.

Lucy shook her head slightly as the mirror dematerialized in her hands.

"Neither do I. This shouldn't be happening to you," she said. Irritated confusion bubbled in his chest.

"What do you mean, 'this shouldn't be happening'? You know what this is?" he asked, trying to mask the building frustration in his voice.

Lucy nodded and gestured for Brian to sit back down. He did not.

"Your soul is being drawn to the bank. It has a way of pulling in any soul that enters Hell. If that soul is still attached to your body, then it takes longer. Along with the physical changes, your out-of-character strategy had me worried that bits of your soul were starting to get mixed in with the lot." Lucy frowned as she thought. "But you shouldn't be affected. Your contract stated that your soul would remain protected for the time that you're here."

Brian's mind was racing. Images of the photo taken by Marie when he and Dallas visited the office weeks ago; his blurry reflection in the mirror only a few days ago. How long had this been happening?

"Why do I look normal now?" Brian asked, trying to make sense of everything.

"It comes and goes. I noticed it the other day when we were talking in the courtyard. I thought I might have been seeing things. That's why I wanted to talk about this plan – I needed to see if your judgment was becoming impaired." She looked at Brian seriously. "You need to return to the human world."

"What?" Brian's heart sank. "What do you mean?"

Lucy raised her hands. "I mean you need to spend some time out of Hell to let your soul heal. Right now, the bank is attempting to pull your soul from your body and mix it in with the rest of the souls in there. If you stay too long the bank might have a strong enough pull over it and your body will start to...."

Lucy's explanation trailed but Brian was sure he already knew what words would have followed. He wasn't sure if the sudden revelation was making him feel hollow, or if the feeling had been there the whole time and he'd been drowning it out with work and Dahlia.

"How long have I even been here? I'm sure people in the human world would have considered me missing at this point. I can't exactly walk back into a circus like that without question."

The hollow feeling seemed to deepen as he thought of his old life –
Amanda and his office that was likely being filled by one of his traitorous
co-workers; his apartment that had been vacant since his arrival in Hell.
Brian thought of his family. His mother and father had probably been
worried sick about him. He wondered what sort of chaos he'd caused
back in his normal life for the few people that were involved.

"Maybe you should visit them." Lucy stampeded her way through
his thought process.

He looked at her angrily. The lack of mental privacy while trying to
cope with the realization that his soul was being sucked from his body
was not a good mix. Brian tumbled back onto the sofa behind him,
sucking in deep, exasperated breaths in an attempt to calm his mind.

"I guess I don't really have a choice. How is this going to work?
There's a project rollout to worry about. That's going to get pretty
complicated. I can't work on it from the human world," Brian thought
out loud, trying to fit the pieces together.

Lucy shrugged, stood and extended her hand. "We'll figure it out.
I'll pull your contract from the Records department and try to sort out
why your protection isn't working," she said sympathetically.

Brian took her hand and got to his feet. The doors to the office
opened as they walked.

"Collect what you need from your room. I'll have Dahlia see that
you get through the gateway to wherever it is you need to go."

★   ★   ★

A soft knock at the door startled Brian after he reached his room.
His nerves felt shot since his meeting with Lucy and the pit in his
stomach became more cavernous with every thought of home.
The handle clicked and the door opened gently. Dahlia entered the
room and shut the door behind her. Brian turned fully to face her.

"Did you notice?" he asked her.

The question erupted in a more accusatory tone than he meant it to.
But then, why shouldn't it? His slow transformation had come to light

only as he gave the particulars of his plan. What use did Lucy have for him now? Was this all part of some scheme?

Dahlia shook her head and walked toward him, tugging him into a warm embrace.

"I had no idea. You never seemed any different with me."

He scanned her face for any sign of deceit. He wasn't sure why, but Brian wanted there to be something sinister at play. As long as it resulted in a concrete answer, Brian could plan. Strategize. He didn't deal in what-ifs very well. Yet, all he saw when he looked at her was worry. He saw what he was scared to see – someone he might lose. Brian squeezed her around her waist briefly before collapsing backward on the bed.

"I don't know where to go. My life back in the human world isn't exactly something I can just step back into. Not since I disappeared, and I really don't have the energy to try and explain that I've been working for the Devil since I vanished," he whimpered.

Brian closed his eyes, which made the thumping in his chest all the more apparent. He wasn't sure if his increased heart rate was a side effect of the anxiety associated with his awkward homecoming or a sign of his body trying desperately to cling on to his soul. He felt the bed sink slightly as Dahlia sat close to the edge.

"Well, if you want to hide, you can always stay at my beach house," Dahlia said in a sheepishly coy tone.

Brian's eyes shot open and he quickly sat upright.

"I'm sorry, your 'beach house'?" he asked skeptically.

He turned to see Dahlia wearing a smug look on her face.

"A little something I picked up on my travels. I don't use soul energy for materializing menial shit. I do, however, use it to create money that I can then use to purchase a beach house in California," Dahlia said proudly.

Brian couldn't help but stare at her while he absorbed the offer.

"What would you need a beach house for?"

"Because my mom can be a bitch and when I visit the human world I tend to prefer not being homeless."

"Fair enough." Brian stood from the bed with a new supply of vigor. "And I can just stay there?"

Dahlia nodded sweetly and then stopped.

"I'm coming too," she said, sounding as though she were being left out of her own plan.

Brian smiled, amused, and extended his hand to her.

"Obviously."

★   ★   ★

Waves crashed gently in the backdrop of the coastal night sky. The salted air was fresh and cool. Brian couldn't believe how different he felt being back in the human world compared to being in Hell. The hole in his core seemed to be slowly filling as he inhaled deeply on the cliffside balcony of Dahlia's beach house. The house was contemporary, sporting an open-concept sunken living room attached to a dining room and kitchen. There was an absurd number of tall windows that lined the back half of the house. The balcony rested at the edge of a cliff that hung over the ocean. A hallway connected the balcony to the master bedroom, which shared the same view. The interior was doused in a very warm, yet simple, scheme of maple wood on white. For a large house it felt incredibly homey. Dahlia stepped out onto the balcony beside Brian, handing him a cool glass.

"Ice water is somehow less impressive in the human world," he jabbed.

She threw him an unimpressed look and put her hand out.

"I can take it back, if you like?" she said.

Brian downed the water quickly. It coated his insides, invigorating him from head to toe. Brian thought about how long it had been since he'd had a glass of water. He then considered how long it'd been since he'd eaten anything. The ache of his stomach clearly chose hunger over any other emotion Brian decided to pin to it earlier.

"I'm starving," he said as he lifted the glass from his lips.

He looked at Dahlia. She glanced back to the kitchen as if she were considering making a meal, then returned her gaze to Brian.

"Pizza?"

★　★　★

The pair sat in front of the fire as the ocean played softly in the background. Empty pizza boxes lay strewn across an old oak coffee table in the center of the living room between the two. Brian had never felt as full as he did at that moment. As he devoured slice after slice, his thoughts returned again to his eating habits in Hell. It seemed like weeks ago that he did anything but sleep and work. He wasn't sure whether or not his lack of appetite was a cause of his inadvertent Hellion transformation or if the concept of time in Hell was so skewed his body couldn't grasp it.

"How are you feeling?" Dahlia said, breaking the silence that followed the pizza-massacre.

Brian took a deep breath, letting it out slowly.

"Better," he replied. He looked at her with a hint of disbelief. "So, you really didn't notice anything?"

Dahlia shook her head. "To be fair, most of the time we've spent together didn't involve the lights being on," Dahlia said innocently, batting her eyes.

Brian chuckled. He reached over and tugged at her wrist, pulling her into him.

"That's true. It might be all this humanity I'm suddenly feeling, but I'd like to spend more well-lit hours with you. You know, on a regular basis."

Dahlia feigned shock as she leaned away from him. She pressed her hand to her chest as her mouth hung open.

"Mister Lachey, are you asking me to go steady with you? Are you asking me to be your – gasp – *girlfriend*?" she said with a thick southern accent.

Brian's face screwed at the sound of whatever character she was attempting to embody.

"Not if you intend on doing *that* all the time. Did you actually just say the word 'gasp'?"

"Take it or leave it, accent and all."

Brian smirked and pulled her back into his arms.

"Is that a yes?"

"Only if you let me do the accent."

"Deal."

★　★　★

Brian was woken by the soft calling of gulls rolling in through the window. He opened his eyes to find that he was alone in bed. With an effort that felt like more than should have been needed, he dragged himself out of the bed. He didn't understand it, but he felt more solid than he had in a long time. His existence in Hell was beginning to feel more fictional and ethereal as the morning sunlight kissed his skin and he felt a warmth he hadn't from the sunshine of the courtyard. His life might have been in shambles, but Brian was starting to feel very glad to be back in the human world.

He made his way from the bedroom to the kitchen, the smell of fresh coffee pulling him along the whole time. He finally saw Dahlia. She stood behind a floating island, slowly pressing coffee. A light robe hung loose and open off her shoulders, revealing a tank top and underwear beneath. Her hair was still messy from bed, but Brian couldn't help but think how beautiful she looked in that moment.

"Good morning, Mister Lachey," she said with a sleepy smile.

"Good morning to you, too."

"How do you feel?"

Brian took a quick moment to ask himself the question, feeling out as much of his body and mind as he could in that short time.

"Whole, I think," he replied honestly.

Dahlia's smile widened. She spun around to the cupboards behind her and retrieved two mugs, placing them on the counter.

"So, what's your plan today?"

"My plan is to figure out a plan," Brian said.

Returning to Hell made him feel uneasy. There was too much up in the air, and he didn't know who to trust.

"You thinking about staying here long term?" Dahlia asked sheepishly.

"By 'here' do you mean your place, or the human world?"

"Both?"

"The human world? Maybe. Your place? Well, as long as you'll have me, I suppose," he said with a playful smile.

She returned it and handed Brian a mug of piping hot coffee. "I give you another night. Tops."

★ ★ ★

After they shared their coffee in the sunshine on the balcony, Dahlia suggested they spend some time at the beach. An opportunity for exercise and relaxation all in one, she said. Brian was content with the idea and Dahlia left him on the balcony to pack them a couple of bags for the day.

Brian eventually wandered to the bedroom down the hall, wondering what he would use as a bathing suit. His clothes from the night before were strewn on the floor, reminding him that he had brought his phone with him when he and Dahlia left Hell. His battery seemed to somehow still be alive, despite the length of time that he was in Hell. The thought made him feel uneasy. The feeling worsened when he retrieved it from his pocket and unlocked the screen.

Impossible....

What felt like weeks – months, even – in Hell had turned out to only be a few hours in the human world. It was about ten in the morning on the day after his last shift at his consulting firm. A message from Amanda waited on the screen for him.

```
9:17 a.m.
Your 9 o'clock is here waiting. Where the hell
are you??
```

The sense of time made Brian dizzy. He had spent a seemingly incalculable amount of time working for Lucy that equated to nothing more than an overnighter in the human world. The idea that he was being tortured now seemed far more possible, and certainly more unsettling. What bothered Brian most, however, was how easily he could slip back into his old life if he chose to. His morning absence could be explained away by an emergency off-site client meeting, and just like that, Brian could be back in the human world. The idea made his stomach turn. He wasn't sure which seemed more like torment.

"I don't have anything for you to wear," Dahlia said, entering the room with two small bags on her shoulder, "but there are a couple little shops on the strip before the beach. You can probably find something there."

Concern scrawled her face as she saw Brian. "What's wrong?"

Brian wasn't sure how to explain his dread. Worse, he wasn't sure how much of a part of Lucy's torment Dahlia was – willing or unwilling. He shook his head and tossed the phone aside, the sick feeling still clinging to his skin.

"Nothing," he said, slapping on a fake smile. "Are we ready to go?"

★   ★   ★

The day was beautiful. The burning sun was rejuvenating, and Brian eventually let the lingering fear and anxiety roll off his shoulders with repeated dips in the salt water. The day wound down and the sun began to kiss the horizon in a warm blaze of orange and lavender. The pair were tired and happy when they returned to the house before night swept the sky.

"I'm starving," Dahlia said, her skin sun-kissed and glowing.

Brian nodded. "Pizza?"

"Again?"

He shrugged. "It's weird, the things you miss when you've been without them for so long."

Dahlia shook her head, an amusingly disapproving look on her face. "Fine, but tomorrow I get to choose dinner."

Brian smiled. "Tomorrow. I like the sound of that."

★   ★   ★

A muffled disturbance of the ocean sounds nudged Brian from his sleep. He sat up, bleary-eyed in bed next to Dahlia. The cool, white sheets of the bed barely clung to his body to protect him from the glow of the fireplace in the master bedroom. He looked down at Dahlia sleeping on her front. Her face was turned away from him and her bare body clung to the sheets that she'd unconsciously torn from him in the night. Brian looked around the bedroom. The fire crackled and warmed the maple of the room while the moonlight streaming through the windows illuminated the whites.

Another rustle came from the living room, causing Brian's attention to turn to the door. Down the hall, the balcony doors were still open from before dinner. Brian wondered if an animal had found its way inside and was attempting to steal the leftovers. He rose from the bed and sleepily walked to the living room. The pizza boxes were undisturbed; the coals of the fire struggled to glow a little longer; and a shadowy figure stood at the front door of the house.

The blood in Brian's veins instantly ran ice cold, wrenching him from whatever was left of his grogginess. His heart pounded into his throat as his eyes darted for a place to hide. As quietly as he could, he lunged behind the couch, ducking down. He swallowed the drumming of his heart. Steadied his resolve. He slowly raised his head over the back of the couch to catch a glimpse of the figure. His chest compressed as he struggled to find the figure once more. He resumed cover, his focus now on the hallway leading to the bedroom. His heart dropped like a rock. A concoction of fear and anger filled his lungs as he inhaled deeply.

He tried to barrel down the hallway toward Dahlia but was shackled to the spot. The hands that held him in place were many. Brian couldn't tell how many were holding him, but the moonlight glinting from their multi-eyes betrayed them to be Hellions. Had Lucy sent a group to finish him off? He ran, and she chased. He turned his head to see who was holding him but his cheekbone was met with the force of a hammer. A ringing erupted in his ear as his sight was doused in a percussive shade of white. Pain rooted at the source of collision. He found that the hammer was, in fact, a fist – and that fist belonged to Dallas. The Hellions lifted him off the ground and suspended him horizontally between them. Brian's head turned once more to the hallway. His mouth opened but the shout to Dahlia was muffled by the heel of Dallas's shoe.

CHAPTER FIFTEEN

Blood pounded behind Brian's eyes as they opened. The strikes that his face endured from Dallas were hard and his head was making Brian profanely aware of that fact. His head swung loose as the Hellions carried him hurriedly across barren stone, kicking dust into his face with each step. His hands were restrained with thin rope and his mouth was bound shut with a torn piece of fabric – likely from Brian's own shirt, based on the draft on his exposed midsection. As his vision returned through the blurred mosaic of his temporary unconsciousness, Brian found himself staring at a clear night sky – framed by the shuffling bodies of six or so Hellions. Muffled whispering and exasperated grunting chorused the hurried pace to wherever it was they were taking Brian. He began to correct the limpness of his neck by tilting his head forward to see if he could catch a glimpse of the posse's intended destination.

Through the cracks of the shuffling figures, Brian could see Dallas leading the pack. He was draped in a dark, silky suit and, by the looks of his collar, a white shirt. He strode as though he hadn't a care in the world. He occasionally looked up to the sky to take in the sight of the starry night. He seemed fairly content with himself.

After a few more minutes of Brian's face being showered in dust from the scrambling feet around him, he was relieved to hear the footsteps muffled by grass. With the sound of the steps dulled, the soft trickling of water began to swell the further they progressed.

"Here's fine," Dallas said softly to the group that followed.

His words were laced with gleeful notes. Brian's body was quickly wrenched upward and he was placed on his feet. His knees nearly buckled when confronted with the unexpected weight of his own body. The Hellions lined up behind Brian, creating a barrier at his back. He turned and noticed that most of the faces he saw belonged to the Sales team. He hadn't met any of them beyond initial greetings, save for Jeremy. The shy, young Hellion stood at the left end of the barricade. His multi-eyes did not lift higher than Brian's exposed belly button. Brian frowned from the disappointing reveal and winced at the pain the frown caused his quickly bruising face. Brian's attention was taken by his surroundings. Finally, being able to get a full view, Brian was surprised to find himself standing in front of the ivory fountain in the courtyard of Hell. Dallas sat at the lip of the basin, one leg crossed over the other. A wide, carefree smile was plastered on his face as he scanned the courtyard. His gaze moved from the sky, to the arched pillars of the walkway, and finally to Brian.

"It's amazing, isn't it?" Dallas said to Brian.

The smile refused to leave his face, making Brian feel infinitely uncomfortable. Dallas didn't seem to notice that the ripped fabric still muffled Brian's mouth – he also didn't seem to care.

"This place always gets me. It's so peaceful here." Dallas dipped his hand into the water of the fountain, cupping out a small pool. "'It's hard to believe this place is Hell'. I bet that's what you thought the first time you came here," Dallas said as he released the water from his palm back into the fountain.

He stood up from the edge of the basin and stood face-to-face with Brian. "I don't blame you. Hell shouldn't look like a prestigious university campus, right? We have a reputation to maintain. Fears to instill and all that."

Brian flinched as Dallas quickly swung his arm around Brian's shoulder. Dallas pulled Brian in tightly to his body and began ushering him on a leisurely stroll around the fountain.

"That's why you're here, right? You're here to maintain the reputation of Hell. You're here to keep those souls corrupted and keep the business going." Dallas halted abruptly and placed a firm hand on Brian's chest. "Don't get me wrong, I think you're doing a great job. You've come up with some ideas that I never would have dreamed of."

There was no hint of dishonesty in his words. He genuinely sounded grateful. This was incredibly concerning when juxtaposed with the current state of affairs.

"However, there's more to it than that. See, the problem is," Dallas said, continuing to move the pair around the fountain, "you are *very* good. In fact, in all honesty, I believe that, in your care, Hell could see the dawning of a new age. There's so much potential behind those calculating little eyes, isn't there?" Dallas said as he pinched Brian's cheek.

He assumed it was supposed to be intimidatingly endearing; it was, instead, incredibly painful on the tender swelling that was now most of his face. "So now, here's my predicament." Dallas stopped their circular route on one of the pathway stones leading toward the fountain with Brian's back facing the basin. "I want you to keep on making Hell better and better. However, *I* want to rule Hell. I know I can't have it both ways." He stood in front of Brian and crossed his arms. A look of contemplation draped his face. "I tried to make it work, but without this—" Dallas reached inside the breast of his blazer and pulled out a stack of papers, "—sitting safely in the Records department, it looks like your body can't hold up to being in Hell for long periods of time. That, sadly, nixed my plan of having you do all the work before killing you and taking Hell for myself."

Brian's eyes lingered on the contract held firmly in Dallas's grip. His heart began to drum faster and his breathing became rapid.

"Trust me, killing you now is *not* how I wanted things to go. Not filing this damn contract stumped my plan, but filing it meant you're protected from whatever I could do to you," Dallas said as he threw Brian's contract into the fountain behind him. "Oh well, I have to be adaptable. Actually, funny enough, I learned that from watching you. I was so caught up with how Hell should be, and not how it is. I think I needed you to show me that the hard way – by showing me that you're much better at this than me. But now it's time for me to take the wheel." He smiled a disturbingly sincere smile. "Thankfully, I'm not starting from scratch. Your plan and presentation gave me plenty to go on. I think I can get it off the ground with enough elbow grease. So, thank you for that – I really appreciate all your hard work."

Brian's indiscernible muffles shook Dallas from what Brian could only assume was his gleeful gloating. Dallas's eyes went wide before he chuckled to himself. "How silly of me, here I am ranting away to you and you can't say anything back. I was wondering why you were being so quiet. Forgive me – I was wrapped up in my own little world."

Dallas tugged the swath of tattered shirt from Brian's mouth. Brian opened his jaw wide, stretching the throbbing reminder of Dallas's heel. He looked sternly at Dallas, trying not to let his rage take him over and go at Dallas's face with his teeth. There were more important things to do first.

"Where's Dahlia?" Brian asked, gritting his teeth in order to keep his rage bound.

Dallas smiled and clapped Brian's shoulder firmly.

"See, it's those kinds of questions that make this such a hard choice for me. You seem like such a nice guy." He drummed on Brian's shoulder quickly with his fist. "Dahlia is fine. I wouldn't do anything to hurt my own sister. How evil do you think I am?"

Brian refused to answer the question at that particular moment.

"So, what now? You just kill me and leave my corpse here in the courtyard so everyone knows you are a better Devil than me?"

Dallas's face dropped, disappointed. "You really think I'd bring you all the way back here just to leave your corpse lying around all willy-nilly?" He shook his head. "No, I don't want anyone to know you're gone. It'd be best if you just, you know…disappeared."

A new smile crossed his face, but the genuine nature had been replaced with a sinister one instead. Brian felt the impending threat but, as always, he was too curious for his own good.

"How exactly do you plan on having me just *disappear*? I'm standing feet away from your mother's office."

Brian's own observation was enlightening. He was so caught up with the surprise of being back in Hell that he hadn't considered Lucy might be able to help. Then again, who's to say that she wasn't part of the coup?

"Brian, Brian, Brian," Dallas said as he took a step toward him, "the disappearing will happen but first, remember when you were asking me about Hellions and when they lose their forms?"

Brian's mind snapped back to the conversation in the lobby of the office building.

"Is this our field trip then?" Brian asked, feeling as though he already knew the answer.

Dallas smiled and gripped his shoulder firmly. "Watch closely," he whispered.

Brian felt a soft rumble at his feet. He looked down to the moonlit grass in time to watch each individual blade slip from its place and slide downward into the earth. The descending blades radiated inward toward the fountain. The rumbling continued as a cloudy burnt orange began to bleed through the dark of the night sky. As the last patch of grass evaporated into nothingness, the stones of the pathways were revealed to be the tops of stone spires that rose up from an unsettlingly colored river. The fountain, as far as Brian could tell from his suddenly elevated vantage point, seemed to be the elaborate stopper of a large, glass ampoule emitting a brilliant blue-white light. Running down the glass were thick bands of leather, casting striped shadows in all directions.

This felt *much* more like Hell.

"So, to answer your question," Dallas said once the transformation was complete, "that is the bank." He pointed to the ampoule.

The light pulsed and swam like an absurdly large lava lamp. Dallas wrapped his arm around Brian's shoulders once more and pointed to the river of thick red that surrounded the bank. "See the icky gooey stuff all over? When a Hellion's soul has been ripped apart and replaced too many times, it forgets what it used to look like. The soul, however, is a stubborn thing. Even when there are fractions of fractions floating in the bank, they still try to take some kind of form. The pieces all call to each other and try to make a physical housing for themselves. When the soul is broken enough, that—" Dallas gestured to the blood-colored sludge below, "—is usually all that can materialize."

Brian swallowed hard. His disturbing glimpse behind the curtain was enough to send chills through him. Dallas explaining it all to him now slowly opened the door to the horror of Brian's situation. He looked from Dallas to the Hellions, who seemed to be standing on thin air behind them. Brian couldn't see any means of escape that didn't involve him plummeting into an amorphous sludge of soul fragments. His heart raced. His skin went clammy.

"Let me guess," Brian's voice quivered from his throat, "that's what's going to happen to my soul?"

Dallas removed his arm from Brian's shoulders and patted him on the back.

"I think so? Honestly, I'm not sure exactly what will happen after the soul fragments find a physical container for them to inhabit," Dallas said.

Brian's eyelids peeled back as far as they could. His head whipped around to look at Dallas flashing a menacing grin before Brian felt a hard thrust between his shoulder blades that threw him from the pillar.

Brian's body dropped quickly from the peak but it felt as though his heart and lungs hadn't caught up with the rest of him. He gave a loud but short yell. The tension in his chest and gut refused to give any leeway to allow the passage of any more oxygen to extend it to a full scream. Wind rushed past his ears attempting its best to flood them from the pounding of his heart as he dropped.

His mind was a blur of panic and impulsive thought. He felt the sheets of Dahlia's bed against his skin. The smell of freshly brewed coffee. He heard the sounds of the creaking fourth step in the staircase of the house he grew up in. Brian was never as accomplished as he would have liked. He never reached the peak of his potential, nor did he slack off enough to truly enjoy the hedonism life had to offer. The smaller brushstrokes painted a canvas of regret, one that Brian careened through on the way to his fate. The briefest glimmer of rage flashed across his heart as the gap between Brian and the surface of the river closed. The crimson goo below started to illuminate in pockets like a lightning storm brewing beneath the depths. Just at the moment Brian felt as though he'd been falling for far too long, the remainder of the drop seemed to accelerate and Brian impacted the river of souls.

The feeling was something akin to dropping face-first into a pool of whipping cream covered with a layer of plastic wrap. Brian submerged what could have been only a few feet before the liquid around him began to congeal and flicker uncontrollably.

A brief moment passed where the words 'that wasn't so bad' skipped across Brian's frontal lobe. That moment heralded another that brought with it the worst sensation he had ever experienced. He felt as though the air was being ripped from his body outward through the walls of his lungs. The sensation of the skin on his chest and back being peeled slowly off the muscle by tiny fishhooks accompanied the absurd drowning. All the while, strobing flashes of soul fragments fired like synapses through the surrounding liquid. Brian's heart drummed a fully automatic procession in his ears that slowly gave way to the newest horror presented by the river.

Screaming.

Millions of voices wailed and screamed in Brian's ears. Some sounded like they were miles away; others sounded as though they were screaming through faulty sound equipment. Most of them, however, were clear and terribly shrill. The voices of the soul fragments were in pain, desperately clinging to Brian's flesh in hopes of making him a new vessel for their mismatched pieces. The voices, Brian soon realized, were bypassing his ears and psychically barraging his consciousness – a consciousness that was beginning to slip away.

The air trapped in his lungs finally released through his mouth. His chest felt dense and his shoulders slouched limply. The crimson light show before his eyes slowly began to sink into a steadily growing vignette of fuzzy blackness. Brian's fingers twitched as the last pinhole of red was swallowed up by the dark. The screaming was the last element that lingered. Brian's consciousness slipped from him somewhere between the screaming growing louder and the feeling of having each molecule ripped forcibly from his body one by one.

124 • BRAD ABDUL

CHAPTER SIXTEEN

The ground was solid, and the sky was a crisp, light blue, pocked by the occasional fluffy cloud. The blades of grass had resumed their former position and danced gently in the warm breeze that lazily swept the courtyard. The calming sound of the fountain was disturbed by the fierce gasp that emitted from the body that lay next to it.

Fresh air careened into Brian's lungs, hitting him in the chest like a bowling ball. His chest heaved as he gulped lungful after lungful of oxygen. His body tensed as his fingers dug into the soft earth beside him. The feeling in his fingers and toes slowly crackled back to life and sent signals proclaiming their utter disdain for having been dead in the first place. A small hand slid under Brian's back and began to gently prop him forward.

"Easy does it," Lucy whispered as Brian's vision spiraled outward from darkness and into the brightness of the courtyard.

His head pounded, making it feel several times too large for his shoulders to support. Compared to the screaming he'd fallen into, the serenity of the courtyard was deafeningly quiet.

"What happened?"

The words grated on his throat like sandpaper and the movement of his jaw reminded him that the strike from Dallas's heel still begged for its own attention among the rest of his wounds. He placed his palms on the ground behind his back to help support his body. Lucy remained crouched next to him, supporting his back.

"Broad strokes? You almost died," she said, trying to lighten the mood.

One of Brian's hands moved from the grass to his forehead.

"Where is Dallas?" he said through closed eyes.

"I don't know. I got out here just in time to see you swan dive into the river."

Her concerned look would have been heartwarming if Brian had been able to open his eyes past the immense pain his body was still in.

"The Sales Reps – they helped him get me," he said somewhere between attempting to formulate a plan and recalling the events that almost led to his death.

"I know." Lucy nodded. "Sal reported some of his Hellions had gone into the human world off the books and haven't come back."

"Oh, they definitely came back," Brian said.

He pushed his body further forward into a slouching sitting position. "Is Dahlia okay?"

"She's fine, she didn't know you were gone until a few minutes ago," Lucy said.

Brian opened his eyes and took in his surroundings with a clearer head. The day was in full swing.

"How long have I been out?" he asked.

"A few hours."

"How long was I under for?"

"A few seconds at most."

"It felt longer than that."

Brian's mind slipped back to the sound of screaming and the feeling of his flesh being forcibly removed from his body, slowly, torturously. His gaze dropped to the soft, lush grass dancing in front of him. "So, that was Hell – the *real* Hell," Brian said.

Lucy sighed and sat next to him. "Part of it, yes."

★   ★   ★

Dahlia bolted from the gateway. Wisps of white flame still clung to her as she arrived in the foyer where Lucy and Brian were waiting; the latter was curled up in a ball on the sectional.

"Jesus Christ, Brian, are you okay?"

Her voice was elevated with concern. Brian gave a slight and very painful nod. He felt like he was coming off of the worst hangover he'd ever had.

Lucy looked at Dahlia with a face of concern that began to border on anger.

"Do you know where Dallas is?" she asked firmly.

Dahlia shook her head and looked menacingly at her mother.

"If I did, I would have dragged him through that gateway with me – one piece at a time if necessary."

Her voice dropped a handful of octaves as she replied and Brian couldn't help but feel like the Devil part of her was something he hadn't gotten a chance to see in their time together.

"I'm hurt enough," Brian said, his voice a raspy crackle. "I don't need you hunting Dallas on my behalf and making me worry about you at the same time."

"I'm not some helpless girl. I am the daughter of the Devil."

"And I would still worry about you," Brian said.

Dahlia stared sternly back at him.

"No one knows what he's capable of – what he's willing to do. That worries me. I don't want you to *ever* experience what I just went through."

Brian slowly unfurled his body so that he was sitting normally on the cushy sectional. He rested his elbows on his knees and his head dangled so his gaze was on the floor before him.

"Besides, if anyone is going to dismantle Dallas, it's going to be me."

Menace tinted his words, giving Dahlia a shiver and Lucy a sly smirk. Lucy rose from her seat next to Brian and made her way to her office. The doors opened and she disappeared behind them for a moment. The clacking of her shoes echoed closer as she left the office once more with a package of papers in her hand. She resumed her seat next to Brian and crossed her legs, handing Brian the stack.

"If you're plotting revenge then you'll need to do it where Dallas can't reach you," she said as Brian took the package.

He flipped open the cover to see the contract that Dallas had thrown in the fountain.

"Is it the same as before?" Brian said as he looked sideways at Lucy.

She nodded. "Once it's signed, you and I will both take it to the Records department and file it ourselves. That way you can continue to stay in Hell without worry of your soul being drawn to the bank like it was before."

Brian's chest tightened at Lucy's words. The experience of being dropped into the river would not be one that went away any time soon and Brian did not enjoy having slivers of it being inserted through his day.

"You don't sound concerned for the safety of your son," Brian said in a grim growl.

Lucy reclined in her seat, throwing her arm over the back of the sofa.

"He's a grown man who made a poor choice. Far be it from me to intervene on what's coming to him."

Brian glanced to Dahlia. The way Lucy spoke of Dallas was the complete opposite of how she spoke about Dahlia. Her words in the courtyard when Brian revealed their relationship were more indicative of motherly concern than her seemingly cavalier position on Dallas's life at present.

Almost reflexively, Brian poised his hand and a thick fountain pen materialized in his fingers. He turned to the last page and signed his name before passing the pages to Lucy. Her eyes went wide in surprise at Brian's conjuring. She took the pen and signed, her gaze remaining on Brian all the while. She closed the package and handed it back to Brian.

He stood from his seat and grabbed Dahlia's hand from her side. Her face was draped in astonishment as well. He smiled at her and squeezed her hand gently before releasing it and turning back to Lucy.

"So, where's the Records department?"

★   ★   ★

Unsurprisingly – yet also disappointingly – the Records department of Hell was just as boring as any other Records department in any other office. Rows upon rows of filing cabinets filled the room, which was attended by a single Hellion named Margaret. She looked like a sweet, old lady and Brian had an easier time imagining her baking cookies in a flowery apron than cataloguing contracts for souls in Hell. When his contract was stored safely in a cabinet near the front of the large office, a sudden and overwhelming feeling took Brian. His insides tingled as though he had just downed a glass of warm milk. The sensation contrasted with the severe pain that still echoed in his bones, and he felt he was being made whole once more.

Brian returned to his room where he found Dahlia waiting for him. Her eyes locked on to Brian the moment he walked through the door. She stood and walked over to him, placing her head on his chest. He winced slightly at the phantom pain of his flesh being torn from his body. He wrapped his arms around her tightly, took a deep breath and exhaled slowly.

"How are you?" she asked, speaking into his chest.

He rested his chin on her head and stared into space. "Alive."

She released him and looked at him. Brian caught his own reflection in her wide eyes. He looked terrible – his eyes were sunken and a deep bruise was fully formed on one side of his face. He was gaunt and looked as though he had not slept in days. "How are you?" he asked, sensing her assessment of his appearance.

She shrugged. "I hate myself for not hearing you wake up. I hate myself even more for not being able to bring Dallas back to Hell in sandwich bags," she said angrily. "I am also not a fan that my house was broken into. Needless to say, I'm selling it and moving somewhere more private now that he knows where it is."

"That's a shame, I was just starting to get comfortable there," Brian said in a weak attempt at levity.

She half-heartedly smirked at him. Both were exhausted and at a loss of how to proceed after the events of the previous night.

"Seriously though," Dahlia said, "how are you feeling?"

Her green eyes looked deep into Brian's and he couldn't help but feel like she was looking into them for something particular.

"Other than being in pain, I'm fine," he said honestly.

Dahlia shook her head. "Not what I meant."

"Want to clarify then?"

"What was with the pen?"

Brian's eyes narrowed as he remembered summoning the pen. He recalled being angry when he did it but there was something else there. The same 'something else' that Brian felt faintly beneath his skin since he woke from his drowning. He attributed the sensation to his continued recovery from the river; in truth, the feeling less resembled a side effect and more of an innate feeling that had been introduced since his forcible baptism.

"I'm not sure. I have this strange feeling running through my body. I don't really know how to describe it."

He raised his hand with his palm up and his fingers curled around. He concentrated and a single rose materialized in his palm.

"I feel like I've always known how to use soul energy. It's almost like muscle memory. I don't have to think too hard about what I want; I just concentrate on something and there it is."

Dahlia's face sank slightly at Brian's explanation.

"It's like a swarm of ants made of light marching up and down your veins. You can't always feel it, but if you think about it, the feeling is there." She looked at him with sad eyes. "Is that what it feels like?"

Brian thought for a moment, letting the rose de-materialize in his palm.

"That's scarily accurate," he said.

She sighed heavily. "Then it looks like you and I are more similar than we thought," Dahlia whispered as tears welled up in her eyes.

Brian quickly moved to her and directed her to sit on the bed. He put one arm around her shoulders and his hand in her lap.

"What does that mean?" he said, worried.

Tears slowly began to roll down her cheeks. "I think the exposure you had to the concentration of corrupted soul fragments in the river might have corrupted your own."

Brian recoiled slightly. He felt as though there were a physical – if not metaphysical – difference since his swim in the river, but he didn't any less like himself.

"How can you be sure?" he asked.

"Because my soul was created using the fragments of the bank. That swarm feeling is how I feel all the time."

Dahlia seemed as though she were in mourning, yet Brian felt somehow comfortable with the revelation that his soul had now been corrupted beyond saving.

"Why are you upset?" he asked.

Brian couldn't understand why Dahlia was so impacted by his sudden change. Despite her origins and lineage, for all intents and purposes, Dahlia seemed normal enough even after her corruption. The tears stopped rolling and their tracks were drying on her cheeks.

"You have a human soul. There are so many possibilities to that. You're capable of good and evil equally – you get to choose which you act on." Dahlia put her hand softly against his chest. "At least, you *did*. Your soul isn't human anymore. It's something different now, and it's unfair that something so important was taken from you."

Brian started to understand. She was mourning the loss of his humanity because she wished so strongly to have it for herself. She never had the chance, being made of corrupted souls, so it made sense that she yearned for a taste of humanity. Brian finally realized that it hurt her to watch his humanity be stripped from him.

"I get it," Brian said quietly. "At least, I think I get it."

Despite all that had happened, Brian found himself the least concerned by the loss of his humanity – whatever that truly meant.

He pulled Dahlia into his chest and hugged her as tight as his aching body would allow.

"If there's a way to fix what's been done to me, I'll find it."

Dahlia pulled away and looked at him in disbelief.

"There isn't a way to 'fix it'," she said.

Brian shrugged. "Has anyone ever tried?"

CHAPTER SEVENTEEN

In the days following his return to Hell, Brian spent most of his time recovering in bed. The feeling of the illuminated ants beneath his skin – which he began affectionately referring to as 'The Swarm' – persisted during his recovery.

Lucy treated Brian's security as top priority, stationing Hellions at the entrance to the tower where his room was at all times. The only people allowed through the barricade were Dahlia, Lucy and, on one surprising occasion, Sal.

His visit was short and forced. Brian assumed he came to show face and to make it clear that he had no involvement in his kidnapping. Brian was content with believing him and ending their forced exchange quickly but, on his way out, Sal lost his composure.

"I can't believe that Jeremy would do somethin' like that to you," he said with genuine frustration in his voice.

"I'm surprised by it as well," Brian said. "I guess I really must have crossed a line with him when we first spoke."

Sal nodded slowly with a contemplative look on his face. "Jus' another minion for Dallas to use. That Dallas – he had us all fooled."

★   ★   ★

When Brian recovered enough to stay conscious for most of the day, he began to dig into the preparations he and Dani had drafted for the kickoff of S.I.N. Industries. In contrast to before, Brian felt that there was a pending due date on increasing Hell's profits. The threat of Dallas reappearing to finish what he'd started was unsettling, especially now that Brian's contract was properly filed in Records. He was sure the next time Dallas attempted to take his life he would do so more efficiently.

Brian also started devoting time to understanding the properties of a corrupted soul. His sudden and complete corruption had become a point of interest regarding the fundamentals of soul composition. When he felt capable enough, he took trips to visit the Twins to figure out how it worked.

"Ain't so simple," Peter said as he clicked away furiously at his mouse, "corruptin' a soul all the way. You sure tha's wha' happened to ya?"

His beady multi-eyes peeked over his computer monitor at Brian.

"From the sounds of things, I think that might be what happened. I was hoping you fellas could tell me if it's true," Brian said.

Paul stood from his seat and stared at Brian with an evil grin.

"You want us to look at yer file, then?" he asked deviously.

Peter chuckled from across the room.

Brian acquiesced. "If that's how you check how much someone's soul is corrupted, then sure."

The Twins looked at each other with devilish glee and giggled like school boys. Paul resumed his seat and began clacking at his keyboard.

"Lessee, then…" he started.

"Stole candy as a lad. Tsk, tsk," Peter continued.

Paul shot him a glare. "Oi, I thought *I* was lookin' up 'is file?"

"I've had 'is file open since 'e walked through the door," Peter confessed before the two broke out into preteen chuckling once more.

Brian sighed with annoyance and rolled his wrist for the two to continue their investigation.

"Ya scratched someone's car and di'int leave yer insurance info."

"Lied and told yer college girlfriend you were gay cuz ya di'int know how to break up wiv 'er."

"Jesus, that's in there?" Brian asked as his cheeks flushed red.

"Jus' about ev'rything ya do is in 'ere. S'how we know how corrupt you are," Paul clarified.

His multi-eyes returned to the screen and squinted slightly, searching for more intrusive details of Brian's shame.

"Is there not a way you can just tell me, in numbers, how corrupt my soul is currently?" Brian asked, becoming impatient with the humor that his life was bringing the Twins.

Peter grunted and turned his monitor out to face Brian.

Brian's list of infractions was small. Among the more embarrassing entries the Twins decided to vocalize, Brian saw snippets from his life and the corruption value they were assigned. At the top of the page, a simplified breakdown was represented in a table:

Subject	Brian G. Lachey
Offense Entries	11
Average Corruption Rate	2.4%
Total Corruption	100%

Brian's demeanor became stern as he assessed the table.

"Doesn't the total corruption rate look off to you?" Brian asked aloud to whichever of the Twins cared to listen.

Peter shot him a confused glare. "Ay? Whatchu mean?" he asked, turning the screen back.

"The amount of offenses I have with the average corruption rate. The math doesn't work for it to equal out at one-hundred-percent corruption."

Peter squinted again at the screen.

"Lookin' at the entries, an' if I'm doin' my maths right, you should on'y be 'bout twen'y-four percent corrupted," Paul said from across the office.

Brian considered the information for a moment.

"Do you have files on Dahlia and Dallas?" Brian asked.

Being able to compare his data with people made from corruption and raised in Hell could give him a benchmark in which to measure his own status.

Paul exhaled annoyedly through his nostrils and turned his attention to the computer once more. After a few additional clacks he turned the screen to Brian.

Subject	Dahlia Fair
Offense Entries	3
Average Corruption Rate	6.8%
Total Corruption	100%

Out of respect for Dahlia's privacy, Brian looked away from her list of offenses. One innocuous glance made a smirk cross his face as he saw an offense listed under *Fraud – Real Estate*. Still, Brian was surprised to find that Dahlia had less than half the number of offenses he did – fairly impressive for the daughter of the Devil.

Brian frowned as he turned his attention to the breakdown table at the top of the page. It resembled his own, including the incalculable math that added up to pure corruption.

"Okay," Brian said after analyzing the screen for a few moments, "what about Dallas?"

He turned to Peter, who adjusted his screen for Brian's viewing.

"What the hell?" he said under his breath.

Subject	Dallas Fair
Offense Entries	72
Average Corruption Rate	18.2%
Total Corruption	0%

Brian stared at the screen for longer than a few moments. Lacking any respect for Dallas, he skimmed over the listed offences. Entries including assault, extortion and harassment were among the list. Brian's eyes snapped back to the breakdown table once more and lingered on the total corruption percentage.

"How is this possible?" Brian asked.

Peter turned the screen back to himself and considered the table. He stroked his chin and shook his head slowly as he scrolled through the information.

"On'y way this could be possible would be if he atoned," Peter said suspiciously.

Surprised crept onto Brian's face. "You mean he asked forgiveness from God?" he said, hoping that Peter would tell him otherwise.

Peter nodded silently.

Brian crossed his arms over his chest. The illuminated ants beneath his skin felt as though they were frenzying to break their fleshy confinement.

"Thank you, gentlemen," Brian bellowed deeply. The rumbling in his chest would have concerned him if not for the drumming of The Swarm marching the feeling down.

The Twins' multi-eyes widened in surprise at the sound of menace in Brian's voice before he left the office.

★   ★   ★

"You're kidding," Lucy said as she slouched against her desk.

Brian shook his head. He distributed his weight evenly and crossed his arms as he exhaled the fire from his lungs.

"How the hell did he convince God to absolve his sins? *His* sins. Dallas, the son of the Devil," Brian thought out loud.

Lucy drummed her chin with her fingertips. A dumbfounded look draped her face as she stared blankly past Brian.

"He's a smooth talker. He always has been," she said pensively. "He must have gone to her and spun some story to get on her side."

Lucy absentmindedly bit her nails as she spoke.

This was the first time Brian had ever seen her react like this to anything. His frustration bubbled to the surface.

"So, what now? If he's atoned then he's likely got some kind of plan involving God, right?" Brian said impatiently.

Lucy lingered. "If she's involved then this could get ugly," she said finally after considering the situation. Life returned to her eyes as they found Brian's. "How quickly can you and Dani launch this project of yours?"

"Provided I'm given free rein on staff and full access to the bank, we can get it off the ground within the week," Brian replied.

Lucy nodded. "Let's get this moving. The more energy we have in the bank to fund a potential defense strategy, the better."

The doors to Lucy's office opened behind them. Dahlia poked her head through the gap and cleared her throat softly.

"There's someone here to see you," she said, anticipation etched in her gaze.

Lucy frowned. "I don't have any appointments today. Who is it?"

Lucy made her way to the doors with a frustrated stride. Dahlia moved back through the gap just as Lucy pushed the doors open fully to scan the foyer. She looked back at Dahlia when she discovered the room was empty. "Well, where are they?"

"She's waiting in the courtyard," Dahlia said sheepishly.

Annoyance took over Lucy's demeanor.

"You let someone in?" she hissed.

Dahlia shook her head. "She was already there. I don't know how long she's been waiting."

Lucy's eyes went wide. She took hurried steps around the receptionist's desk toward the double doors of the courtyard.

Brian glanced curiously at Dahlia. "Who is it?" he asked.

Dahlia gave a look of astonishment. "Someone we haven't seen around here in decades."

CHAPTER EIGHTEEN

Brian and Dahlia hurried to catch up with Lucy as she pushed open the double doors to the courtyard. Brian wasn't sure whether or not his new connection to the bank had provided him with some level of extrasensory perception, but he felt as though he could sense Lucy's heart beating in his chest.

The sunlight glittered off the trickling water of the fountain. The dazzling light danced around a dainty figure sitting on the lip of the basin.

Her slender form was clad in a flowing white gown that looked like it had been stitched from wisped smoke. The dress was an elegant mix of mermaid bridal gown and nightie, hugging her figure and allowing the pigment of her skin below to show through the sheer material. Her dark skin contrasted beautifully against the undulating white smoke. Vagrant mist from the fountain lit her tight curls that parted off-center, making her locks glitter with a similar brilliance as the streams of water that rose and fell in the sunlight. Her pale blue eyes dreamily glided from underneath their smoky lids to find Lucy.

Lucy took slow steps toward the woman. As Brian watched, Lucy's appearance began to shift before him. Her once shoulder-length wavy brown hair became saturated from root to tip with an orangey-red. The waves grew longer as they dropped loose and elegantly around her shoulders and hung in front of her bosom and down the middle of her back. The black business suit that she wore (less now because it was a temptation for Brian and more because she liked the way it looked) transmuted from silk to the same wisped smoke that her guest wore, but of a darker variety. The smoke retained the shape of the suit for a brief moment before spilling down Lucy's body to form a simple, low-cut, low-back, long-trained dress. The shadows of the courtyard seemed to shiver as Lucy completed donning her new form.

The woman at the fountain watched in sultry amusement as Lucy approached. She rose to her feet in a fashion that suggested that the white smoke of her dress had simply lifted her from her seat.

"Gabrielle," Lucy began, "how are you?"

Lucy's voice was pure silken lust. The smoke of their respective gowns twisted together as she embraced Gabrielle.

"I'm alive," Gabrielle said as the two separated.

Lucy smirked. "You never get tired of that joke, do you?" she said, giggling softly.

Gabrielle smiled and leaned to peer around Lucy's shoulder.

"And who is this?" Gabrielle said as her eyes found Brian.

Lucy hesitated for a moment, seemingly experiencing difficulty in finding the words to describe Brian.

Dahlia sighed at her mother's flustered demeanor.

"This is Brian," Dahlia said as she hooked her arm into Brian's. "He's been helping out in Hell lately."

Gabrielle raised an eyebrow at Dahlia and Brian's linked arms. "Helping indeed," she said deviously.

Dahlia's cheeks went slightly rosy at the comment. "Brian, this is Gabrielle," she said, directing his attention with her hand. "Better known by her working name – *Death*."

Brian's eyes widened and began darting from Dahlia to Gabrielle to Lucy. A playfully surprised expression took Gabrielle's face.

"I can't recall the last time you called me that," Gabrielle said amusedly. Her gaze moved once more to Brian. "Brian, was it? You're alive, aren't you?"

Brian's words nearly got caught in his throat. "For the moment, yes," he said cautiously.

He felt more hesitant meeting Death than he did in his first meeting with Lucy.

"That's interesting, I can't say I've seen any living service in Hell in quite some time," Gabrielle said with a hint of surprise and whimsy in her voice. She turned her attention to Lucy once more. "Can't find any decent help these days?"

Lucy's fingers rose up and massaged her temples as she sighed in annoyance. "You have no idea."

"Actually, I think I might," Gabrielle said as she resumed her seat at the lip of the basin.

Lucy sat next to her, their dresses ebbing and flowing into one another.

"I saw Dallas."

Lucy glared. "How? Where?" she asked.

Gabrielle raised her hand gently between them, a gesture that looked like it was meant to calm Lucy down. Lucy recoiled but retained the look of concern on her face. Brian and Dahlia found themselves taking unsure steps toward the conversation as Gabrielle started again.

"One of my Reapers found him. He was asking to meet with me and, from the sound of things, wasn't very shy about flaunting who he was in order to make that happen." Gabrielle explained. "Seems he and a few Hellions used their influence to start a school shooting, hoping to get my attention."

"Son of a bitch," Brian blurted, now far closer than he last remembered being while listening to the story.

The red-headed Lucy shot him a dirty look. He cringed as he considered his words.

"Sorry, no offense."

Dahlia smacked his chest with the back of her hand for his awkward intrusion. Lucy shook her head at the pair and resumed her conversation.

"What did he want?" Lucy asked.

Gabrielle donned a worried expression. "He wanted me to bring him to Allanah."

"Fuck," Lucy let slip.

She glanced back to Brian, who returned it with an inquisitive one.

"Who's Allanah?" Brian asked.

Gabrielle gave him a sympathetic yet patronizing expression. "Lucy's sister," she said.

"God," Lucy corrected quickly.

Brian's eyes felt as though they were about to roll out of his skull.

"God is your *sister*?" Brian hissed. "I've been down here this whole time and you didn't think that was important to mention?"

"No, because it's not important," Lucy said harshly at Brian's criticism. "It doesn't matter what we are to each other. Where we stand with one another is far more important."

Brian looked back at Dahlia, whose nonchalance was clear.

"She's not wrong," Dahlia said.

Brian sighed in annoyance. Lucy returned her attention to Gabrielle.

"Do you know what they talked about?" Lucy asked, hopefully.

Gabrielle shook her head softly, her tight curls gently bouncing.

"I wasn't around for their conversation. I think the correct term is that I was 'shooed away'." Gabrielle paused for a moment and took a deep breath. "I did hear *one* thing before I was forced to exit," she said hesitantly.

"What?" Lucy probed.

Gabrielle's face scrunched slightly in confusion.

"'Dear, sweet aunt. I've come to repent,' I think were his exact words."

"Well that confirms your theory on Dallas's soul being cleaned," Lucy threw back to Brian.

Dahlia's eyes narrowed at the comment.

"Wait a damn minute. Dallas isn't corrupted anymore?"

Her gaze darted from Lucy to Brian.

"I just came back from talking with the Twins. We pulled up his file and it looks like he's clean," Brian explained.

Dahlia's face started to flood red as the words sank in.

"Son of a bitch," she spat.

Lucy looked back at her, less in a critical manner and more in a sympathetic one.

"Lucy," Gabrielle interrupted, "I wouldn't have come here in person just to tell you that." She placed her hand on Lucy's. "I've noticed Angels making some strange moves lately. My Reapers have been reporting to me on any movement on any side, and Dallas kept on showing up in those reports. He's been making frequent trips to the human world. I think something is coming your way."

Lucy fell silent at Gabrielle's words. Brian couldn't figure out whether Lucy was scared or furious.

"What are you thinking, Lucy?" Brian asked hesitantly.

"I think we've all been giving Dallas less credit in the smarts department than he deserves," she replied.

Brian frowned at the thought. "What does that mean?"

"It means that I think Dallas is working for Allanah to take over Hell," Lucy replied through gritted teeth.

Concern etched Brian's face. "So, what do we do?" he asked.

The thought of Dallas alone was enough to set Brian on edge. If he was being supported by God, that was a far more terrifying prospect.

"Is it fair to assume that you came to tell me all this because you want to help?" Lucy asked Gabrielle.

Gabrielle gave a soft, knowing smile.

"There's a delicate balance that needs to be kept between Heaven and Hell. Part of my job is to keep that balance. Plus, let's just say that things would be less interesting without you around," she replied.

Lucy smiled and stroked the top of Gabrielle's hand that held her own.

"Then we need to prepare," Lucy said as she stood from her seat next to Gabrielle. "Can you have your Reapers keep an eye out for any other strange happenings in the human world?"

"They're already on it," Gabrielle replied.

"We need to get your project off the ground as soon as possible," Lucy said to Brian.

"Wait, Dallas might be spinning some kind of story to Allanah to get her support, but she doesn't know him. She doesn't know how long he's been vying for the throne. More importantly, she doesn't know why he hasn't been chosen to take over. Maybe we can talk to her? She might not want Dallas in charge if she knows the details," Dahlia interjected.

Lucy shook her head. "Allanah doesn't want someone capable. She wants a puppet."

"Tipping her off that we know something is up might also prompt her to launch an attack before we're ready," Brian added. "I'll work with Dani and Sal to get things moving ASAP."

Lucy turned to Dahlia. "I need you to do research and find out which Hellions Dallas has on his side. We need to cut off as much of his support as possible. Pull their contracts from Records and destroy them."

"Losing that many Hellions, that much soul energy, that will be a huge hit on the bank," Dahlia replied.

Lucy gave a stern look in reply. "It's too much of a risk having them out and about while being able to use the gateway whenever they please. Work the numbers with Deborah and figure out how much of a loss we'll take. See if there are any other corners that can be cut to preserve energy in the event of an emergency," Lucy commanded.

Dahlia nodded dutifully. "Should I prep Sal, Marie and the others for emergency protocol?"

Lucy paused for a moment before locking eyes with Dahlia and giving a sharp nod.

"What emergency protocol?" Brian asked.

"Any Hellion with a history of extreme violence, or who contracted their soul for violent means, are given special provisions in the event of an invasion," Dahlia clarified.

"What kind of provisions?"

"They return to their original form and are provided augmented weapons in order to defend Hell. It's a big strain on the bank to actively pull all the original fragments of their souls back together, so it's not a strategy used very often."

Brian was surprised to hear the countermeasures that Hell had and wondered how often Heaven and Hell warred with one another.

Gabrielle touched Lucy's arm gently, bringing her back to their conversation.

"If it's all the same to you, I'll stay in Hell for a while and coordinate my side from here," she said.

Lucy turned to face her in surprise. Her brief militant nature was stifled by Gabrielle, and Lucy seemed as though she wasn't sure how to respond.

"Excellent. I love when Aunt Gabbi sleeps over," Dahlia said in a patronizing tone.

Gabrielle gave Dahlia a snarky smile while Lucy shot her a dirty glare.

★ ★ ★

Brian tossed in his sleep. The events of the day seemed to have the intention of catching up with him in his dreams. Elements of his corruption, Dallas's murderous – and now, apparently, benevolently sanctioned – schemes, and the coming frenzy that was the S.I.N. Industries kickoff all intertwined in Brian's head into horrendously transmuted versions of themselves.

A sharp breath hit Brian's lungs, jolting him up in his bed. He attempted to claw his way from the fog of his dreams and into the comfort of his darkened room, chest heaving like he'd been drowning. As the remnants of the subconscious demons dripped slowly once more into the back of Brian's mind, he noticed that he was alone in his bed. He then recalled specifically not being alone when he first fell asleep.

After donning a thin robe and slippers (that wardrobe never ceased to amaze Brian), he opened the door to his room, allowing moonlight to flood in from the window across the hall. He stepped out and was drawn to the shapes of two figures sitting in the courtyard. Brian's chest clenched instinctively when he remembered the last time he saw nondescript figures in the night. The tension in his solar plexus released slightly when he realized that the figures belonged to Dahlia and Gabrielle.

Brian exited the stairwell that led down from the tower and entered the courtyard. Dahlia was wrapped in a robe similar to the one Brian was wearing. The waves of her hair were bound in a ponytail, and she sat cross-legged on the grass. Next to her was Gabrielle, who was dressed in very much the same clothing (if it were, indeed, clothing) as

Brian saw her in earlier that afternoon. The pair turned to look over their shoulders as Brian made his approach.

The moon illuminated the trickling streams from the fountain and the sound of the water dribbling into the basin echoed softly across the courtyard. Gabrielle smiled at Brian as he arrived next to the pair.

"I hope I'm not intruding," he said hesitantly.

Gabrielle shook her head softly, the smile still across her lips.

"Not at all," she replied.

"I was just catching up with Aunt Gabbi. It's been *decades* since we last chatted," Dahlia said, offering up the patch of grass next to her for Brian to sit.

"Decades?" Brian repeated as he took a seat. "You're going to tell me how old you actually are one day, right?"

Dahlia dramatically made a hair-flipping motion with her hand that touched none of her actual ponytailed locks.

"Age is just a number. All that matters are these devilish good looks," she said in her mock-southern accent.

Gabrielle giggled at the exchange.

"So, what have you two been talking about?" Brian asked.

Gabrielle smiled warmly at him. "As a matter of fact, we were talking about you," she said.

Brian shot Dahlia a look.

"What about me?" he asked cautiously.

"Only the worst things," Dahlia mused.

Gabrielle giggled slightly once more. "Dahlia was just telling me what brought you here. Lucy can be a convincing individual," she said in an amused tone.

Brian smirked. "You'd know, I'm sure. From what I hear, you two have quite the history."

Gabrielle's smile was suddenly draped in nostalgia.

"You have no idea." The nostalgia shifted into melancholy and the smile faded. "That's why I'm so worried about what could be coming," she confessed.

"You mean God? I still can't believe they're sisters," he said.

Gabrielle's mouth curved into a slight frown.

"Believing doesn't get any easier even after knowing both of them as long as I have. They've never seen eye to eye."

"Why not?"

"Probably because of me," Gabrielle said pointedly.

Dahlia's head cocked. "This is the first I'm hearing of this. What happened?" she asked.

Gabrielle took a deep breath and slowly released it into the night.

"As far as Allanah sees things, Lucy corrupted me." The melancholic tone had now fully laden her words. "I used to be one of Allanah's Archangels."

"As in the Archangel Gabriel? That was you?" Brian asked.

Gabrielle smirked. "It's always ever been Gabrielle, however, the male-centric world you live in couldn't allow one of God's most powerful and dangerous Angels to be a woman. That would threaten the veil of their superiority too much." She shook her head at the thought.

"Why does Allanah think Mom took you away?" Dahlia asked.

Gabrielle leaned back and propped her torso up by her palms on the grass.

"When the Archangel comes around, sinners get punished. Your mom and I worked very closely together for a long time. Eventually she and I became closer than any immortal beings should. Allanah was not pleased with that and my title was revoked. "Lucy got the worst of it. Allanah went full-force on a campaign to disavow anything to do with Lucy. Organized religion as a concept was basically created as a large-scale propaganda attempt at making people fear the Devil. Allanah wanted to try and convert enough of humanity so that Lucy would be starved of energy and eventually fade from existence."

Brian donned a pensive look as he listened to the story. He knew God was a force to be reckoned with, but he never expected her to be so systematic in her actions.

"I hadn't heard the whole story until now," Dahlia said softly.

Gabrielle seemed unsurprised.

"It's not one your mom likes to talk about. She doesn't do well with girl troubles." Gabrielle attempted a chuckle but was more saddened by the ridiculousness of her words.

"So, you're not, you know, *amorphous* like Lucy?" Brian asked. "You just seem fairly comfortable with referring to yourself as a woman."

"I've always been a woman," Gabrielle replied. "If you're familiar with the Archangel Gabriel, then you'll definitely recognize my original identity. I was *Eve*."

"You're kidding," Dahlia said as her jaw dropped.

Gabrielle shook her head, sending her curls bouncing around her face.

"After we learned what we did from Eden, Allanah and Lucy couldn't have us rejoin the world, so we were given our roles," she explained.

"So, Adam is an Archangel now too?" Brian guessed.

"It's *Michael* now," she corrected.

"Wow. I should have paid more attention in Sunday school. Or, you know, *gone* to Sunday school," Brian replied, dumbfounded.

"There's no Sunday school in Hell," Dahlia added, equally dumbfounded.

Gabrielle shrugged. "Most of what you would have learned is garbage anyway. Best to hear the stories from the source than try to make sense of misconstrued propaganda from centuries ago."

Brian sat with Dahlia and Gabrielle for a while longer. After her revelation, they returned to talking about events from their recent lives. Brian resigned to listening as the two caught up like family. He could tell that, though Gabrielle and Lucy were not together, she was still part of the family. He wondered what she thought of Dallas's betrayal but didn't have the heart to bring up another depressing topic amid the lighthearted recounting the two were enjoying.

After some time, Brian excused himself from the conversation and returned to his room. His mind had somehow equally been eased of the thoughts that had woken him from his sleep and simultaneously abuzz with the new information he'd learned from Gabrielle. He had just slid under the covers as the door to his room opened slightly and Dahlia slipped through the crack. She quietly slid under the covers and nestled into his chest like a cat.

"She seems nice," Brian whispered.

Dahlia nodded. "It's crazy to think of all the things she and Mom have been through together. It's even crazier to think that they're not still together after having been through all of it." She wrapped her arm around Brian's ribs tightly and squeezed.

"That's true. Her story also makes me realize how little I really know about everything that's going on," Brian said softly.

Dahlia let out a small, melancholic sigh.

"Me too."

CHAPTER NINETEEN

The hue of the apple seemed to glow brighter tonight. Lucy sat in the gallery and stared up at the painting, drinking in the brushwork as if it could suture the reopened wound in her chest. Decades had passed since Lucy and Gabrielle were in the same place yet it was as though she could still smell the honey-crisp sweetness on her lips like she had back in the garden.

With great effort, and in a bid to stifle the ache inside her, Lucy tore herself away from Leonardo's imagery and made for her room. The heavy door clacked shut, and Lucy turned to find Gabrielle sitting on her sofa flipping through *The History of Hell*. The sudden fluttering feeling in her stomach caught Lucy by surprise, her organs jumbled up like a lovesick game of fifty-two pickup.

"I hope I'm not intruding," Gabrielle said softly, responding to Lucy's surprise.

Lucy shook her head and made her way around the banister, down toward the sofa and the crackling fire.

"I don't think there is any way you could intrude on me," Lucy replied.

Gabrielle closed the book on her lap and placed it on the arm of the sofa.

"Are you sure? There are some pretty personal things written in here," Gabrielle said, nodding to the book.

"Nothing untrue, and nothing you weren't there for too," Lucy said.

Gabrielle smirked playfully at the comment and invited Lucy to join her.

She hesitated for a moment before taking a seat next to Gabrielle on the sofa, making sure to leave enough room between the two of them to maintain the unclear boundaries that had befallen their relationship in the past century.

"I just had a wonderful chat with Dahlia and Brian," Gabrielle said, changing the subject. "Brian seems like a bright one, though it still surprises me that you outsourced a human. Again, I mean."

Lucy swallowed a developing lump in her throat. "He told you why he's here, I imagine?" she asked.

"Dahlia did."

"All of it?"

"As much as she felt appropriate. The rest I figured out on my own." Gabrielle took a deep breath and exhaled slowly. "I know how this must make you feel, my being here."

"You say that like you don't feel any differently being here," Lucy replied somberly.

"This visit isn't about us," Gabrielle said.

Her words, as well as her conviction, sounded weak.

"None of our visits in the past century have been."

"Lucy—"

"I'm doing this for us," Lucy declared, leaning in toward Gabrielle. "For the chance to have what we used to have."

"Lucy, I love you to death," Gabrielle started.

"Har har," Lucy rebutted, turning her gaze to the fireplace instead.

Gabrielle's hand grazed Lucy's chin, pulling her attention back with the simplest of gestures.

"But I need you to focus on the real reason for my visit if you want to survive long enough to retire."

Lucy looked into Gabrielle's eyes. She swam in them, getting lost in the glimmer of the fireplace that reflected in their depths, and found a sorrowful undertow that pulled her in further. She considered Gabrielle's words and attempted once more to keep the rupture in her chest from widening.

"So, what do you suggest?" Lucy said, trying her best to keep her head above the swells.

"I think Allanah might be considering Dallas as a suitable replacement for you. He knows the inner workings of Hell, and he would be easy to manipulate. I think an invasion is coming, and I think it's coming soon." Her words were filled with worry.

"I still haven't heard a suggestion," Lucy pressed. She could see Gabrielle struggling to find the right words.

"It's not an easy suggestion, but we need to eliminate Dallas somehow."

Lucy's shoulders went rigid as she leaned away from Gabrielle.

"I don't mean *kill him*, just take him out of the game somehow. Detain him. He is Allanah's access to Hell. If he's not involved, that takes away a huge advantage she has."

Lucy fell silent.

Dallas certainly deserved whatever came his way for the choices he'd made. That being said, she had no intention of letting him die. Brian made a fairly convincing threat after his swim in the pool of souls, but she knew he would never have the conviction to see it through. A strange feeling enveloped her. Something primal. Lucy had never felt maternal at all during her time as a parent – especially not toward Dallas. He was headstrong and stubborn, even from a young age, so she never saw the need to coddle him. However, the thought of any harm coming to him prodded a beast within her, and she was unable to translate its roaring into sensible thoughts or familiar emotions.

"Dallas is an impressionable kid. If Allanah has her hooks in him, it's not going to be easy to pull him out." Lucy chewed her thumbnail as she thought out loud. "Especially if he thinks he's going to take my place when this all shakes out. He will want to be on ground level."

"Is there any way we can find him in the human world? We could try to detain him before he even makes his move," Gabrielle spitballed.

"He's got access to the gateway, and he's used to slipping in and out of the human world. Worse, if his soul has been purified, he doesn't rely on the bank anymore for vitality, so he can play as long of a waiting game as he wants and take us by surprise." Lucy racked her brain, trying to think of a way to get around Dallas, all the while involuntarily admitting how airtight his approach was.

"I don't think we have any other choice but to wait until he comes back home."

Gabrielle collapsed into the back of the sofa. Her curls bobbed as her chin dropped to her chest in defeat. Silence hung in the room for a while with the crackling of the fireplace the only thing stopping it from being deafening.

"If it means stopping this invasion, and saving you, I'll do what I have to," Gabrielle said into the fire.

Lucy's eyes widened at the declaration. Her body clenched, and her instincts took over.

"I love you, Gabrielle," she said, "but if you hurt him, I can't guarantee I won't hurt you back."

Gabrielle's gaze lifted and met Lucy's, already fixated on her. There was no malice in her eyes, no menace – only a convicted stoicism, spiked with insecurity. With a pleading stare, she begged her lover one last time.

"Please, don't make me do that."

CHAPTER TWENTY

Brian's recovery was going slower than he would have liked. What felt like weeks slipped by as he lay in bed, his mind going miles per minute. His security detail was forcibly told to back down a bit and, with that, Brian started receiving some other visitors. It was strangely comforting to know how many of the residents of Hell seemed to care for his wellbeing.

Dani came by, talking like an auctioneer about ideas she had on the upcoming launch of S.I.N. Industries. She was in her glory, and Brian neither had the strength, nor the heart, to cut her short of her mostly incoherent ramblings.

Deborah also stopped in for a visit, which was a surprise. Brian never imagined them to be too close. She was pleasant enough while they worked together, but she always struck him as very guarded when it came to talking about anything but work. Her visit was brief but courteous. She checked on his condition, wished him well, and went back to the Finance department. Enough of a gesture to let Brian know that she was in his corner.

★   ★   ★

When he wasn't getting visitors, Brian was practicing. His dip in the river of souls had changed him. He knew that. What he didn't know was in what ways. The tingling sensation of insect legs under his skin came and went. More than the feeling, however, Brian felt something different. It was as if his senses were heightened, but not in any traditional way. More accurately, Brian felt attuned to the environment around him. The crackling of the fire in his room, the feel of the sheets against his skin. Brian was sure he was even beginning to sense when his wardrobe materialized clothes for him, or when the mini-bar at his bedside restocked the water bottles. It was like a vibration that tremored through his body. It also gave Brian the idea to test out some more of his Hellion abilities.

He recalled the feeling of summoning the fountain pen when he signed his new contract. The tingle at his fingertips that bled into the feeling of the metal barrel pressed between them. It took him a few tries to summon the pen on command rather than impulse. He eventually got familiar with the associated sensations, prompting him to try other objects. A drinking glass. A shoe. A leaf. Always materialized in his hands. He needed to 'feel' the object before he was successful in creating it. Another few days' work, and Brian was able to materialize things across the room. He drew on his memories of his first days in Hell, summoning a plastic chair across from his plush armchair in front of the fireplace.

★   ★   ★

When he was feeling a bit better and moving around a little easier, Dahlia came up with an idea to help speed up his recovery.

"You want us to go to the human world?" Brian asked, making sure he heard her right.

She nodded happily. "I think it could do you some good. You felt loads better only after a night at my place."

A shiver coursed through his body as Brian recalled the last memory he had of Dahlia's beach house. Particularly, the moment Dallas's shoe came in contact with his face.

"I don't know," he said, looking for a way to avoid Dahlia's place without offending her. "Dallas and his crew could be waiting for a chance to finish me off up there."

"That's why it'll be a short trip and we'll go to a place he'd never expect you to go."

Brian's curiosity was piqued. "Where exactly would that be?"

She smiled in return. "I want you to show me your old office."

★   ★   ★

Brian and Dahlia exited the gateway at an abandoned building a few blocks from Brian's old consulting firm. Curious, Brian pulled his phone from his pocket to check the time and date. Eight forty in the morning. Again, despite weeks in Hell, he found that he'd only been out of the human world for two days since his abduction. A flurry of messages barraged his phone as the network connected. His parents, Amanda, and his boss had all been trying to connect with him. From his first arrival in Hell, he had been missing for almost a full work week at this point. He made a mental note to answer the important messages later, and offered his elbow to Dahlia as they set off into the morning.

The downtown streets were busy. Worker bees in business suits all zigzagged their way through, carrying coffee cups, the odd one muttering something about the amount of time they had before their shift started. Brian and Dahlia strolled casually through as the waves of bodies parted around them like a stream around a stone. Unfortunately, Brian didn't feel the instant release he did when he first stood on Dahlia's balcony. Presumably, his condition was no longer exclusively a human one, and the human world wasn't the remedy it was last time. The thought should have bothered him, but it lingered on Brian's mind for only a moment before passing, allowing him to enjoy the stroll with Dahlia.

Before long, they reached the building where BS Consulting leased out the third and fourth floors for their offices. The pair made their way up to the fourth, exiting the elevator to the muddy teal carpet that Brian not so fondly remembered. They walked the still mostly deserted aisles of cubicles, until they reached the office in the northeast corner. Outside of the office, Amanda was sitting at her desk, casually sipping her coffee as she logged in to her computer. She nearly choked when Brian approached.

"Where the hell have you been?" she demanded.

"Good morning, Amanda," Brian replied with a smile.

"'Good morning' my ass, answer the damn question. Have you not gotten any of my messages?"

"Cell reception hasn't been great where I've been staying. By the way," Brian stepped aside, bringing Dahlia into the conversation, "this is Dahlia."

Amanda looked over her glasses at Dahlia – an action that he could see put her off quite a bit.

"Dahlia, this is Amanda. She was my assistant."

"Pleasure," Dahlia said flatly.

Amanda looked as though she were about to snap back before catching what Brian had said.

"Hold it a minute, what do you mean 'was' your assistant?" she asked, half angry and half worried.

Brian smiled a carefree smile. "I'm only showing Dahlia around briefly. We'll be out of your hair in a minute."

Without giving her a chance to respond, Brian maneuvered past Amanda, Dahlia in tow, and shut the door to his office.

Dahlia immediately made her way to the row of windows alongside Brian's desk. The skyline of the business district sprawled out before her.

"Nice view," she commented, looking down at the street below.

Brian nodded, taking in the remainder of the office. He had no pictures. No personal touches. Nothing but his old computer, an uncomfortable desk chair, and a plant that would have been dead by now had it not been part of the cactus family.

"It's about the only nice thing in here," he commented.

The door to Brian's office whooshed open and a short, stocky woman entered. She was dressed in all gray, including some of her shabbily kempt hair. She looked tired and had a fake smile plastered across her face.

"Good morning, Dianne," Brian greeted his boss.

She smiled wider and faker in return before directing her gaze to Dahlia.

"Are you in with a client, Brian?" she said demandingly.

"Oh, I wouldn't work with this firm if my life depended on it," Dahlia snorted.

Brian choked back a cackle.

Dianne's cheeks flushed red as she redirected her attention back to Brian.

"You gave us all quite a scare, Brian. I hope you're doing well."

Brian nodded in consideration. Despite the lingering aching from his forced baptism, Brian had to admit that he felt pretty good.

"Better than ever," he replied with a genuine smile.

Dianne inhaled sharply, looking as though she were trying very hard not to let her rage break through.

"We've been trying to get in touch. We weren't sure what had happened. Your clients hadn't heard from you either. Lots of missed appointments," she continued, letting her annoyance slip slightly.

Thinking the human world didn't make him feel any better earlier was premature. In that moment, Brian was feeling great.

"Yeah, some things came up. Got another job. Met this lovely young woman. I just stopped in to do a once-over on the office before telling you to go fuck yourself."

Amanda let out an audible snort from her desk on the other side of the wall.

God, that felt good.

Dianne's face twitched.

"Excuse me?" As she spoke, the fake smile shattered into a million angry pieces.

"Sorry, let me dumb it down for you," Brian said, leaning fully into the dream resignation he never thought he'd get, "I'm tired of doing all the work for this bullshit firm and making you ridiculous amounts of money for nothing. I quit. You and those miserable assholes out there that call themselves my colleagues can all go to Hell." The sentiment slipped before Brian noticed the irony of it. He smirked, more to himself than Dianne. "I'm sure I'll see you there."

Her rage seemed to leave her dumbfounded. She tried to formulate words, but only guttural sounds came out. Brian was sure her incoherent sputtering was meant to be some scathing rebuttal, but he really didn't have the time, nor did he care to hear it. He looked back at Dahlia and extended his hand to her.

THE DEVIL'S ADVISOR • 157

"Shall we?"

Dahlia smiled and took his hand, and the pair left the office while Dianne furiously emulated the sounds of a broken lawnmower. Brian stopped once more in front of Amanda's desk. She looked at him with shocked eyes and a lingering smirk.

"Thanks for everything," Brian said, extending his other hand to her. "Don't let this place ruin you."

She took his hand and gave it a single shake. Her amicably stunned look hung on Brian for a moment longer.

"Take care of yourself, Brian."

He smiled warmly. "You do the same."

Brian and Dahlia made their way back down the aisle. Curious heads poked out of cubicles as Dianne finally got her motor running and bellowed curses and threats after him. He looked to Dahlia and grinned.

"You were right, this did make me feel better."

Dahlia hugged Brian's arm as they stood waiting for the elevator.

"I like this office," she replied, "it's so lively."

CHAPTER TWENTY-ONE

Danika had been busy. While Brian was recovering from his brush with death, Dani had completed the necessary preparations to launch the adult entertainment portion of S.I.N. Industries. Domain names were secured, copyrights were written and notarized, and necessary paperwork, including their business license, was filed for the full launch of the company. Once he felt ready enough, Brian jumped headlong into the proceedings as he met frequently with Sal and the remaining Hellions of the Sales team. Sal seemed eerily well suited to directing low-budget adult entertainment and took the reins uncomfortably quickly from Brian. His directorial instincts took over and seeing him barking orders about lighting, sound, and camera angles became a frequent sight in the shipping bay.

Brian and Dani met with Stephanie to iron out the final kinks of the Terms and Conditions clause that would be added to the website's landing page before entry.

"I had to reword this thing at least five times before it was both witty and legally binding," Stephanie said as she turned a sheet over to Brian and Danika for revision.

A single line near the bottom of the page was highlighted—

The content hosted on this domain is the property of Sinful Media, a subsidiary of S.I.N. Inc. All persons depicted are legal employees of Sinful Media and have met the minimum age of eighteen (18) years old. All acts were consented to by all parties involved, regardless of depiction. All Content is copyrighted and protected by the DMCA.

By entering, you are confirming that you have reached the minimum age of majority in your jurisdiction or are eighteen (18) years of age or older, and you are in agreement with Sinful Media's terms and conditions.

Sinful Media is a free adult entertainment hosting site. There is no cost for enjoying our content; however, by entering you agree that no more than 10% of your soul will be surrendered over to Sinful Media upon entry.
It's okay, we're all Sinners here.

If you're ready to enjoy our Sinful content:
-Enter-

"I think it looks great," Brian said after he scanned the disclosure. "The ten percent line looks like a fluff piece that panders to the branding."

"And I added the little jab about the ten percent being owed up front. We'll have to work out an intermediary system with Death's Reapers, but now we shouldn't have to wait 'til these pervs expire before we rake in our profit," Stephanie said proudly.

Brian nodded in approval and handed Dani the disclosure.

"Think you can have this posted to the site for me?"

"On it."

★   ★   ★

While Brian clocked seemingly endless hours in the time vortex that was Hell, Dahlia pulled the files of all the Hellions that Dallas had swayed to his side. She met with Lucy to confirm her intention to destroy their contracts.

"We're giving them a free pass," Dahlia said in a lazy protest.

Lucy shook her head, making her now seemingly permanent ginger locks dance about her shoulders.

"I don't care, we need to disarm Dallas. He can't have subordinates who have access to Hell," Lucy said, brushing aside Dahlia's concern.

A dull knock rattled the door to Lucy's office and Gabrielle poked her head through. Her curls popped in moments after.

"There's something you may not have considered," she said.

Lucy gave a disapproving look. "Were you eavesdropping?" she asked.

"Absolutely," Gabrielle replied, unashamedly. "I'm glad I was, though. I've been thinking about your problem with the Hellions and I think it might cause a bigger issue."

Lucy gave an unhappy sneer at the pending problem. "What issue?"

"Dahlia's soul is composed of souls from the bank. Hellion souls." Gabrielle spoke the last words hesitantly.

Dahlia's face dropped as she spoke.

"Shit," Lucy said as she seemed to arrive at the same issue Gabrielle had.

"Some of those Hellions might be part of Dahlia. If you destroy them, you might be harming pieces of her." The energy in the room sank. "But I might have a solution."

★　★　★

"You can do that?" Dahlia said as Brian entered Lucy's office.

"Do what?" he said, startling the room with his sudden presence.

"I can get rid of Dallas's Hellions without affecting the energy in the bank," Gabrielle explained. "I think."

"That's amazing," Brian's face lit up. "How?"

Gabrielle cringed slightly. "That's the tricky part. I need to find them first. Theoretically, after that, I can strip the life that's attached to the soul and they shouldn't be able to take form anymore."

Brian was elated to hear the news. With the impending invasion, more energy in the bank was certainly better than less. If Gabrielle's solution was a viable one, they might be in a better position for the plan Brian had been formulating since his late-night chat with her and Dahlia.

"I think it's worth a shot," Brian said conclusively. He looked to Lucy. "Do you think we can swap Sal out of the director's chair for Dani instead? He might have some insight on how to find the missing Hellions."

"Good luck pulling Sal out of that chair," Lucy snorted, "he seems quite comfortable behind the cameras of the particular brand of entertainment you have him making."

"I'll be convincing," Brian said. He turned to leave the office.

"Wait, why did you even come in here?" Lucy shouted to him as he swung the doors open.

"It can wait," Brian said, disappearing through the gap.

★　★　★

It took a bout of linguistic gymnastics to convince Sal to relinquish his newfound passion for film. Comments involving 'taking a step back to see the bigger masterpiece' and 'getting a woman's point of view to the production' were integral in convincing Sal to pass the reins to Danika – however reluctantly that passing may have been. Once he was wrestled away, Sal sat with Brian in the small, cramped office of the shipping bay.

"So, what's so important that you need to pull me away from your precious project?" Sal asked, attempting to make Brian responsible for his obvious and sudden interests.

"I need your insight on the Reps that went missing with Dallas," Brian said.

Sal rubbed one of his chins and surveyed Brian.

"What do you need to know?" he replied cautiously.

"I'm hoping that the Reps that went missing had some habits when they were out in the human world. Places they liked to visit or were frequently stationed at. Any ideas on where we could find them?"

"Not exactly," Sal said. His multi-eyes left Brian while he thought. "Most of the Reps that Dallas took were old-timers. They'd been everywhere from California to Shanghai."

Brian frowned. He was hoping for something more conclusive.

"Well, do you at least have the location of each of their last few leads?"

"How will that help?"

"I'm not sure, but at least it gives me a place to start. If you can round up the last three or four leads for each Rep that went AWOL on us it would be a big help."

Sal scratched at his stubble while he considered Brian's request.

"All right," he said finally, "I'll pull the files. You get 'em, I can go back to the project?"

Brian shook his head in disbelief. "Yes, Sal. You can go back to the project but Dani will stay on to help you, just in case I need you for something else."

"Deal."

*   *   *

Brian sat with several folders spread across the floor of his room. There were six Hellions in total that escaped with Dallas. Each of them, as Sal had mentioned, were fairly versatile regarding their abilities. They had donned the appearances of gang members, business executives, ex-lovers, celebrities – the list went on.

The locations they pulled their leads from were equally diverse. There seemed to be no pattern that classified the leads they took. Brian exhaled in frustration as he pressed his back against the large armchair close to the fire.

Dahlia stepped from the shower and wrapped a towel around herself. She pulled her wet locks away from her face and tucked loose strands behind her ear.

"No luck?" she asked.

He let out an exasperated groan. Dahlia frowned as she made her way over to the mess of pages radiating from Brian.

"Did you look over their contracts that I pulled from Records?" she asked.

Brian reached behind his head and grabbed a set of folders from the seat of the armchair he rested against.

"Most of these Hellions sold their souls decades ago for things that were, more often than not, completely unrelated to the types of leads they pulled. At least, in the last four lead files I have for each of them,"

Brian said. He went limp on the floor, dropping the folders down to his side and slumping his head backward onto the seat.

Dahlia's head cocked as she looked down at the lead folders.

"You have twenty-four folders on the floor."

"Uh-huh."

"And how many Hellions did you say are working with Dallas?"

"Six."

"Then why are you holding seven contracts?" Dahlia asked smugly.

Brian's head shot off the seat and he raised the contracts up.

"Jeremy," he whispered to himself. "Jeremy was never a fully fledged Rep. He never pulled any leads."

"Meaning he was never allowed in the human world," Dahlia added. "So, where do you think Jeremy would go if given the chance to be out in the human world for the first time since he died?"

Realization dawned as Brian recalled the conversation he and Jeremy had on their first meeting.

"Did we ever find out what school Dallas shot up to get Gabrielle's attention?" Brian asked frantically, his brain putting the seemingly arbitrary pieces together.

Dahlia thought for a moment.

"Caltech, I'm pretty sure," Dahlia said.

"Shit."

Brian flipped open Jeremy's file and leafed through a few pages. He pulled one from the folder, turning it to face Dahlia.

"Jeremy went to Caltech. That's where he met his girlfriend."

"Holy shit," Dahlia breathed.

"Jeremy still has memories of his human life. He's still a fresh Hellion. Dallas probably used his insight of Caltech to orchestrate the shooting. If Jeremy still remembers his school, maybe he's hiding out somewhere else familiar from his past life."

Brian put the page back into the folder and flipped through the pages once more. He stopped after a few more turns. He looked it over before handing the page to Dahlia.

She nodded. "Yeah, this might be the place."

CHAPTER TWENTY-TWO

The list of locations that Jeremy would visit on his first trip back to the human world after his death was short. Jeremy's old apartment, his school, and his parents' house were among the few places that he could go. Brian and Dahlia, however, felt the search would result in Jeremy being found at the place where his life came to an end – the same place that his girlfriend's life ended in the car crash he told Brian about.

He wasn't sure why but Brian felt as though he needed to confront Jeremy himself. The alternative – having Jeremy dragged back to Hell by his heels, kicking and screaming all the while – was less digestible than seeing the young Hellion in the flesh. Or, rather, in the corporeal projection of flesh.

However Hellions actually worked.

Escorted by a small platoon of Hellions – and further supported by a small, hidden contingent of Gabrielle's Reapers for good measure – Brian made a trip to the human world. The sun had settled comfortably behind the city skyline and night was in full bloom. Brian strode casually along the grass at the top of a hill. The grass rolled down to a rocky ditch that was straddled by a lonely overpass leading away from the major metropolitan cluster of buildings. The lights from the streetlamps were few and far between and, as the moonlight was intermittently covered by vagrant clouds, Brian felt as though he were feeling the full immersion into the night of Jeremy's accident.

The grass began to thin as Brian approached the steep drop of the ditch to the right of the overpass. The sound of tiny stones uprooted by his footsteps echoed down the solitary gap. He wasn't sure if the sound he heard amidst the clacking of the stones trickling down the drop was closer to a whimper or panicked breaths. Either way, Brian knew he was in the right place.

He looked to his left and noticed a shivering mass that huddled in a small gap between the overpass and a piece of level boulder. He looked around to find footing that would take him to the mass, testing stones with a nudge of his foot before placing his weight upon them. The Hellions and Reapers hid silently nearby in case there was trouble. Brian suspected they wouldn't run into any.

"Hey Jeremy," Brian said as he approached the shivering mass.

It flinched as he spoke and Jeremy's face slowly leaned out from the shadow of the overpass. "How you doin'?"

"I don't know where they are," Jeremy said defensively.

His voice was shaky and his eyes were wide with fear. Brian balanced his weight on two boulders and crouched to get closer to eye level with him.

"Can we talk?" Brian asked softly.

Despite Jeremy being involved with Brian's attempted murder, he couldn't help but feel sorry for him. After all, Jeremy was just a scared kid.

"I don't have anything to say," Jeremy replied.

"Look," Brian said, attempting to sit on one of the boulders without toppling over, "I'm going to be honest with you. I've come looking for you because you need to come back to Hell. I don't want to force you but I will if I have to." Brian attempted to sound as nonthreatening but as firm as possible. "You have information that we need. In return, I might be able to help you."

Jeremy shot Brian a skeptical look.

"'Help me'? How exactly would you do that? Bring me back to Hell so I can go back to my life as a Rep?" He shook his head fervently. "There's nothing there for me. There never was."

Brian's shoulders slouched as he listened. His eyes left Jeremy for a moment to survey the ditch.

"So, this is where it all happened, huh?" Brian said in a soft tone. Jeremy looked at him curiously. "This is where her life ended. Where yours ended too – eventually."

"How did you know?"

"The location of your suicide was in your file. It seemed like an odd place. I just assumed that you would have wanted to end things where they should have ended the first time." Brian turned to look sympathetically at Jeremy. "You wanted to die with her that night, right?"

Jeremy's body tensed as Brian spoke.

"I was the one driving that night. It wasn't fair that she died. It's not fair that I made it out alive. It's not fair that I'm still living." Jeremy's eyes roamed over his arms that wrapped around his knees. "Sort of."

"You're right," Brian said as he stood up from his perch on the boulder. "It's not fair, but maybe I can change that." He extended his hand to Jeremy. "When I said I might be able to help you, I didn't mean you returning to be a Hellion. I mean that I might be able to help you die. For real this time."

Jeremy looked up at Brian in astonishment. His mouth slightly ajar.

"Before that, I need you to help me with a few things."

★   ★   ★

The gateway opened slowly and Brian stepped through the white flames into the foyer. A troop of Hellions followed shortly after surrounding Jeremy. Dahlia looked up from her desk as they walked in and she shot out of her chair in surprise. She jaunted over to Brian and whispered frantically.

"Holy shit, I didn't think you'd get him that quickly," she said, gripping his arm tightly and pulling him further away from the Hellions at his back.

Brian shrugged and smiled.

"We make a good team. I wouldn't have thought to look there if you hadn't pointed out his folder to me. I'd like to get this over with though. Where is Gabrielle?"

"In Mom's office," she replied, throwing a look over her shoulder toward the doors.

Brian cringed.

"Maybe knock first. We'll be waiting in the courtyard," Brian said as he motioned back for Jeremy to follow him to the double doors. The perimeter of Hellions surrounding Jeremy moved with him and Brian raised a hand for them to stop. He shooed them away before he and Jeremy made their way through the doors.

The night sky was clear and perforated with the bright whites of the stars above. The ants under Brian's skin crawled slightly as the pair entered the courtyard and made for the fountain. His memory was cast back to the last time he and Jeremy both stood on the grass in front of the fountain – a likely reason why his nerves were set on edge.

"Why are you doing this?" Jeremy asked quietly as he strode a few paces behind Brian.

Brian looked back over his shoulder noticing Jeremy was looking everywhere but at him.

"I have a hunch that you didn't want to be involved with Dallas's plan. I think Dallas smooth-talked you into helping and you got in way over your head," he said as they reached the fountain.

Brian stood on one of the white stones of the pathway that radiated from the fountain. Jeremy fell silent for a brief moment.

"I didn't want to help them," he started, his voice weighted with shame. "I was so angry the night that we met."

Brian exhaled softly through his nose.

"I had a feeling that I went too far that night," he said guiltily.

Jeremy shook his head in disagreement.

"That's not it at all," he said. "I was angry at myself. Talking about what happened made me so furious with what I had done and how it all ended up. I was furious with Lucy for constantly rubbing the shame in my face every time I saw her." Jeremy finally directed his gaze to Brian. "Dallas just picked up on it all. He asked me if I wanted to do something about it. He told me that if I helped him, Lucy wouldn't be in charge anymore and that I could finally forget about it all."

Brian sat on the edge of the fountain and rested his elbows on his knees. He hung his head so that all he could see were his black Oxfords against the white stone.

"I get it, Jeremy. I can't imagine living with what has happened with you. I don't want any kind of explanation, I just need your help." Brian's head raised and he locked eyes with Jeremy. "I need to know what Dallas is planning. I need to know whatever you can tell me about where they are and what they're doing."

Jeremy winced as though Brian's lack of anger were painful. His eyes didn't leave Brian's as he stood quietly, seemingly waiting for the 'gotcha' moment that Brian knew wasn't coming.

"Dallas met with God," Jeremy said finally.

His voice quivered as though he were holding back tears. Brian nodded slowly.

"I know. Do you know what they talked about?"

"No, we weren't allowed in where they were talking. The only thing I heard was at the end when Dallas came back."

"What was it?" Brian asked.

Jeremy hesitated for a moment. His eyes darted around the courtyard, still looking as though he were about to be unpleasantly surprised.

"When they finished meeting, Dallas told us all that we were to go into hiding. He would find us when he needed us. Before we left, God thanked him and said she looked forward to seeing him again soon. She called him by a different name, though."

Brian's brow creased as he listened.

The doors to the courtyard opened and Lucy, Dahlia, and Gabrielle all walked out onto the grass. Jeremy tensed as they appeared, to which Brian stood and extended his arm to the trio to cease their approach.

"Jeremy, look at me. It's fine, no one is going to hurt you. They're here to help." He put his hand on Jeremy's shoulder. Jeremy looked at him in terror as his body recoiled. "Jeremy, focus," Brian said, trying to calm him by getting him back on topic, "what did she call Dallas?"

"She called him Gabriel," Jeremy said in a terrified voice.

Brian's heart sank when he heard the words. He looked at Gabrielle, who returned his stare with one of shock.

"She made Dallas her new Archangel," Gabrielle squeaked in a mousey tone.

Her hand rose slowly to her lips as she continued to stare blankly in surprise.

After many attempts and much coaxing, Jeremy lowered his hackles and calmed to the presence of the immortal women that entered partway through his conversation with Brian. They discussed further the details (or lack thereof) that Jeremy knew of Dallas's plan and finally came to the next phase of Jeremy's return to Hell.

"Thank you, Jeremy," Brian said genuinely. He gripped Jeremy's shoulder firmly and smiled. "You've done great."

He released his grip and stepped aside to allow Gabrielle room to situate herself between them. Her shock over Dallas's sudden incarnation as an Angel of the apocalypse was mostly dulled now and she was able to focus on the task at hand. She looked back at Lucy and Dahlia.

"I'm not sure if this is going to work," she said with hesitance.

Lucy raised her hand up to her mouth and tensed her fingers. A sleek, black handheld radio receiver materialized in her palm.

"Only one way to find out," she said as she depressed the button on the side of the receiver. "Deborah, you there?" she spoke into the microphone.

A crackle of static preceded the speaker flickering to life.

"I'm here, ma'am." Deborah's voice rang through the receiver in a tinny quality.

Lucy pressed the button again.

"Twins? Can you hear me?" She spoke once more into the mic.

"Oi, loud 'n clear," Peter or Paul replied.

Lucy nodded.

"We're about to proceed. Are you all ready?"

"Yes, Ma'am."

"Waitin' on you lot."

Lucy nodded to Gabrielle, signaling her to carry on. Gabrielle took a deep breath and turned her attention to Jeremy.

"This might tickle," she said as she reached for Jeremy's chest with her hand.

She gently poised her fingertips around the center of his chest, sparking five small buds of light where they touched. Jeremy drew a sharp breath and his posture straightened where he stood. Slowly, his multi-eyes shuddered into one another. After a few more moments, the multi-eyes became normal eyes. His head tilted forward and he smiled at Gabrielle. His gaze drifted to Brian as his figure began to fade into nothingness before them.

"Thank you," he whispered softly.

The Hellion known as Jeremy slowly faded from existence and left nothing but cool night air in his stead.

After a brief moment, the radio crackled to life followed by Deborah's voice.

"Good news," she said, elation clear in her tone, "we actually *gained* soul energy from whatever it was you just did."

Lucy's eyebrows rose as she lifted the receiver to her mouth.

"How is that possible?"

"My best guess is that, since some of the energy was devoted to creating a corporeal figure and personality, now that he no longer exists the energy has been freed up."

"On a more complica'ed note," the radio crackled once more to one of the Twins' voices, "the file on Jeremy shows that 'is soul went from one-'undred-percent corrupted to zero percent. Wha'ever you did musta cleansed his soul, so the energy's prolly sittin' as a neutral mass in the bank."

Lucy looked at Gabrielle in surprise.

"That shouldn't matter. The energy is housed in the bank with other corrupted souls, so it will likely re-corrupt over time just by contact."

"Does that mean that if a soul is cleansed this way and *isn't* housed with other corrupted souls it will stay cleansed?" Dahlia spoke as she stared off into space.

Brian's eyebrows rose and his eyes trained on her as she thought. Gabrielle put a finger to her chin and directed her gaze upward as she considered the query.

"I suppose it would," she said. "Though, I don't see where else you'd store a Hellion's corrupted soul if not in the bank." Gabrielle raised her eyebrow at the thought. The realization dawned on her a moment later. "You." Her eyes lingered on Dahlia.

Dahlia nodded.

"Dahlia's soul was made of fragments from the bank," Lucy clarified.

"So, if we cleanse all the fragments in Dahlia like this, she would be purified?" Brian asked.

The excitement in his voice was beginning to echo in the growing expression on Dahlia's face.

"It makes sense," Gabrielle said pensively.

"No, it doesn't," Lucy said. "Dahlia is made up of fractions of fractions. Her soul is composed of thousands of others. For that to work, we would need to strip the remaining life from all of those pieces."

Brian's excitement shattered.

"The toll that would take on the bank would be immense."

Lucy nodded.

"With an invasion at our door, can we really justify taking that kind of hit on the bank?" Lucy asked.

Brian was sure that he heard a note of pleading in her voice. It was as if she were asking him to do the math himself in hopes she were wrong, and she could grant Dahlia her wish.

"No," he said solemnly, his eyes looking mournfully at Dahlia, "we can't."

CHAPTER TWENTY-THREE

The launch of Sinful Media was a booming success. The amount of traffic the website saw in the first few days alone was enough to boast a six percent increase to the energy in the bank. Sal used the positive influx of energy as justification to put his directorial ambitions in overdrive, pushing the Reps harder – in more ways than one – to produce more content. Dani's eyes were already set on the next phase of the plan and she began working with Stephanie to draft the necessary documents to launch S.I.N. Industries' own liquor brand – aptly named *Corrupted Spirits*. Meanwhile, Brian was battle planning. He knew that with the successful launch and the increased revenue, if Dallas had an ounce of intelligence, he would figure out that this was the ideal time to attack. Hell was primed for a forceful takeover as it now had a constant and steady stream of soul energy coming in but still barely enough to scrape together a comprehensive defense. Even if the bank was tapped dry, the steady income would be at work to constantly, if slowly, recoup the losses. It was dangerous, but not having the revenue from this project was even riskier. Preparing for a conflict required considerable resources, the kind Hell didn't have access to without the launch of S.I.N. For the first time in a very long while, Brian found himself in a situation in which he knew very little about: defense strategy.

A new room had been manifested that jutted off to the right of Lucy's office. The small space was dark, save for a fluorescent light that illuminated a lengthy table that stood in the center. Lucy, Brian, Gabrielle, and Dahlia surrounded the table and looked down onto a map carved into the gray marble of the tabletop. The carvings shifted and moved occasionally based on the conversation and what strategy was the most logical at the time. Brian's eyes were glued to the map. He analyzed the layout of the buildings he knew of and had visited frequently in Hell. Now that they were represented in cartographic fashion, he couldn't fathom how they took up such a small piece of the area the group was planning on defending.

The main compound of Hell consisted of Lucy's office, the reception area, Brian's tower, and the office building adjacent. Outside the gate there were patches of varying terrain spread across arbitrary distances, just as Dallas had once told Brian. Swatches of desert were placed near thick jungle forests. Waterfalls tumbled down into deserted suburbs. A women's shoe section of a department store was situated inexplicably next to a high school cafeteria. The existence of the unique environments made Brian's head spin as he tried to understand why they were located in Hell.

"They're the remnants of old portals," Lucy explained. "Before the gateway we have now, there were portals to Hell littered all over the world in various places. They were how Hellions got in and out of the human world. They shouldn't be active anymore but I think Dallas may have figured out how to get some of them working again. That's how he got you back into Hell after kidnapping you without anyone noticing. If Dallas has backup coming from Heaven, they'll need to use one of these physical portals. The gateway only works for residents of Hell."

Brian recalled the night he regained consciousness in the indelicate arms of Dallas's Hellions. He remembered the dust and stone being kicked into his face as they all moved.

"The desert might be one that's active. I think that's the way we came in the night Dallas got me," Brian said, pointing to a section of the map to the southeast of the main compound.

Dashed lines etched into the marble and circled around where Brian's finger indicated on the map.

"That makes sense," Dahlia added. "That portal's in California, where my beach house is. *Was.*"

Her 'was' oozed through her irritated snarl. Brian nodded.

"California is where Jeremy went to school and where Dallas

orchestrated the shooting to get Gabrielle's attention. It's a fairly safe bet that he used the same portal to get out of Hell after trying to kill me."

"So, we need to focus on shutting this portal down," Lucy said as she tapped the circle on the map. The dashed lines of the circle joined and became a solid perimeter.

"It's amazing that he even got the portal running again. That must have taken years," Gabrielle said in airy astonishment.

Brian considered for a moment.. "What's required to get a portal running again?" he asked.

"The portals are exact copies of their twin locations in the human world," Lucy explained. "Everything at the portal lines up exactly as it does in the human world. If a rock moves there, it moves in our version down here. However, if someone moves a rock down here, its copy won't move in the human world. If the portal isn't an exact copy of its twin in the human world, the portal doesn't work."

"That seems incredibly volatile," Brian commented.

Nudging a rock, moving a chair, or knocking a high heel off a display seemed like things that could easily happen if one were not careful.

"It is. That's why we moved to the gateway instead."

"So," Gabrielle chimed in, addressing the original question, "Dallas and his Hellions must have arranged things exactly the way they should be for the portals to line up again. If even a single rock was turned a fraction of a millimeter off its mark, the portal wouldn't work."

Brian considered the desert and how difficult it must have been to make sure everything was exactly the way it should be for the portal to re-open. It must have taken an immense amount of time and diligence to complete. He couldn't help but wonder what sort of progress Hell would have made if Dallas directed half of that drive toward helping to fix things.

"So, how do you want to get rid of the portal?" Dahlia asked the room.

Lucy sighed annoyedly. She rubbed her forehead with her fingers as her eyes clenched.

"I could do it but I wouldn't feel comfortable leaving the Compound open. We'll have to use Legion," she replied in an aggravated tone. She looked at Dahlia, who was already becoming giddy.

"Now?!" she shrieked excitedly.

Lucy reluctantly nodded. "Better to close off access now than when it's too late." She pointed a stern finger at Dahlia, who was nearly bursting at the seams. "I'm trusting you to keep him in line," she said firmly.

Dahlia nodded furiously and practically skipped from the small room toward Lucy's office.

★   ★   ★

"So, what's Legion?" Brian asked as he stepped quickly to keep pace with Dahlia, who was glee-speed-walking.

She threw back a beaming smile.

"You'll see."

They arrived at the main doors of the foyer. As they opened, the common sight of the white flames of the gateway were gone. Instead, a mixture of sounds and sights that Brian had seen on the map, but was not prepared to see in person, met his senses. Dahlia skipped through the doors and headed off to the left. Brian followed in bewilderment.

The terrain outside of the compound was an unbelievable sight. Though Brian had seen the juxtaposed landscapes mashed together on the marble map in their meeting room, it was a completely different sight to behold in person. The sound of a large waterfall rumbled off in the distance and was accented by the screeching sounds of jungle life only a few meters away. The vague sounds of big-city traffic glided occasionally through the air as the pair walked. Each portal varied in size, some being only a few meters in diameter, while others, Brian estimated, spanned kilometers. The pair arrived at the base of a short mountain made of red stone. The mountain, unlike the other sights, looked to be a fixture belonging to the natural cartography of Hell. At the base stood a monolith made of obsidian. The quadruped figure was a carved, hulking mass of muscle, tails, and teeth.

Rows of teeth.

Rows of teeth below its two crescent columns of eyes.

Brian had a hard time making sense of the creature. It was an unfathomable fusion of mythology, exoticism, and nightmare.

Intricate carvings ran across the glossy black surface of the stone. The characters were closer to language than pictographic but Brian had not seen any characters similar to them in the human world.

"This is Legion," Dahlia said as she gently stroked the stone.

She turned back to see the confused look scrawled across Brian's face.

"I still don't get it," he said. "What is this? Is it an animal?"

Brian's eyes couldn't settle on a specific feature of the carving. They bounced from the talon-like mantis claws/paws at its front, to its dinosaur-esque, medieval dragon-style spinal spikes that rose out of an exoskeleton that was only 'exo' around the creature's midsection.

"Legion is a vessel for the river," Dahlia said as her fingertips traced over some of the carvings on the beast. "These markings imbue a sort of functionality to the stone. They tell the stone how to act. They're like step-by-step instructions on how to be a living creature. He couldn't function or move without them. The souls from the river then get injected into the stone and provide energy for these instructions to work."

"Why does it have to be souls from the river?" Brian asked, suddenly terrified at the thought of this monstrosity moving about freely.

"The souls in the river have lost all concept of what they used to look like or how they used to act. They still try, instinctively, to make a shape, but they can't, so they fill the void of any shape they can as an alternative. They're just a pure energy source now. That's all we need for Legion to work. Think of them like liquid batteries."

"So, this thing is going to destroy the portal for us, huh?" Brian said, assessing the many tools of destruction the creature had at its disposal.

"Legion isn't a thing," Dahlia shot back defensively, "he's a living being. Well, once we put some juice in him. After that, he's a living being."

She leaned in and hugged a section of razor-sharp talon lovingly as she spoke.

"Why do I get the feeling that this was your household pet growing up?" Brian said, genuinely hoping it to be no more than a joke.

Dahlia shrugged. "I'm the only one he's ever listened to." Her lack of direct answer was answer enough for Brian.

This was Hell's version of a puppy.

Dahlia rubbed her hands together eagerly. She placed her palms onto the mass of muscle that Brian assumed would be called a calf. Her fingers outstretched and tensed, prompting a trace of white-blue light to encompass the perimeter of her hands on the stone. Brian felt a gentle rumbling in the soles of his feet. He looked back in the direction of the compound and noticed the clouds floating gently overhead had become tinted with burnt orange at their bottoms. A shiver ran through his body as The Swarm beneath his skin danced. A moment later, a vortex of orange fog gently swirled up above the compound and drifted toward the mountain where Brian and Dahlia were standing. The fog narrowed to a point as it descended into the stone of the creature's flesh. The carvings closest to the fog's contact point slowly illuminated in a cherry-red tone that continued downward as the fog continued to fill the creature. The black stone bleached in certain areas, accenting the spikes and exoskeleton, talons, and, of course, rows of teeth. The six eyes atop the beast's head flickered to life as the last of the fog filled the final void of the carved characters. A sound rattled from within the creature, signaling its return to life. A mixture of ghostly wailing, bass-filled prehistoric growls, screaming – which Brian recognized instantly as the same screaming from the depths of the river – and, peculiarly enough, kazoo noises made the air around the mountain shudder like thunder. Legion's head arched backward almost liquidly as it stretched its stone body.

"Hey, buddy," Dahlia said with a grin.

Legion's attention locked onto Dahlia without moving his head. It released a cry that, to Brian's surprise, was fairly recognizable as one of joy. Legion twisted toward Dahlia and nuzzled her with the space between its many eyes. Dahlia giggled as the beast lavished her in affection.

"Uh," Brian uttered.

Legion's six eyes quickly snapped in his direction. Almost instantly, Brian was faced with the teeth of the beast as it unleashed a deafening roar at him. Whether or not Legion considered Brian a threat, or he was just not impressed by his rude interruption, Brian was unsure.

"Legion, no!" Dahlia said sternly.

She tensed her fingers and a flash of light transmuted into a heavy chain that she quickly shackled the beast with. She tugged him backward and Legion plopped into a sitting position.

"This is Brian," Dahlia said as she walked around from behind Legion.

"Hi," Brian said with a voice he borrowed from his years of early puberty.

"Brian is nice. We like Brian. Brian is our friend," Dahlia said calmly and rhythmically as she stroked Legion's leg.

The creature let out a deep rumble from within its chest. Brian assumed that he was hearing Legion purr – if that's what it could be called.

"Hey, buddy, didn't mean to startle you." Brian's voice was elevated several octaves.

He slowly approached and stretched out his arm. The leftmost row of eyes rolled in their sockets and locked on to Brian as he continued to move closer. They narrowed but remained still. Brian's hand touched the stone and his heart almost gave out. The stone of Legion's head gave way to the sensation of touching warm leather. The beast's eyes remained narrowed for a moment longer until Brian began to hesitantly pet his head. Legion groaned slightly and nuzzled into Brian's hand as he stroked. He smirked at the creature and the tension in his body began to release.

"Legion, we need some help," Dahlia said close to a whisper. "We need you to break a portal. Does that sound like fun?"

Legion's body went rigid. He threw back his head and released another joyful howl before descending onto his front knees, offering

Dahlia and Brian the opportunity to climb aboard. Brian couldn't hesitate as Dahlia grabbed him by the collar and hurled him up onto Legion's back, giggling with glee as she jumped up behind him.

CHAPTER TWENTY-FOUR

Lucy's steps echoed through the walkway leading to the office building. Gabrielle trailed behind, her own tread a whisper compared to Lucy's determined stride.

"Are you sure you want to do this now?" Gabrielle asked, trying to keep pace.

Lucy nodded. "There's no guarantee that Dallas doesn't still have eyes on the inside reporting back to him. If he gets wind of Legion being woken up, he'll have to move as fast as possible to make sure his invasion route isn't cut off."

A smug smile crossed Gabrielle's lips. "You're forcing his hand," she said.

"I'm trying to catch him unprepared," Lucy replied.

While she played the militant, in the back of her mind, Lucy hoped that Dallas's impulsiveness would put him at a disadvantage, making him easier to bring under control. As the pair walked, Lucy considered the possible outcomes of the unfolding events, feeling Gabrielle's presence prickle the back of her neck.

Lucy pushed open the doors to the waiting room and made her way to the desk at the front. Waves of Hellions parted in her path, staring on with tense awe. Marie noted her approach and stood quickly from her seat, straightening the wrinkles from her dress.

"Mariko, it's time," Lucy declared.

"Time, miss?" she replied with a wince.

"Emergency protocol. You're on duty effective immediately," Lucy said.

Marie's sheepish stare shifted from Lucy to Gabrielle and back again. Then, all at once, her meek presence evaporated. Her wide eyes narrowed and her posture became rigid. She put her hand up so that her palm faced Lucy. Lucy mirrored her action, touching her palm to Marie's.

With the billowing of a nonexistent gust, Marie's black dress began to tighten around her figure. The silk transmuted to something more akin to spandex, fitting her petite form and clothing her in a modified shinobi shozoku, complete with two katana at her hips.

Gabrielle let out an impressed whistle. "Looking at her, I never would have expected this," she said, giving Marie an up-and-down with her index finger.

"Sato Mariko offered her soul to the akuma in exchange for the ability to avenge the murder of her parents. After that, she became a feared ronin that killed without remorse. Her name was lost to history but she remains one of my favorite and prized contracts to this day," Lucy recited proudly.

"You honor me," Marie said, bowing, her transformation completed.

Lucy nodded before moving around the desk to the back area. Gabrielle and Marie followed in her wake as she made her way down the hall to the shipping bay.

The lights in the bay were dimmed and only a small set with a couch, a desk, and a handful of cameras were illuminated by spotlights. She could hear Sal's enthusiastic direction as she approached. As Lucy arrived at the set, Danika nudged Sal in the chair next to her. He instinctively shot her an irritated look before realizing he had company and quickly hopped from his director's chair. He looked from Lucy to Gabrielle, and then to Marie, the latter of which he lingered on for a moment.

"Remind me later that you have this outfit. I've got the perfect script for you," he said with a cheeky grin.

Marie pushed one of the swords at her hip slightly out of its sheath with her thumb. Lucy raised her hand to give pause before directing a stern glare at Sal.

"It's time, Salvatore."

She placed her hand up in the same fashion she did with Marie. Sal tugged at his collar and shot a glance back to Dani and his vacant chair.

"Youse guys can't take a joke, huh?" he said, placing his palm against Lucy's.

With a similar disembodied gust, Sal's form began to shift. His stout, robust figure stretched upward and leaned significantly. His wrinkled, shabby clothes pressed against his form, tailoring around his new physique and leaving him draped in a smartly cut, dark pin-striped suit. Where Marie's features showed little to no change, Sal was transformed almost entirely from head to toe. He was handsome, lean, and square-jawed. His piercing blue eyes glimmered beneath his stern brow and his slicked-back dark hair.

Dani let out a flirtatious whistle from her seat. "Remind me later that you have this outfit. I've got the perfect script for you," she said.

Gabrielle choked back a laugh at the comment. Lucy smirked.

"Salvatore Maretti, notorious hitman working under the Russo family syndicate. Merciless, relentless, and unrivaled. Remind me, what did you sell your soul for again?" Lucy asked.

Sal reached into the breast of his blazer and retrieved a long-barrel pistol. He admired it for a moment before returning it to his shoulder holster.

"Took a gut shot on my last contract and was bleeding out. Wanted to make it home to eat my wife's gnocchi," he replied.

"That's not a euphemism, is it?" Gabrielle jabbed.

Dani's snort was audible to the group from her chair.

"Danika," Lucy said, making her jump from her seat and to attention. "You're in charge. Get the Reps armed with anything they can find and get ready to defend. We're going into lockdown."

Lucy turned on her heel and made her way from the room. She strode back down the hallway and through the lobby where the gathered Hellions requesting reassignment were still waiting and dumbfounded. Her trio followed behind her, Marie stopping briefly to prop a *Be Right Back* sign onto her desk. As they entered the walkway back to the courtyard, a distant tremor shook the ground beneath.

"What the hell was that?" Sal asked, reaching again for his shoulder holster.

"Sounds like Legion is up," Lucy answered.

Her movement quickened as they rounded the corner to the wrought iron around the courtyard and the river of souls that was opened below. Another tremor was unleashed, this time much closer and much more violent. Lucy stopped in her tracks. Her head whipped back around to the office building they had just come from. A strange illumination glowed from the greenery outside of the walkway, sending a nervous chill through her body. In the reflection of the glass walls, Lucy caught glimpses of fluttering shadows. Urgency chilled her skin as she tore into a full gallop to the foyer.

"Lucy!" Gabrielle called out.

She didn't stop. She couldn't.

She wrenched the doors open to find a lone figure standing in the lobby. He was waiting casually, hand in his pocket, hip bent. He held a flaming sword in his hand, the blade resting on his shoulder.

"Hey, Mom," Dallas said.

Gabrielle, Marie, and Sal came bursting into the room a moment later. Gabrielle let out a sharp gasp as the light of the flaming sword flickered and danced across the marble of the room.

"Gabrielle, the lockdown switch is at my desk," Lucy said through gritted teeth.

Gabrielle nodded and hurried around the reception desk to Lucy's office. A moment later, the walls of the foyer shook and began sinking into the ground below. The roof folded back, dousing the room in the burnt orange of the courtyard beyond. As the walls continued to shrink, Lucy could make out the fluttering wings of Angels swarming and converging around the group below. Cookie-cutter residents of Heaven, all clad in the same crisp white robes covered in golden armor. Shields strapped to their backs, swords at their hips. Their features were obscured by helms with ostentatious red plumes erupting from the top. Their appearance a mix of Medieval battle garb and ancient Greek casual wear.

"What the hell have you done?" Lucy scolded.

Dallas shrugged, swinging the flaming blade from his shoulder and dangling it at his hip.

"What's necessary. I can't let you hand the family business to that idiot."

The Angels converged at Dallas's back, poised to attack.

"You think Brian is your only problem? You haven't thought about how you're going to stop me. Remember, it's my damn throne you're trying to take," Lucy said.

She squared her hips and shoulders. Her eyes flashed with fury.

Dallas chuckled. "I have no chance in hell of stopping you. I do, however, have an entire army who can hold you off just long enough for me to kill Brian. I can think of what to do after that. I'm good at improvising."

With a devilish grin and a descending sweep of his free hand, the chorus of Angels at his back all flooded past him and rushed Lucy.

She was met with the feeling of hands gripping every part of her body they could reach, trying to restrain her. Through the mass of bodies, Lucy watched as Dallas's silhouette sprouted its own pair of wings and took off in the direction of Brian and Dahlia. As the gap in the bodies closed in around her, she was given just enough space to see Gabrielle take off in pursuit of Dallas. Her chest clenched. Trying as best she could to turn her face in the direction of Sal and Marie, she unleashed a wild scream.

"Stop them!"

CHAPTER TWENTY-FIVE

Brian held on tight as Legion galloped along the abstract painting that was the landscape of Hell. Dahlia hooted with joy behind him. Brian imagined the feeling to be what riding on a lion would feel like. Provided, of course, that the lion did not realize you were there and decide to eat you instead. That fear was still not entirely alleviated regarding Legion, but Brian assumed he was relatively safe with Dahlia.

With loud scraping and a plume of dust, Legion came to a screeching halt at a patch of desert. Dahlia swung her leg back and dismounted him gracefully. Brian was significantly less graceful as he attempted to dismount without impaling himself on the collection of various sharp objects that was Legion. He landed unsteadily on his feet and surveyed the desert before them.

Shy of a few boulders and the odd budding cacti, there was nothing in sight. Through the desert rolled a soft wind that refused to drift outside the borders of the portal and into the remainder of Hell.

"So, how do we do this?" Brian asked.

Dahlia looked up at Legion, also surveying the area. She pointed a finger across the desert.

"All right, boy, do your thing," she said, patting his shoulder.

Legion rose on his hind legs, exposing his belly, which was distending rapidly. His head arched back as it did when he first woke and the bulge that had collected in his gut slowly began to creep up his body. His muscles flared and flexed as the mass traveled closer to his throat. Legion threw himself back onto all fours with force and opened his jaw wide. A monstrous roar bellowed from the creature's chest. With it, a burst of white fire careened toward the desert. The air around the burst spiked in temperature and Brian felt as though his face had been seared.

The ball of flame tore through the desert. Boulders melted where they stood. The cacti were erased entirely from existence. The flames carved a trench into the ground that looked like a hot scoop dug into rapidly melting ice cream. As the flash of white and the heat that accompanied it dissipated, the desert was left melted, smoldering, and, more pointedly, destroyed.

Brian moved to step closer to the awe-inspiring destruction but decided otherwise when the sole of his Oxford liquefied slightly as he hovered it over the massacred desert. He looked at Dahlia, who beamed back. He looked at Legion, who puffed out his chest with pride.

Hell never ceased to surprise him.

"That was…efficient," Brian said to the pair as his gaze drifted back through the destruction.

The moment was cut short by the feeling of the ground rumbling beneath. Brian looked to the destroyed terrain, then back to Dahlia and Legion. They seemed equally as confused.

"Aftershock?" Brian guessed.

Dahlia shook her head and began to look for the source of the tremors. She stopped when she turned in the direction of the compound. Brian peered over her shoulder as she squinted across the distance. The walls of the compound were slowly sinking into the ground beneath. The clouds above still sported the burnt-orange shade that signified the river being open. What looked like a mass of insects was spouting from the ground and up into the sky, blotting out the setting sun. The rumbling in the ground came to a crescendo as the walls of the compound completed their submersion. Dahlia turned to Brian, her eyes wide with terror. Brian wasn't sure what was happening but the ants beneath his skin felt as though they would soon find a seam and come bursting through. Legion howled, bringing the two back to reality. Dahlia's terror solidified into resolve as she launched herself atop Legion's back. Brian followed suit and the three galloped quickly toward the chaos at the compound.

As they approached, Brian slowly became aware of the sound of shouting. Angry, resolute, determined shouts and screams echoed from the compound and, soon after the swell of the noise peaked, Brian was able to see the cause.

The insects that erupted from the ground were not insects at all. To his astonishment, Brian witnessed as hundreds of Angels ejected from the earth and took to the skies around the compound. Where the normalcy of the Hellions' appearance was a surprise to Brian, he was unimpressed at the generic and obvious look of the Angels. They were all clad in crisp, white robes, their bodies held aloft with fluffy, white wings; their characteristics almost entirely interchangeable from one to the other.

They were met by squadrons of Hellions battling from the ground. They fired arrows into the sky, launched grapples, and used rocks in an attempt to bring their invaders down to the ground so they could better deal with them. The Angels, in turn, lashed wildly with swords in great, swooping slashes from above. As Legion approached the opening of the river, Brian was surprised to hear gunshots coming from where his tower would have been. He looked over to see a tall, lean man in a dark suit and slicked, dark hair aiming an absurdly large pistol up toward the swarm of Angels. He darted around, expertly firing off shots into the sky, each one rewarded with the sight of a winged body dropping from the cluster and onto the ground beneath. Dahlia tugged Legion toward the man. As they approached, Brian was able to see his face. His cheekbones were high and his jawline was square. He looked as if he were an actor plucked from a mafia film.

"Sal," Dahlia yelled over the sound of the battle, causing both the man and Brian to direct surprised looks at her, "where's my mother?"

Sal threw his head in the opposite direction, firing his gun into the sky all the while.

"You'll see her. She's got her hands full," Sal said.

The voice of the stout, out-of-shape Hellion came from the man.

Dahlia nodded and steered Legion toward the chasm of the river.

"That was Sal?" Brian asked.

Dahlia nodded. "That's what Sal looked like originally," she said over her shoulder. "Emergency Protocol, remember? We need to find my mother."

Legion galloped toward the chasm. Brian braced himself for Legion to leap to one of the stone pillars that rose from below. Instead, Brian's heart dropped as Legion continued to run across the gap, the beast's feet dashing through thin air as they did so. When they reached the other side of the ridge, the battle cries of the Angels and Hellions slowly faded into screams of terror. Brian raised his head to get a better view over Dahlia's shoulder.

Streaks of lightning carved into the sky, sending bodies tumbling down. The figures shattered into pieces as they collided with the ground. The Angels continued to rush in but Brian could tell that their resolve was wavering after seeing their comrades being turned to stone and subsequently crumbled. Regardless, they rushed at Lucy, who fired another whip of lightning that sent a section of Angel statues to their disassembled fate.

Lucy's hair glowed orangey red and looked as though it were caught in a constant updraft. The green of her eyes mimicked the glow and her black dress danced around her as she released wave after wave of electricity from her open palms. Despite the power she unleashed, the sheer mass of bodies that descended upon her kept her pinned down, only able to defend herself from the onslaught.

Only a few meters from reaching her, a sharp noise rattled below Legion's torso and his front knees buckled suddenly. Dahlia and Brian were thrown from Legion's back as he collapsed and rolled across the ground, rattling the immediate surroundings. Brian connected with the ground, the hard thud causing him to see white and deafening him to the sounds of conflict around him. He palmed his head in an attempt to soothe the throbbing. He shakily rose to his feet and looked around for Dahlia. She was on all fours with blood dripping from her forehead. Brian hurried to her side and wrapped his arm around her while swinging hers around his shoulders.

"I was really hoping you guys wouldn't wake Legion up for this," a voice said behind the dust cloud that began to settle from their impact. Dallas stood before them, pristine white wings sprouted from his back, and clutching a flaming sword. His face held a look of genuine disappointment. "I don't want to have to hurt him."

Legion rolled over and rose from the ground. His haunches tensed and he let out an earth-trembling roar at Dallas. Dallas tilted his head at the creature's threat and raised his sword. With a turn of his wrist, the sword morphed into the shape of a bow and Dallas tugged back the string, notching an arrow made of fire that appeared as he retracted. He took aim at Legion and loosed the arrow. The sharp arrow screeched across Legion's shoulder, making him buckle on one side. Dahlia let loose a feral growl as she dashed toward Dallas. Dallas notched another arrow and corrected his posture to draw the string back. The arrow dropped as his body recoiled from Dahlia's fist on his cheekbone. Dallas stumbled backward and the bow reformed into its original sword shape. His eyes drifted to Dahlia. Before he could register anything other than surprise, Dahlia balled her fist and struck him hard again. Dallas tumbled onto one knee before rising quickly and stepped back a few paces to gain some space.

"Well, this isn't very good communication, Dahlia," Dallas said as he wiped a drop of blood away from his lip with the back of his hand.

"You traitorous asshole," Dahlia spat back.

Dallas smirked at her outburst. "More self-preservation than betrayal, really. Mom clearly wants this asshole in charge of Hell. Where does that leave us, the creatures made for the exact purpose of ruling Hell? You get to stay in the picture since you're screwing him. I'm just looking out for me, just like you're looking out for you."

Anger flashed across Dahlia's face as she lunged toward her twin. With a roar, Legion lurched forward between the two siblings. Brian wasn't sure whether Legion was protecting Dahlia or if he just wanted the fighting between his owners to cease. Either way, the sword of flames meant for Dahlia plunged into Legion instead. Dahlia gasped as the flames re-emerged on the other side of Legion's body.

"Sorry, buddy," Dallas whispered as he retracted the blade from his liquid obsidian form.

Legion roared at Dallas, who wound up for one more swing with his sword. Once again, his actions were interrupted as Brian threw his body into Dallas's, sending both of them tumbling over. Dallas swung his sword at Brian. The Swarm took over and (feeling more powerful being closer to the open river) manifested a round, Greek-style golden shield. The sword collided with the shield, sending vibrations down Brian's arm and toppling Dallas over. Brian quickly steadied himself while brandishing the shield against Dallas. Excluding the occasional bar fight when he was in university, Brian was never one for physical violence. He was a thinker, and thinkers would use logic to think their way out of their problems, so he applied logic to the situation. Brian's logic came to the conclusion that physical violence was the only way his conflict with Dallas would end.

The ants under his skin concurred vehemently.

Dallas scrambled to his feet and swung his sword again. The sound of the collision bellowed through the air as Brian was pressed to one knee but kept his guard. He peered over the ridge of his shield to see Dallas smile confidently back at him. Brian was being toyed with and he knew it. He had no skill with a sword, so manifesting one would only make him worse off than he was.

As if reading his mind, Dahlia lurched into the conflict. Brian saw a glimmer of light from her palm that morphed into a sword of similar shape to Dallas's, minus the flames. She swung at her brother with a ferocity that removed the smug smile from his face. He parried her attack and masterfully drew his blade to slice across her midsection. Brian threw his arm forward and blocked the strike with his shield. Dahlia looked down at Brian, who smiled apprehensively in return.

Amidst the skirmish, Brian became acutely aware of the mass of Angels that continued to flood into Hell. He searched for their origin point and found them emerging from the forested area located just outside the glass walkway to the office.

"Legion, you need to destroy the portal that the Angels are using!" he shouted over his shoulder to the Hell beast.

Though he was wounded, Legion suffered no damage to the carved characters that dictated his movements. He roared and galloped toward the source of the Angels' invasion, where the office building had been.

Brian recalled his trip to the office with Dallas and the lush greenery he saw outside the windows of the walkway. Of course, the forest outside of the office was another portal. It made sense Dallas would use a portal close to the Sales department where his Hellions worked. The desert had been bait. The moment they destroyed it, Dallas invaded through the unsuspecting portal. Brian couldn't help but think that Hell hadn't given Dallas enough credit. He was intelligent – cunning, even. However, all his cunning was emotional. He truly embodied the malevolent side of the ruler of Hell. In that moment, Brian felt sorry for Dallas. He was well suited to rule Hell; he just lacked refinement. There was no question why Dallas felt betrayed by Brian's presence.

That revelation, however, didn't matter when compared to Brian and Dahlia's own survival. The pair kept their cooperative attack pushing forward on Dallas, allowing Legion enough time to get to the portal.

"Enough of this!" Dallas screamed. He slashed with his sword hard enough to knock Brian into Dahlia.

The pair slid back a distance and came to a stop just at the edge of the chasm to the river. Brian's heart lurched as he glanced at the drop. His muscles tensed and he instinctively rose his shield as quickly as he could. He glanced over the rim of the shield to see Dallas advance once more. Dallas launched himself into the air, materializing another blade wreathed in flame in his free hand. He brought them down hard in an overhead strike.

The Swarm twisted through his limbs, throwing Brian onto his back and tucking his knees to his chest. He quickly covered as much of his body with the shield as he could before Dallas's downstroke collided. The impact concussed his knees, forearms, and tremored through his whole body. The ground cracked beneath him and Brian tasted blood in the back of his throat as his chest groaned in agony.

Dahlia threw her shoulder into Dallas's exposed ribs from the side. The siblings tumbled. Dallas lost his second sword, but Dahlia clung to hers for dear life. She rolled back toward Brian so the pair could regroup. Before they could recover, Dallas was upon them. He kicked the shield from Brian's reach and into the chasm. It de-materialized as it fell. He repeated the action with Dahlia's sword. The confident coolness that draped Dallas's face earlier was gone and replaced with anger and determination. He lifted the sword overhead and threw his upper body down with the blade, making its impact with the ground that much harder.

The ground split where Dallas struck and the section that Dahlia and Brian lay upon started to slide backward into the chasm. Brian's heart began to beat up into his throat. The ants under his skin frenzied to the point of pain. His breath was left somewhere between where the stone was connected with the earth and where it was currently dropping into the river. He felt as though he could already hear the screams of the soul fragments in his ears. The Swarm crawled beneath his skin, feeling like they would burst from any seam they could. No flash of sensations this time. No time for regret or anger. Just panic engulfing his body. His terror numbed him to the sensation of a small fist grabbing him by the shirt and tugging him to safety.

Brian collided with solid ground and rolled a handful of times in the dust before he came to a halt and glanced up. Illuminated in the now moonlight were the tight black curls and dancing white dress of Gabrielle. Her back was turned to Brian and Dahlia still lying on the hard stone. Before her stood Dallas. He smiled wickedly and brandished his sword of fire at its previous owner.

CHAPTER TWENTY-SIX

"Hi, Aunt Gabbi," Dallas said, a cocky smile curling onto his lips.

"Stop this, or I'll stop you," Gabrielle said sternly – a vast departure from her usual light and airy demeanor.

Dallas grinned again and lifted the flame sword, reminding her that it was still there.

"I get that you have a history with my mother but don't you think you're going a bit far? Death is supposed to be a neutral party between Heaven and Hell. It looks a lot like you're picking sides right now."

"You can't begin to understand how serious keeping the balance of Heaven and Hell is." Gabrielle stepped toward Dallas. "If you rule Hell, Allanah rules you. Allanah is the real heir in that scenario."

Dallas shuffled backward, keeping his distance. Quickly, he raised the sword over his shoulder and swung it diagonally. Gabrielle stepped aside with ease, the wisps of her dress curling from the flames at the last moment. Dallas readjusted his stance and swung again. Again and again, Dallas continued his attack on Gabrielle, who evaded each attempt. Dallas's breath became labored and the confident smile dropped from his face, giving way to frustration.

"You haven't had that very long. You clearly don't know how to use it," Gabrielle chided.

Dallas grimaced and launched another assault on her, swinging faster and more furiously than before.

"It's a bit demeaning that you haven't presented a weapon of your own, don't you think?" Dallas said through heaving breaths.

Despite his frustration and fatigue, on some level he seemed to still be enjoying himself.

Gabrielle tilted her head in confusion. "All this time you've known me and you still haven't figured out that I *am* a weapon?" she said with a hiss.

Dallas swung his blade single-handedly down the center of Gabrielle's body. As before, she stepped to the side but was stopped short of completing her movement. Dallas quickly produced a second blade with his free hand and caught Gabrielle in her evasion. The second blade plunged into her core and through the other side.

Gabrielle took in a sharp breath, her eyes widening with surprise.

"I'm better at this than you think," he whispered venomously to her as he retracted the first blade back into his palm.

Gabrielle's expression neutralized. Getting over the initial shock of the wound, she seemed unimpressed and, for someone who had just been stabbed with a holy weapon wielded by an Archangel of the apocalypse, bored.

"There's a lot you've still to learn, little Dallas," she said smoothly.

Her hand lifted to Dallas's wrist that gripped the fiery hilt. Her fingers wrapped around it tightly, sending a wince across his face. A shriek of pain erupted from Dallas as the spot where Gabrielle gripped turned black and began to crumble. He pulled back, removing the blade from her stomach, and cradled his arm just above the decomposition. The black looked a mix of sand and ash. It ran up Dallas's fingers and crumbled to pieces quickly after. In a few short moments, Dallas was on his knees screaming and clutching his forearm.

A rumble off in the distance sent tremors through the ground and to the edge of the chasm where the group stood. Brian glanced in the direction of the quake, seeing the remains of white flame and a plume of smoke wisp into the air. The Angels that surrounded the area were all cascading backward from the explosion and Brian assumed that Legion had done his job and destroyed the portal near the office. Dallas seemed to come to the same conclusion. His screams of pain were muted with a wide-eyed look at the destruction and the image of his slowly failing invasion. He shot panicked glances around the battlefield, looking as though he were hoping to see his Angels triumphing over the Hellions. If that was what he sought, he would be sorely disappointed.

The Hellions, though grounded, were successful in defending against the attack even as their numbers thinned. The peculiarly youthful Sal dashed with inhuman speed from conflict to conflict, firing rounds from his seemingly infinitely loaded weapon. To Brian's surprise, Marie was included in the emergency protocol and matched Sal's movements. She ran in his wake, wielding a katana in each hand. She leapt and sliced down Angel after Angel, dropping them for the masses of Hellions below to finish the job. Legion had found Lucy after destroying the portal and the two were laying waste to the majority of the force. Bursts of lightning and white flame spouted from their central location either turning their foes to dust, melting them where they stood, or a mixture of the two.

"You didn't think it through," Dahlia said as she took in the same sight as her brother. "You brought a lot of Angels, but you bottlenecked them through one portal. The ones attacking Mom had no clue how strong she is. You also didn't plan on Legion being awake, or Aunt Gabbi coming to Hell and supporting us."

She looked sympathetically at Dallas. Despite his efforts, his betrayals, and his justification, he'd failed.

"You and I would have made a good team, sis," Dallas whispered through the quivers of pain. "This is what you're good at – the fine details. You're a scalpel and I'm a hammer. This is how Mom made us. We were supposed to work together and make this place ours one day. Why throw your lot in with him?" Dallas asked, nearly pleading, as he threw his head in the direction of Brian.

Dahlia fell silent at the question.

Brian did not.

He stepped toward Dallas and crouched beside him. He wasn't sure whether it was the adrenaline, the anger of having almost been killed again by Dallas, the fact that he threatened Dahlia's life, or just plain old revenge; Brian was in no mood for sympathy or mercy.

"If you knew anything about your sister, you'd know she's not interested in living a prescribed life. She's not throwing her lot in with me, she's just in pursuit of her own freedom. Her own happiness." The words angrily rumbled from Brian's chest. "Now, if you're wondering why your mother chose me over you," Brian grabbed Dallas by the collar and dragged him to the edge of the chasm, "it's because I can be both the scalpel *and* the hammer."

Dallas's moment of weakness passed in a flicker that returned his cocky smile. He rose to his feet with Brian still gripping his collar.

"Are you planning on throwing me in the river? I guess you do have some hammer in you after all. However, I can't say that your scalpel is as sharp as my dear sister's."

Dallas's shoulders rolled forward slightly, flexing his back and extending his wings.

Brian replied with his own vicious grin. "I beg to differ."

Brian released Dallas's collar and swept to his side.

He threw his arms around the joints of Dallas's wings, hugging them hard to restrict their movement. He bent his knees and launched hard off the edge of the chasm, down toward the river.

Dahlia screaming his name was the last thing Brian heard before the rushing air filled his ears. The fall to the river was different this time. He was prepared for the drop. He was prepared for the impact. He was prepared for – though, not exactly pleased by – the screams of the soul fragments as he submerged into the viscous mass. He was confident that Dallas was not nearly as prepared for the fall as Brian was – evident from the violent, panicked thrashing of his wings both above and below the surface. The ants in Brian's skin danced gleefully as they reunited with their source. It felt as though their reunion was followed shortly by the opening of all the doors to Brian's body. The memory of the pain Brian experienced as a result of his plunge last time was a shadow in comparison to what he felt this time. With the increased adrenaline in his system from the fight before the fall, Brian's mind refused to relinquish consciousness, allowing him to feel the full extent of agony.

A short, yet seemingly infinite moment later, Brian felt a familiar small fist grab hold of the back of his collar and jolt him upward. He tightened his grip around Dallas's wings, hugging them close to his chest to ensure he didn't slip as they were pulled from the river. The pair broke the surface and were thrown back up the chasm, landing on the hard ground at the edge.

Having not been conscious the last time he was rescued from the river, Brian found it a peculiar sensation to be dry as a bone. He looked to Dallas, who was also dry and in a severe amount of pain. Dahlia ran to Brian's side as he tried to shake his own pain from his body. Gabrielle glided gracefully from the pit and landed next to the pair.

"What was the point of that?" Dallas rolled over onto all fours and spat through a mixture of immense pain and violent anger. "You didn't even kill me." The triumph in his voice masked his confusion.

"Your sins had been forgiven. Your soul was pure," Brian said through the pain. "If you died like that your soul would have just gone to Heaven. I needed to re-corrupt you," he explained.

The gloating that was creeping over Dallas's pain-riddled face quickly faded at the sound of Brian's words. The wings on his back fluttered slightly. The feathers began to tint gray.

"I needed to make sure that when you died, the value of your soul would belong to Hell. We don't have the budget to write off that kind of loss."

Feathers started to drop to the ground as they turned pitch black. They smoldered to ashes as they landed until Dallas's wings were nothing but a smoking mess. His head swiveled slowly as he watched the remainder of his plan literally go up in smoke around him. As the last feather disappeared and the smoke blew into nothingness, Dallas chuckled to himself.

"Clever son-of-a-bitch," he said quietly, smirking at the singed marks on the stone around him. He looked to Brian once more, pain giving way to a glimmer of admiration. "I loved the website, by the way. Very tasteful."

Gabrielle walked over to Dallas. She paused for a brief moment before placing her hand on Dallas's head. He fell still – his heaving breaths and shudders of pain halted as the outline of his figure illuminated for the briefest of moments before his form began to disappear entirely. Slowly, his body faded into transparency. Before long, the only thing that remained of Dallas, the son of the Devil, was an ashen silhouette of unmarked stone where he last knelt.

★ ★ ★

With the portal irreparably destroyed, the Angels that found their way into Hell under misguided orders were soon wiped out. Being similar to Hellions in their makeup, though the physical elements of their bodies were destroyed, their soul energy was still that of Heaven, and so they would return – excluding, of course, the odd Angel that fell into the river and became corrupted before their death. While Hell was lucky to survive any sort of invasion unprepared, they were only lucky enough to corrupt two Angels by way of plunging them into the river. Their added soul value would be miniscule in comparison to how much was spent during the defense of Hell. Where the ampoule of the bank typically shone a bright blue-white, after the onslaught, the glass had dimmed significantly. The energy that reverted from Dallas after his passing was a bigger saving grace than Brian wanted to admit.

As the last of the Angels were rounded up and disposed of, the Hellions that fought in defense of Hell began to congregate around Lucy. The effects of the energy shortage were already noticeable in the mass. Their bodies flickered in and out of existence; some lacked any defining attributes short of limbs and eyes.

As they reached Lucy, she waved her hand and removed their physical forms. Brian assumed she knew how big of a hit they took and saving energy by removing the Hellions' forms would be a momentary fix. It seemed that Brian still had a long road ahead in getting Hell running at optimal performance.

That was, after he recovered from his dip in the river – a feat that was already even less forgiving on his body the second time around. Everything from his skin to his bones screamed at him in agony. Every breath he drew felt as though it were rupturing more of Brian's organs.

As Lucy relieved the last of the Hellions from their physical form, she and Legion approached Brian and company. The grass of the courtyard began to appear out of nowhere as it filled the gap of the chasm inward. Dahlia and Gabrielle slung Brian's arms over their respective shoulders and dragged him onto the now solid, lush ground. As the last blades of grass shot into place, Brian felt the tension begin to slip from his body into the blades beneath. As Lucy and Legion reached the party, the walls of the compound rose up around them. In a matter of moments, the courtyard was exactly as Brian had last seen it save for the crisp moonlight that bathed the inhabitants below. A reverent silence took the group, broken only by the gentle trickling of the fountain. Brian fought to stay conscious in the sudden lull and cease of adrenaline.

Lucy looked at Brian. Her eyes and hair had lost their luminescence and her dress weaved from shadows moved about as much as a normal dress should.

"I saw what happened with Dallas," she said, speaking to the group.

The three remained silent. Despite the betrayal and their façade of disownment, Lucy had lost her son, and Dahlia had lost her twin brother. There was no downplaying a loss of that magnitude and it felt as though no words could express the proper emotion to match the feeling that hung in the air of the courtyard.

"I'm sorry, Lucy," Brian said genuinely.

Lucy didn't respond. Her face was stern and she seemed to be on the brink of unleashing the kind of rage she'd exhibited in the battle earlier.

"It's not your fault, Brian," she said through gritted teeth. "It's someone else's." She looked to Gabrielle. "We are going to see Allanah."

"We're coming too," Dahlia added.

Lucy shook her head and shot Dahlia a blunt look.

"Look after Brian." She turned and walked to the foyer, Gabrielle trailing behind her.

"Are you sure you don't want them to come?" Gabrielle whispered to Lucy.

Her eyes flashed a terrifying violence. "Allanah is the reason my son is dead. This is between her and me."

The doors to the foyer closed, leaving Dahlia and Brian alone in the moonlit courtyard – neither was sure how they survived or what to do next.

CHAPTER TWENTY-SEVEN

The walk was dead silent. As Lucy and Gabrielle traversed the Hellscape, even the various sounds of the environments couldn't seem to penetrate the deafening tension.

Two forests and a New York borough later, Gabrielle finally attempted to extend an olive branch.

"I'm sorry, Lucy," she said as the pair crossed into a massive library.

Silence hung. Lucy couldn't bring herself to respond in any way other than unbridled anger and violence.

The pair weaved their way through twisting bookshelves and dust-thick air.

"I asked you not to," Lucy said at last. "I begged you."

"He wouldn't have stopped."

"I told you what would happen if you hurt him," Lucy said.

Gabrielle paused as she thought back.

"So, are you going to hurt me?"

Lucy quickened her pace through the musty volumes.

"I wouldn't ask that if I were you."

★ ★ ★

The pair walked in silence for what felt like an eternity. The various scenes slowly trickled into the natural, barren landscape of Hell.

Then they walked some more.

On and on until, finally, an object on the horizon began to emerge. After one more eternity, the object came into view, and Lucy and Gabrielle found themselves standing in front of a sequoia.

It was old and weathered. The trunk looked as if it were embedded

202 • BRAD ABDUL

with bones of various limbs. Lucy extended her hand and ran her palm down the dead wood, feeling a nostalgic twinge emanate from the knots beneath her palm.

"I've seen this before," Gabrielle said, sounding very unsure on whether she should speak or not.

Lucy nodded. "Alannah has one as well. It's an old portal – the very first, in fact. The only portal in existence that ties the human world to Heaven and Hell."

The deadpan of Lucy's words sent tremors of memories through her body from the base of her skull. Memories of family. Memories of siblings.

Then, as if the portal knew that she tiptoed too close to the most painful of the memories, the barren landscape of Hell began to fade. Only the tree and the dried earth around its roots remained. The fading soon turned to illumination. The bright light drowned everything from vision. Quicker than it came, the light dimmed and revealed the pair's new location.

A small path carved along the base of a cliffside mountain. The path turned to a narrow shelf that led to the archaic ruins of what seemed to be an old temple facing the water. The stone was dark and plain other than various carvings on the rubble.

"What is this?" Gabrielle asked, raising her voice against the sound of the crashing salt water below.

"The house of my father," Lucy replied.

Gabrielle's brow raised at Lucy just as the light began to fade in once more. In another flash of blinding light, the drab gloom of the gray stone and water was replaced with a lush expanse of a grassy field.

The field stretched for miles in every direction – the sequoia and its visitors the only thing disturbing the canvas. The sun shone brilliantly in the washed blue sky above. Lucy removed her hand from the trunk and awaited the welcoming party. Only a short moment after their arrival, the luminescence of the sky was blotted by dozens of bodies.

An army of Angels came crashing down around the pair, sending tremors through the perfect landscape. They were clad in alabaster armor trimmed in gold. They brandished rounded rectangular shields and spears of white marble. The winged soldiers created a perimeter around the sequoia, parting only to let two Angels through to meet Lucy and Gabrielle. The armor they wore was a stark obsidian but still trimmed in a vibrant gold. Flaming swords, similar to the one Dallas wielded, were strapped to their hips.

The pair approached Lucy and Gabrielle. Neither party looked pleased by the meeting. The Angel on the left removed his helmet, revealing chiseled features beneath a curtain of flowing brown hair. The Angel to the right followed suit, letting his blond locks drape around his own square jaw.

They were handsome, if not unimaginative.

"You have no business being here," Lefty addressed the women.

"Tell my dear sister that I'm here for a visit," Lucy replied, disregarding Lefty's defensiveness.

Righty scowled. "Do your ears not work, demon?" he spat.

Lucy's gaze slid to Righty, venom igniting the green glow in her eyes. "Have you ever seen a demon, you cockless piece of shit?" she whispered.

Righty stared back at her sternly.

"Demons were monstrosities. Mindless hulks of mass built for nothing more than providing the most torturous punishments Hell has to offer. They were nightmares incarnate – the living embodiment of damnation."

The blue sky above began to darken with thick clouds. Lucy's hair flickered with light and danced in a steadily rising updraft. Worry crossed Gabrielle's face as she watched the rising tide of chaos swell before her. All the while, the army of Angels looked on stoically.

"I am no demon," Lucy said, her voice a feral rumble. "I am what demons were terrified of. I'm the fucking Demon Queen."

Lightning webbed its way across the dark clouds that now blotted the sun from the sky. The Angels began to shift awkwardly in formation at the display of power and fury before them – all but Lefty and Righty.

Righty leaned forward, bringing himself to eye level with Lucy.

"You are nothing," he said.

A razor-sharp grin tore across Lucy's lips. A rumble of thunder rolled across the sky.

"Thank you," Lucy replied genuinely. "I really needed this. I have a lot of coping I need to do."

Lightning ripped down from the sky, gashing a trench through the Angelic defenses. Arms were presented and the forces rushed in.

"Lucy..." Gabrielle cautioned.

"Let me cope," Lucy said, hunching down, poised for an attack.

She erupted from where she stood, tearing limbs, throats, eyes, and tongues from various bodies. Lefty and Righty attempted to flank her, forcing a blood-drenched giggle from the depths of her mourning. She led them, dancing around the spear thrusts so that each one found its way into the body of a fellow soldier. Each step was masterfully executed, every Angel maliciously exterminated. She drifted across the battlefield leaving a trail of gore in her path while continuing to command the strikes of lighting that barraged the forces below. As Lefty lurched forward for a strike with his spear, Lucy found the hilt of his fiery sword. She pulled it from its sheath and took off his left arm at the shoulder in the process. She spun as he fell, finding Righty at her back. He unsheathed his own blade and advanced on Lucy, locking his gaze with hers. She parried, dodged, and countered with ease but the soldier pressed forward, keeping her moving and continuing his assault. Had she not been so inconsolably pissed off, she might have commended him for the decency of his efforts. But she was – so she didn't.

Instead, she noticed that her patience with the display of power was wearing thin, and her onslaught was becoming tedious. The glee slipped from her face and with it, she began to slash wildly at Righty. She forced him onto the defensive, pushing him back while what remained of his battalion looked on in awe. With a side step, Lucy gripped the hilt of Righty's sword. With a twist, her own found the throat of the confident Angel. With a swipe, his head departed from his shoulders, leaving Lucy with both flaming swords.

If she were human, her chest would have been heaving with

adrenaline in her heart and fire in her lungs. If she were human, she might have processed the grief of losing her son in a more calculable or predictable way. If she were human, she might have begged God to bring her son back to her so she could tell him all the things she never did – all the things she never knew she felt until she lost him. Instead, she stood in a blood-soaked field of Angelic limbs and entrails, daring God to show her face so that she could slice it off.

As if her prayers were answered, the dark clouds that canvassed the sky split, allowing the blinding light above to illuminate the grotesque scene below. The light itself sublimated and became rigid, zigzagging from above. As the clouds diffused against the protruding light, Lucy spotted her.

She descended the stairs of light, her gown flowing about her. It looked as though she were clad in the sky itself, her chestnut locks cascading down her shoulders, bouncing around her heart-shaped face with each step. Her cheeks were so rosy, she could almost be drunk. She dismounted the stairs in front of Lucy, drifting slowly to the ground, her toes pointed like a dancer's. As she connected with the grass below, a burst of golden light spread across the field, sweeping the horror away with it. The few Angels that remained all bowed to her before taking flight, leaving only Lucy, Gabrielle, and Allanah standing under the sequoia.

"Okay," Allanah said dreamily, "you have my attention."

Lucy's brow dropped, her anger flaring once more.

"You cocky bitch."

"Pot, kettle, don't you think?"

Lucy's jaw clenched. Her grip tightened on the hilts of each sword.

"I just wanted to have a damn conversation with you," Lucy said through gritted teeth. "Your Angels need to learn their place when it comes to immortals."

"They're fine with respecting immortals, they're just not so keen on intruders," Allanah parried, shattering Lucy's last remaining fragment of patience.

"You killed my son. I'll intrude if I damn well please!" Lucy screamed, her rage bleeding into her grief.

"No, she didn't." Gabrielle stepped forward. "I did."

Lucy shook her head. "You were right, Dallas would not have stopped. He would have kept coming. He would have kept on trying for control of Hell—" Lucy raised one of the swords, pointing it to Allanah's throat, "—because *you* used him."

Allanah shrugged. "Your son was his own person. He took full advantage of all that free will you covet so much."

Her words lacked empathy. She spoke as if she hadn't a care in the world. It didn't seem to bother her that Lucy stood before her, brandishing weapons.

"Bullshit," Lucy spat back. "He was a win-win for you. If he got rid of me and took control of Hell, you would have controlled him and reigned over it all. If he lost and died, you knew it would be another wound you could deal to me without lifting a finger. You made him a fucking Archangel, gave him an army, and sent him to his death – all because you have a problem with me. All because you want to win this *game* of ours that ended millennia ago."

"So I saw an opportunity to get rid of you," Allanah replied. "Can you blame me?"

Lucy dropped the swords at her sides and slowly walked so she was face to face with Allanah.

"Dallas would have told you about my retirement. He would have told you I was handing Hell over to someone else. You didn't just want to get rid of me. You wanted control. Just like you always do – and you didn't mind sacrificing my son to get it."

The brilliant light from above did nothing to stop the shadow of malice crossing Allanah's face. Her carefree demeanor evaporated.

"So what do you want, an apology?" Allanah asked, the sweetness in her voice turned sour.

Lucy stared into Allanah's eyes. She stared an unblinking stare.

"I want out," she said finally. "I want to be done with all of this. The fighting, the feuds, the bullshit between you and me. I want to be free of it all and just exist." She turned to look at Gabrielle, a wanting ache etched in the lines of her face. "I'm done with this endless competition."

The building violence in Allanah's look receded for a moment as she considered her sister's words. She cocked her hip and crossed her arms over her chest.

"So you want out that badly?" she asked.

Lucy returned her gaze to Allanah, the pain in her look pressed back into anger.

Allanah let out an annoyed sigh.

"Tell me about this replacement of yours."

CHAPTER TWENTY-EIGHT

Similar to his last dip in the river, Brian spent the majority of the following two days recovering in bed. Dahlia remained by his side, recovering from her own wounds – physical and otherwise. Lucy and Gabrielle had yet to return from their visit with Allanah and, after the sun had set on the second night, panic started to appear in the compound.

"They'll be back soon," Brian said as he propped himself up against a pillow.

His body seemed to be recovering faster this time around, and he wasn't sure if that was a good thing. The pain had been dialed down enough for Brian to feel The Swarm strumming constantly in its stead.

"They should have been back already," Dahlia said from the armchair by the fire.

She swigged back her vodka water and tossed the empty glass on the side table. Brian had no way to be sure that they were okay other than the fact that Lucy and Gabrielle were literally the Devil and Death. Something terrible befalling both seemed fairly unlikely, logically. However, they were parlaying with God, so that likely threw the numbers out of whack.

Dahlia stood from her seat and made for the door. Brian threw off the blankets and swung his legs over the edge of the bed.

"Where are you going?" he asked, stretching.

"I need to go for a walk. I just want to clear my head," she replied.

"Want some company?"

★   ★   ★

Dahlia and Brian left the main doors of the foyer and exited to the Hellscape beyond. The pair turned to the mountain to the north and started walking. Dahlia hadn't spoken a word since they left the room. She wrapped her arms around her torso as she walked and Brian threw his own arm around her, pulling her close. For all their disagreements and differences, Brian was surprised how concerned Dahlia was for Lucy's wellbeing. He supposed that the risk of losing another family member so soon after the first was a threat that hovered over a fairly raw wound. The closer they got to the base of the mountain, the more distinct the rumbling of the ground became. After the battle, without Lucy to force Dahlia to return Legion to his hibernation, she let him roam Hell as he pleased. Her only rule was that he was not allowed to be in the compound.

Legion pounced across the various patches of terrain, chasing wildlife, rolling in grass, and generally acting unlike any respectable Hell beast should. As they approached, Legion's eyes locked on to them and he came galloping to meet them. He skidded to a halt a few meters from where they stood and Dahlia smiled a weak smile, extending her arm to pet the beast between his columns of eyes. Brian followed suit, giving Legion a scratch under his chin. Dahlia's hand roamed Legion and found the stone of his body chipped in places where Dallas had fired his arrows and the piercing from his sword.

"I can't forgive Dallas for what he did," Dahlia said softly as she stroked the beast, "but I can't help but feel a little empty now that he's gone."

Tears welled in her eyes and Brian pulled her in tight.

"Of course you can't. He was your brother – your *twin* brother, no less. You were raised together, played together, grew up together, and dealt with Lucy's shit together. Betrayal can break a bond but it doesn't make loss any less painful."

Brian squeezed Dahlia. He shifted his weight in order to remain on his feet as Legion leaned in to nuzzle the couple in silent mourning.

After spending some time playing with Legion and getting their minds off the events of the recent past, Brian and Dahlia returned to the compound. As the pair entered the foyer, Brian's attention was drawn to the courtyard doors settling in their lintel. He looked at Dahlia, who seemed to notice it as well. She shot Brian a glance and they both quickened their pace to get to the opposite end of the room.

The courtyard was bathed in the lingering violets and oranges of the setting sun, sending twinkling reflections across the arching water of the fountain. Lucy and Gabrielle stood in the center along with a young, brunette woman clad in a blue dress. Dahlia and Brian stepped out into the courtyard toward the trio. Lucy turned to the pair as they approached. The rage that she left the courtyard with nights before seemed to have subsided.

"Allanah, this is my daughter, Dahlia," Lucy said as she extended an arm to Dahlia and drew her close. Dahlia stood by her mother's side. "Dahlia, this is Allanah – my sister."

Allanah gave a pleasant smile and nodded in greeting. She seemed to be in her mid-twenties. The sky-blue dress she wore was of a similar make as Lucy and Gabrielle's, and flattered her tanned form. It hung loose around her bust and sunk deep into her lower back. Her hair was thick and voluminous, looking more like finely shaped cotton candy than actual hair.

"Such a pretty girl," Allanah said absently. "I'm sorry for your loss."

Brian saw the vein in Dahlia's neck nearly erupt from beneath the skin. Her outburst seemed to be quelled by a nudge of Gabrielle's elbow. "And who is this?" Allanah said, intentionally or innocently oblivious to the emotions she stirred in Dahlia with her comment.

Lucy looked back and invited Brian to join them.

"This is Brian," Lucy answered.

Brian nodded to Allanah. Professional pleasantries were nowhere near the forefront of Brian's mind. He was displeased to have Allanah in Hell.

"I've heard a lot about you, Brian," Allanah said airily.

Brian snorted. "Is that so?" He made no effort to hide his dislike for her.

She smiled sweetly and unaffectedly. "I hear you'll be running Hell soon. That's a good thing." She looked to Lucy, who shot her a vicious look. "My sister and I do not exactly have an, how you'd say, amicable relationship. This is unfortunate, as Heaven and Hell are very much two sides of the same coin. With you running things, however, I feel as though we may have a chance at a friendly working relationship. I do sincerely hope that we can work together in the future." She smiled innocently – unconvincingly, but innocently.

"Why should I believe you? Not a week ago you allowed Dallas to march an army of Angels on Hell." Brian's words pushed past gritted teeth.

The Swarm beneath his skin began to dance and the bass of Brian's voice swelled as he spoke.

Allanah's eyes widened slightly in surprise at his rebuttal. The moment passed and the sweet and poisonous smile returned to her lips.

"I was simply facilitating a plan that would have resulted in the removal of my dear sister from the throne," she said, playfully jousting Lucy with her fist. "I was interested by the prospect of her being eliminated."

She spoke with no animosity in her voice. There was no anger or disgust – Allanah spoke of the disdain she had for her sister as she might the weather or time of day.

"I have no ill will for Hell. As an institution, your services are irreplaceable. It's my sister I can't stand. Give me no reason to despise you the way I despise her and we should get along swimmingly."

Hate bubbled beneath the surface of Brian's skin. He was infuriated hearing that the invasion of Hell was nothing more than a sisterly squabble to Allanah. The resulting death of Dallas was just a bump in the road and the residual emotional torment it put on Dahlia and Lucy were nothing more than nuisances. Brian's fist balled instinctively. Gabrielle seemed to notice Brian's swelling fury and urged calm by gesturing subtly behind her back with her hand.

"Regardless," Brian said, finding it near impossible to unclench his jaw as he spoke, "I don't see how I can trust you."

"Oh, that's easy. I've brought you a gift," Allanah said cheerily.

She stepped forward and nudged Dahlia's chest with her finger. Dahlia released a grunt of pain before buckling to her knees. Brian moved to aid her but hesitated as he saw a stream of red-orange flood from her back and collect in a ball that hovered just above her torso. Allanah waved her hand as if lazily swatting a fly, forcing the ball to disintegrate into nothingness.

"What the hell did you just do to me?" Dahlia said through labored breaths.

Allanah smiled and cocked her head. "I forgave all your sins, dear niece. Your soul is no longer corrupted. A gesture of good will."

Brian's eyes widened. As Dahlia rose to her feet, he realized the same look was on her face. She looked at Brian who, admittedly, was at a loss for words and seemed to lose the edge of anger that he had not a minute ago. "Now, as I understand it, you are only to take the throne of Hell once certain obligations have been met, correct?" Allanah addressed Brian as if nothing had changed.

Brian turned his gaze to her and returned to his stern demeanor. He nodded.

"I see. So, in the meantime, my sister will continue to rule. You will only be the Prince of Darkness for now. Once you've taken over, I would be willing to sit down and work with you more closely." Allanah smiled sweetly again.

"Isn't Lucy the Prince of Darkness? That's what humans call the Devil." Brian's curiosity got the better of him as he let his sternness slip for a brief moment.

Allanah burst into laughter at his question. Lucy swore at her angrily.

"Allanah started calling me that when we were younger to piss me off. She used to call me the Prince of Darkness because our father was the King. He's been dead for centuries and everyone still knows me only as the Prince. It's infuriating," Lucy spat over Allanah's keeled-over gut-laugh.

"Enough, you two." Gabrielle finally broke her silence and intervened between the shockingly childish immortal siblings.

Allanah corrected her posture and wiped tears of laughter from her eyes.

"All right, all right – I've done all I came here to do. Brian, I look forward to working with you in the future. Lucy, I am genuinely upset by the fact that you're still alive."

"Okay," Gabrielle said as she began to usher Allanah from the courtyard and to the foyer.

"Go fuck yourself," Lucy shouted as Allanah crossed the threshold and the doors to the foyer closed behind her. "It took literally every ounce of willpower in me not to rip off her damn face and drop her in the river," Lucy spat.

"Do you believe her?" Brian asked. "She seemed genuinely interested in working with Hell, just so long as you weren't involved."

"She's always hated me. Even before my thing with Gabrielle. I don't know what her problem is but I wouldn't put it past her to try and pull something over on us if we were to work together."

"What do you suggest?"

"Pulling something over on her first – when the time is right."

★   ★   ★

"Yep, yer clean," Paul said, spinning the screen to face Dahlia.

Her eyes locked on to the breakdown of her offenses:

Subject	Dahlia Fair
Offense Entries	3
Average Corruption Rate	6.8%
Total Corruption	0%

"Holy shit," she breathed as she read the chart again and again. Brian smiled at the numbers.

"Would you look at that. You've got your very own soul with your very own chance to do with it what you will."

He threw his arm around Dahlia and gave her a squeeze.

"One small caveat though," Peter shouted from his desk opposite, "yer soul is clean, which means that the bank don't supply you wiv nourishment no more. Yer human now. Don't cock it up."

Dahlia looked at Brian in bewilderment.

"I don't think I know how to be human," she said in genuine concern.

Brian gave her a smile and kissed her forehead.

"It's not so bad, though you'll have to buy your new beach house with actual money now."

"Don't be stupid, that's what you're here for. You're still corrupted. You can just do all my bad deeds for me."

*　　*　　*

"The numbers finally came in," Lucy said as she handed Brian a folder before reclining on the sofa in her office, "we lost about sixty-seven percent of the bank during the invasion."

"Yikes, that's worse than I thought," Brian said. "I don't suppose my fifty percent increase target can be based off these numbers?"

"Nice try," Lucy replied absently. "Looks like my retirement will have to wait."

"Speaking of, where did Gabrielle go?" Brian asked as he flipped through the folder.

Lucy frowned. "Back to work. She said it was nice catching up but she had a lot waiting for her back at the office."

"That's rough," Brian replied.

Lucy shook her head gently and gave a forlorn look. "That's how it always goes with us. It's nice for a while, then work gets between us. Besides, I think some space right now wouldn't be such a bad thing."

Brian nodded silently, turning his attention again to the folder in his hand. The numbers were definitely lower than he was expecting. Based on the situation Hell was in before his arrival, the amount of work ahead of him was plentiful. The challenge was taunting Brian, daring him. It was challenging the passion he'd rediscovered when he took the job in Hell. A passion that had not died.

No – a passion that burned more furiously than ever.

FLAME TREE PRESS
FICTION WITHOUT FRONTIERS
Award-Winning Authors & Original Voices

Flame Tree Press is the trade fiction imprint of Flame Tree Publishing, focusing on excellent writing in horror and the supernatural, crime and mystery, science fiction and fantasy. Our aim is to explore beyond the boundaries of the everyday, with tales from both award-winning authors and original voices.

•

You may also enjoy:
The Sentient by Nadia Afifi
The Emergent by Nadia Afifi
American Dreams by Kenneth Bromberg
Junction by Daniel M. Bensen
Interchange by Daniel M. Bensen
Second Lives by P.D. Cacek
The City Among the Stars by Francis Carsac
The Haunting of Henderson Close by Catherine Cavendish
The Garden of Bewitchment by Catherine Cavendish
Vulcan's Forge by Robert Mitchell Evans
Black Wings by Megan Hart
Stoker's Wilde by Steven Hopstaken & Melissa Prusi
Stoker's Wilde West by Steven Hopstaken & Melissa Prusi
The Widening Gyre by Michael R. Johnston
The Blood-Dimmed Tide by Michael R. Johnston
Those Who Came Before by J.H. Moncrieff
The Sky Woman by J.D. Moyer
The Guardian by J.D. Moyer
The Last Crucible by J.D. Moyer
The Goblets Immortal by Beth Overmyer
The Apocalypse Strain by Jason Parent
Until Summer Comes Around by Glenn Rolfe
A Killing Fire by Faye Snowden
Fearless by Allen Stroud
Resilient by Allen Stroud
Screams from the Void by Anne Tibbets

•

Join our mailing list for free short stories, new release details, news about our authors and special promotions:

flametreepress.com